THIRTEENTH SUMMER

A novel by
Peter H. Riddle

AmErica House
Baltimore

Copyright © 2001 by Peter H. Riddle.

All rights reserved. No part of this book may be reproduced in any form without written permission from the publishers, except by a reviewer who may quote brief passages in a review to be printed in a newspaper or magazine.

First printing

Cover photograph by Robert E. Rushton

ISBN: 1-58851-776-4
PUBLISHED BY AMERICA HOUSE BOOK PUBLISHERS
www.publishamerica.com
Baltimore

Printed in the United States of America

Dedication

This book is for two special people: my very good friend, sailing instructor, and musical colleague Robert E. Rushton, with special thanks for his BPFs and BFTs; and of course for the prototype for Laurel MacKenzie, our daughter Anne, who still screams during scary movies…

One

Night sounds penetrated the log walls of the cabin, a soothing melody of insect song, gently flowing water and the sigh of wind through the rushes that lined the stream. Normally at peace and better able to sleep in his cabin that at any other place on earth, Eric Kelman lay wakeful. He was troubled by the stiffness and random pain at the site of the breaks in his not yet completely healed leg.

Finally giving up any hope of dozing off again, he levered himself silently out of his sleeping bag. He checked his watch in the soft glow from the dimly lit oil lamp on the table: shortly after two a.m. They hadn't turned in until after eleven. Never a sound nor consistent sleeper, especially in the last two months since the double fracture he had suffered in June, he counted himself lucky to have had almost three hours of uninterrupted rest.

As he pulled on his shorts and sweatshirt, he glanced around the cabin at his companions, all of them sleeping peacefully. His wife of thirty-eight years lay comfortably in the lower left hand bunk against the back wall. Deanna rarely accompanied him on his retreats into the far reaches of their forested acreage. She preferred the relative comforts of civilization, and was also respectful of Eric's periodic need for solitude. This week's outing, however, was a special occasion, the fulfillment of a promise made to a young friend.

Fran MacKenzie occupied the lower bunk on the right, and her husband, Walt, snored peacefully in a sleeping bag on the floor nearby. Although they had met barely two months before, the Kelmans and the MacKenzies had quickly become good friends. Despite the difference in their ages (Fran and Walt were in their middle 30s, while Eric was rapidly approaching retirement) they had soon discovered they shared many interests.

The children slept in the two upper bunks, Laurel MacKenzie above her mother, and her friend, Sara Hancock, above Deanna. Laurel was the reason behind the adults' newfound friendship, the result of an adventure she and Eric had shared in June. That escapade had also resulted in his injury. He crossed the floor and stood beside her bunk, gazing fondly at the child's serene, untroubled sleep.

Eric had been staying alone in the cabin in June, shortly after the close of the university term and the beginning of a summer's respite from his teaching obligations. With Deanna away, visiting with their eldest daughter and her family, he had embarked upon his yearly isolation from society, intent upon long days of solitary contentment in their forested retreat. Upon returning from a day-long canoe trip and the pursuit of his hobby of photography, he had arrived at the cabin to find a frightened but resourceful Laurel MacKenzie, lost and on the run from a deranged young man who had abducted her on the way to school.

Leaving the side of Laurel's bunk, he padded softly around the cabin's single large room, trying to ease the discomfort in his cramped leg. He deliberately stretched the tendons and muscles in an exaggerated stride, although careful not to make any noise that might wake the others. He worked his way around the wood stove, which was still warm from cooking their supper. He circled the rustic but serviceable table and chairs that he had built the summer after he completed the cabin itself, then paced between the pine dry sink and the rows of open shelves along the walls that held their supplies.

On his third circuit, he paused before the dry sink and gazed out the small window that sat midway up the wall above it. He noted with pleasure the improvement in the weather. The sky had been overcast when they turned in, but now the stars shone brightly, accompanied by the barest sliver of an almost-new moon.

Now fully awake, Eric abandoned the idea of returning to his sleeping bag. Almost silently he eased open the cabin door and slipped outside. He lowered himself gingerly, favoring his weakened leg, to sit at the edge of the small porch, and leaned back against one of the poles that supported the overhanging roof.

While neither stylish nor imaginative, Eric's cabin was sturdy and functional. Its handsome symmetry reflected a high level of craftsmanship. Walt had complimented him sincerely on its quality, high praise indeed from an innovative architect whose work had attracted nationwide attention and won him two major awards.

The structure sat upon raised poles, treated with creosote and sunk into the ground well below the frost line. The walls were of dressed pine logs, meticulously notched to interlock at the corners and around the windows and doorframes. Each window was fitted with a set of locking shutters. The door opened onto a raised porch, overhung by wide eaves. A similar overhang at the rear sheltered a storage area for outboard motors and other equipment. Eric had shingled the roof with thick spruce shakes.

Designed primarily as a solitary retreat, the cabin boasted few amenities other than its superior construction. Had Deanna shown an interest in accompanying him more often, Eric would no doubt have installed some rudimentary indoor plumbing, and possibly a generator for electricity. But since he was most often the only one in residence, he preferred the simplicity of a wood stove, oil lamps, and the crude but efficient outhouse that stood behind and downhill from the building. Water came from a hand-dug well on the high side of the land, near the cabin's door.

In keeping with the primitive nature of the accommodations, personal cleanliness was afforded by a simple but ingenious shower arrangement, a barrel suspended overhead and fitted with a hose, a nozzle, and a pull-chain valve. The only major inconvenience was the need to refill the barrel by hand, requiring many trips up a ladder with brimming buckets of water.

There was one other minor problem inherent in this system, one that Eric had failed to consider until they had guests in residence. The shower was not enclosed, and offered nothing in the way of privacy for the modest. Upon their arrival, Eric and Walt had hastily erected a rudimentary and temporary wall to shield one side of the shower from the view out the cabin window.

Eric's good friend Paul VanOostrum, who ran a large general store near the entrance to the national park that adjoined the Kelman property, had helped him to build the cabin years earlier. Together they had felled and shaped the logs, set the footings and erected the walls. They had even dug by hand the well that provided them with pure, sweet water. They were assisted during various phases of the building process by several of Paul's neighbors, and to repay them, Eric gladly gave them the use of his property for their own retreats or vacations.

Sitting on the open deck of the porch, Eric surveyed the clearing around him with pleasure and contentedness. His profession, professor of music at a small-town university, gave his life great focus and satisfaction. But his energy was often drained by the demands of teaching young minds, keeping up with the latest research, and dealing with the ever-present rancor of university politics. In his later years, he sought the seclusion and rejuvenation of the forest more and more often.

The Kelman property occupied the major part of a huge wooded tract from which a logging company, showing unusual restraint for that sort of enterprise, had selectively culled only the more mature hardwoods for the furniture trade a hundred years earlier. They had also later removed partial stands of pine and spruce for the building industry, but without a large river in the vicinity, transporting the trees had proven to be uneconomic. The isolated location of the land had led the company to concentrate on more accessible acreage, and by the time the Kelmans acquired the land, second-growth trees were well established.

Eric derived great satisfaction from his preserve. In recent years, he and Deanna had turned down immense sums of money for logging rights, but no amount could have tempted them. With an ever-increasing population denuding more and more land every year in an insatiable demand for living space, they made a conscious decision to maintain their land as a private sanctuary. Although both Eric and Deanna recognized the overly romantic nature of this somewhat impractical attitude, they considered the forest and its wildlife their personal responsibility, one that they took very seriously.

As Eric sat surveying the night, myriad sounds gradually penetrated his consciousness: the soft murmuring of insects, faint rustling of rodents in the tall grass that rimmed the cabin's clearing, a whoosh of wings as an owl swept into a nearby tree. Off to his left, the starlight sparkled on the slow moving waters of Shrewsbury Creek, well below its high water mark on the banks this late in the summer, but still navigable by canoe or small boat. The creek was their principal access route to the cabin, as Eric had neither bothered nor wanted to cut a road this far into their huge tract of undeveloped land.

He had not been to the cabin since June, hampered by the cast on his leg that made sitting in a canoe virtually impossible. As he surveyed the clearing, he thought back to that last visit, and to his first meeting with twelve-year-old Laurel MacKenzie. The child had been kidnapped by an unbalanced young man and taken deep into the adjacent national park. With courage and resourcefulness far beyond her years, she had escaped from her captor and made her way through the woods, finally coming upon the cabin.

At first wary of Eric, whom she suspected of being a hermit and perhaps a danger to her, Laurel had gradually learned to trust him. And when her powerful abductor traced her to the cabin and stalked them both, Laurel and Eric outwitted and overpowered him to make their way to safety, although not without one final violent encounter, during which Eric's leg had been broken.

In the course of a long night spent in the cabin, sheltering from a vicious thunderstorm, the aging professor had helped his young charge overcome her fears, and to tap her own reserves of courage. As a diversion from the shock she had endured, he shared with her much of his attitude and philosophy about the world, and of his love for nature. In return, he learned much from her about the spirit and resiliency of youth, attributes that had begun to desert him in his later years.

Eric had promised Laurel a return visit to the cabin, along with her parents, under happier circumstances. Although the visit had been delayed while his broken leg mended, finally, true to his word, he and Deanna had invited the MacKenzie family for a week's stay, along with Laurel's closest friend, Sara Hancock. The Kelmans and the MacKenzies had quickly discovered a strong compatibility among them all, and promptly became close friends.

Eric never failed to be amazed at the constant and highly varied noises in the supposedly silent forest, and at the amount of life that surrounded the cabin. Nocturnal creatures of all sizes went about their business, foraging and procreating and preying upon each other, all maintaining a natural balance that too much intrusion by mankind would quickly destroy.

Amid the expected sounds around him, there filtered into his consciousness a soft thump, followed by shuffling footsteps in the cabin behind him. The door eased open, and he saw Laurel's sleepy eyes peek around the doorjamb, blinking to adjust to the starlight. "Gotta pee." She vanished around the side of the cabin, and Eric heard the gentle squeak of the hinges on the outhouse door. He smiled. *When do kids finally outgrow announcing their destination every time they have to go to the bathroom?*

Presently Laurel reappeared, but instead of going back into the cabin, she plopped down at Eric's side, now more fully awake. She drew up her knees and stretched the hem of her oversized sweatshirt over them, against the slight chill in the air. "How come you're up?"

"Couldn't sleep," Eric answered, "but you don't have any such excuse. Scram."

"Nope. Not until you do what you promised."

"And what's that?"

"The last time we were here," Laurel answered, "you said you'd show me the Milky Way. Dad tried to show it to me back in town, but you were right, the lights in town make it too hard to see, and it just looked like a bunch of fog, and you said you can see it better out where there aren't any lamp posts and houses and cars and stuff, and…"

"Hold it!" Eric laughed, amused by her exuberance. "Take a breath once in a while. And keep your voice down, or we'll have everybody up."

"Sorry," Laurel said in an exaggerated whisper. She was gazing off toward the tops of the trees that surrounded the clearing. "Anyway, where is it?"

"Go back inside and look on the shelf over the sink. My binoculars are there, in a brown leather case." Laurel bounced up and headed for the door. "And try to be quiet. The others need their sleep."

"Okay." She eased the door open and slipped inside, then quickly returned with the case. She handed it to Eric, and he removed his powerful Pentax binoculars and adjusted the focus to infinity. He handed them back to her.

"Look up." He gestured overhead, where the lack of moonlight accentuated the blanket of stars. Laurel followed his finger.

"I don't see… I… Oh my gosh!" Eric smiled at her open-mouthed astonishment, reliving the memory of such discoveries in his own youth. "It's amazing! It's so beautiful!"

"Told you so. You town kids miss out on a lot." He turned his face upward, taking in the vast expanse of closely packed stars, billions of pinpoints of light that spread like a ribbon across the sky. *Is there anything more lovely in the universe?* he wondered, not for the first time. Then he looked again at Laurel's rapt face. *Yes, there is: the beauty of an intelligent child who is just discovering the immensity of existence.*

Laurel's voice rose with her growing excitement. "How far away are they?"

"Shhh. Let the others sleep," he whispered. "If you got in the fastest rocket ship ever invented and tried to go to the nearest star, you couldn't live long enough to get there."

"We learned in school that *we're* part of the Milky Way, too. How can we see it like this if we're *in* it?"

"Our solar system, the sun and all the planets around it, including the Earth, is sort of out toward the edge of the Milky Way. When you look out there, you're looking toward the center of it."

"It's so big…"

Eric smiled. "It sure is."

Laurel sat silently for several minutes, her eyes slowly scanning the sky from east to west and back again. "Are all the stars in the Milky Way?"

"Nope. That's just a small part of the universe. The Milky Way is called a galaxy, and there are a bunch of other galaxies, even bigger ones. All together, there are billions of stars out there."

"Planets, too? Like earth?"

"Apparently so. We can't really see them, because they're too small and too far away, but we can tell they're there by the way they affect each other with their gravity. Astronomers study the positions of the stars, and can tell where things are by the way everything moves and affects everything else. Telescopes keep getting better and better, and just recently they've found pretty convincing evidence that some stars have planets, just like our sun. So it's a pretty fair guess that a lot of them do, maybe even most of them."

Laurel stared upward in wonder. Then she turned and gazed at him seriously. "What's it all for?"

"You don't ask easy questions, do you, runt? Wouldn't you rather know how to turn lead into gold? Or maybe how to make brussels sprouts taste like ice cream?"

"Come on, Doc, I'm serious. I want to know."

"Don't call me Doc!"

"Then don't call me runt!"

They glared at each other, and then dissolved into laughter. During that long night in June, as Eric patiently coaxed her back from the shock and trauma of her kidnapping, they had fallen into gentle mutual teasing. Once she had discovered that he taught at the university and had a Ph.D. ("Part Hound Dog," Eric called his degree), she delighted in always being able to get a rise out of him by calling him Doc. In return, he called her runt in honor of her small stature.

Laurel was slight like her mother, gracefully slim at not quite five feet tall, and just beginning to acquire the first signs of a mature figure. Her tiny waist and long, tapering legs gave her an air of fragility and soft femininity. Her small heart-shaped face was framed by fine blond hair, and her eyes glittered with a deep blue, penetrating brilliance that bespoke the intelligence that lay within.

"Now answer my question, please. What's it all for?"

"Okay. Look over there at that oak tree. What's that for?"

"You're doing it again," Laurel bristled. "Instead of answering me, you always ask me another question! I don't know what the darn tree is for, and what's it got to do with what I asked you?"

"Just listen. Listen to the tree."

"Huh?"

"Just sit very still and listen."

She fidgeted restlessly. "I don't hear anything."

"You're too impatient. Wait. Take a deep breath and hold it, so you won't even hear your own breathing. The tree will tell you."

Laurel sighed theatrically, inhaled deeply, then braced her thin arms stiffly against the porch floor and cocked her ear toward the tall, thick oak. Gradually she became aware of the night sounds around her. She turned her face toward him. "What is it?"

"Lots of things," Eric replied. "There's a little wind, so the branches are brushing together. And the little humming sounds are insects."

"What kind?"

"Now you've got me. I'm only a musician, remember, not an entomologist."

"Yeah, but you know lots of stuff."

"That's what comes from reading, runt, and from living too long. You should try it. Reading, I mean."

Laurel countered the jibe. "I read lots! And you're not so old. Anyway, you don't *act* old." She turned her head abruptly at the sound of a sudden splash from the creek. "What was that?"

"Sounded like a frog to me."

They fell quiet again, staring at the oak tree and listening intently for several minutes. Then the upper branches rustled, and in the dim starlight they caught the vague outline of a body plummeting downward. It was followed by a small squeal of terror as an owl locked its talons around its prey. The owl climbed aloft again, its heavy wings beating the air, and settled back onto a high limb to savor its meal.

Laurel whispered in her smallest voice. "Something just died, didn't it?"

"Uh huh, a mouse or shrew or something. That was an owl. They hunt at night. And the mouse had to die so the owl could have something to eat. And now do you know what the tree is for?"

"I guess it's where the owl lives. And the insects, too?"

"Right. How about the frog?"

"Well, it doesn't live in the tree, does it? Frogs don't live in trees!"

"Some do. There are all kinds of frogs, including tree frogs, but that one was a bullfrog, and they live in the creek and in the rushes that grow along the banks. Anyway, have you got the answer to your question yet? What's the Milky Way for, and all the other stars?"

She concentrated. "For us to live in."

"Just us?"

"And frogs and owls and mice, and everything else." She paused and thought. "But is everything out *there* just for us, too? All the billions of stars and planets? That doesn't make sense. We can't go there, can we?"

"Think about it."

"Aliens, right!" She pounded her small fist on his thigh. "All the stars and planets are for all the aliens that live out there, and someday they're going to come here and eat us!"

Eric laughed; she didn't seem too upset at the prospect of being eaten by a space invader. "You watch too much TV," he said.

She turned serious again. "I still don't get it. Who put it all here? And is it all just so we'd have some place to... to *be*..."

"Nobody has the answer to that yet."

Their voices had risen, and the cabin door opened behind them. Deanna peered out. "What are you two doing out here? You're going to wake up the whole neighborhood."

"Yeah, right," Eric laughed quietly. "I'll bet all the bears and deer have been phoning you to complain. I'll have you know Laurel and I have been solving the riddle of the universe."

Deanna eased the door closed and sat down next to Laurel. "Yeah, right, yourself. You, who can't even figure out your own income tax."

"Oh yes I can, but why should I, when by acting dumb I can get you to do it?"

Laurel looked nervously from one to the other. "Are you two fighting?"

Eric and Deanna managed to keep their faces stern. "We sure are," she said, "and we're just warming up. Wait 'til we *really* get started, and get out our weapons."

"Right," Eric said. "Whipped cream canisters at ten paces." Laurel realized they were teasing, and she relaxed again. Their raised voices provoked more noises from inside the cabin. They shushed each other, but it was too late. The door opened, and three faces peered out.

"Join the party," Deanna invited. "You might as well, since these two inconsiderate philosophers have gotten us all up."

"Dad, come out here and look at this. Eric showed me how to see the Milky Way. It's *huge!*" Laurel bounced up and grabbed the binoculars, then tugged on her father's hand, pulling him out onto the porch and down into the yard. Fran MacKenzie and Sara followed close behind, and all three stood gaping up at the heavens as Laurel chattered at them.

Eric slid over companionably beside his wife. "Remind you of anything?"

"Oh, yes," she answered, "but I haven't thought about it in a long time. The girls were around nine and ten the first time we came out here, weren't they?"

"I guess so. I built the cabin the summer you finished taking courses for your degree at the university. Becky had just finished grade four."

"We were here just about this same time of year, after the summer session ended. I still remember how everything seemed so new to them. We could hardly get them to go to bed at night."

"One night we couldn't. Remember? We sat out here counting stars with them, until Amy finally fell asleep leaning against your arm." He sat silently, lost in thought, and then continued a bit sadly. "Where did they go, anyway? I look at Becky, managing two kids and a career on the side, and Amy about to get her Ph.D., both of them so competent... How did they get there so fast?"

Deanna spoke in a whisper. "And you and I are old..."

Eric smiled at her. "Only sixty-one... Not so old yet. I still can't see the end of the road, our road." He paused, then put his arm around her and drew her close. In the clearing, the MacKenzies and Sara Hancock were still enthralled by their surroundings. "And you know what? I wouldn't have missed it, not one day of it."

Two

Despite their impromptu late night party, everyone in the cabin was up shortly after sunrise. This was the morning Laurel had been most excited about, a canoe trip to "Eric's Lagoon" and a two-night campout.

In the area around the northwest corner of the Kelman property, one of the tributaries of Shrewsbury Creek backed up behind a narrow canyon, where it formed a broad, deep and placid lake. The region was virtually inaccessible except by water, and Eric had discovered it almost by accident. When the lumber company had pulled out of the property years earlier, the forest had been allowed to return to its natural state, and all the roads they cut had quickly grown over and become impassable.

An avid canoeist and keen explorer, he had ventured into the upper reaches of the creek to investigate both of its two major tributaries years before. He had discovered a deep cut and a stretch of white water in the western arm, and considered it a personal challenge to defeat the current and travel to its source. Finally fighting his way out of the canyon, he was rewarded by an idyllic and totally unspoiled Eden.

Despite its remote location and the difficult passage upstream to get there, it remained highest on his list of pleasure spots. The water warmed up fairly quickly each summer, affording temperate swimming and total isolation. To Eric, it was the most beautiful place on earth. He had described it to Laurel the previous June, and promised to show it to her before the summer was out.

The lake area was approachable by land only with considerable difficulty. Dense woods separated it from the national park to the east, and Eric had only occasionally found traces of hikers who had made it that far. He had no objection to their presence, provided the trespassers cleaned up after themselves, but he had little patience with inconsiderate vacationers who littered the woods and destroyed foliage and animal habitat indiscriminately.

He always enjoyed the challenge of the approach to the lake, upstream through the canyon against the fast-flowing current. He steadfastly resisted putting in a road, or even breaking a trail to skirt the canyon. In fact, he had even withstood Deanna's pressure to put in an overland access to the cabin, although she had frequently lobbied for him to rough out a one-lane dirt road. Deanna endured but did not enjoy canoe trips.

However, Eric knew that since all roads went in both directions, the privacy he treasured might thus be compromised. The problem was the national park. As long as the forest acreage separated their cabin from the nearest public campsites, only the hardiest campers would penetrate deep into their property. A road would jeopardize this protection.

The lack of land access had made building the cabin somewhat more difficult, however. Even though the walls, footings and roof had been fashioned from trees that grew on site, many commercial items had to be transported. All of the tools, equipment and supplementary materials had been brought in on countless trips upstream in Eric's cargo canoe, which was powered by a small but efficient outboard engine. The heaviest items, such as the wood stove, had been towed in on a rough log raft.

His large cargo canoe was broad and stable, with a squared-off stern and ample freeboard, but it could not carry the four adults, two children and all of their camping gear. For the present outing, they had borrowed a second canoe and outboard engine from Paul VanOostrum. After a quick breakfast, they packed the two craft with food, lightweight tents, sleeping bags and miscellaneous necessities. They were fully loaded and headed upstream by nine o'clock.

Eric led the way in his own canoe, accompanied by Deanna and Fran MacKenzie and with half of their supplies aboard. Walt MacKenzie piloted the second canoe, with the rest of their equipment amidships and the two girls in the bow. He was an experienced sailor, the proud owner of a thirty-foot yacht that he sailed offshore. Although his wife Fran was not avid about boating, Laurel was as keen and capable as her father in anything that floated, and she agitated for a turn at the canoe's tiller.

Most of the trip was relatively easy. The small but powerful outboards coped easily with the heavily loaded watercraft, requiring little more of their captains than careful guidance through the deepest part of the channel. For most of the way, Walt turned this chore over to Laurel, and she in turn showed Sara how to anticipate bends in the stream and keep away from the rushes and shallows along each bank.

When they neared the canyon that separated the creek from the lagoon, Eric called a brief halt, and they beached the canoes side by side to plan the remainder of the trip. With the water level at a seasonal low in August, the current would not be as swift as during the spring runoff, but they would still encounter some rough going.

Eric knelt in a small sandy area on shore, and the others gathered around him. Using a pointed stick, he drew an approximation of the upcoming canyon in the coarse sand, a series of lazy S-shapes that looked something like a fat snake. He explained the route the channel took through the narrow confines, and the location of rocks that would pose a hazard to the unwary. Then he began placing pebbles to show where the most dangerous rocky areas lay.

Sara quickly lost interest and wandered back to the canoes with Fran and Deanna, but Laurel remained keenly engrossed. She squatted down next to Eric and examined the diagram carefully. When he had finished his explanation, she said, "There's a pattern to it."

"Right," Eric replied. "Any idea why?"

"Easy. The rocks are all opposite the wide side, so the water must have cut its way through the softest sand." She pointed to the fatter side of each S-shaped section. "So all you have to do is steer away from the skinny side each time you go around a bend, but not too close to the shore." She turned to her father excitedly. "I can do that!"

Eric's first impulse was to tell her that her father had better do the steering, but then he realized that Walt seemed to be taking her request seriously. "It's not like our boat," he told her. "A canoe turns faster, and you have to watch out that the lower arm of the outboard stays clear of the bottom and the rocks."

"I know. It's just like the keel, only easier because it doesn't stick down so far. So can I do it? Please?"

"You're the captain," Walt answered, smiling at her broadly.

"Yippee!" Laurel erupted from her crouch and ran back to the canoes, eager to cast off.

Eric turned to Walt and raised his eyebrows, some concern showing in his eyes. Walt laughed. "Just watch her. I swear she's got a pirate ancestor back there somewhere. She has a real instinct for boats. Anyway, I'll ride lookout in the bow. She'll be fine."

"The last part is really tricky, Walt. The current is strong, and there's very little clearance at the mouth of the canyon. It's fairly shallow and not really life-threatening, but you could get swamped. She'll have to follow me *exactly* if you want to get through."

"Let's let her take a shot at it. If she can't manage it, I'll take over. But ten bucks says if *you* can do it, *she* can."

"No bet," Eric laughed. "Not after the way she saved my bacon last June. If you say she's capable, I'm not going to argue with you."

The two men returned to the canoes, and Eric gave Laurel one final bit of instruction. "The first time I came through here, I didn't use the motor until the very end, where the current is the strongest. It's easier with the motor, but be sure you follow my wake exactly. Don't cut any corners, or you'll snag the propeller."

She gave him a mock salute. "Aye, aye, sir!"

"And the hardest part is at the end of the canyon," he said seriously. She gave him her complete attention. "Do you want your father to take it through there?"

"What's hard about it?"

"We have to go through a really narrow pass. The lake on the other side is plenty wide, and all the water tries to go through the pass at once, so the current is strongest there. It spills over a sort of ledge, and it's only deep enough in one spot for the outboard to clear the bottom. And you can't let the bow get caught sideways. If you do, you'll tip over."

"How do I do it?"

Eric realized she was not too overly confident, and was concentrating fiercely to absorb his instructions. "The current enters the canyon from the left, then makes a sort of whirlpool at the first S-curve. You'll be able to see it on the surface. You have to steer around the rim of the whirlpool and point the bow toward the left wall, straight into the current. It'll look and feel like you're going to hit the rocks. That's what happened to me the first time. But if you time it just right, the current will catch the bow and shoot you right on through."

"Are you going first?" she asked eagerly.

"Yup."

"Then I'll watch you. I bet I can do it."

"Okay. But ask your dad."

Laurel turned to Walt hopefully, and he smiled at her. "Do you understand exactly what to do?"

To Eric's amazement, Laurel paraphrased his instructions clearly and concisely. She didn't miss a step. "Let's do it, then," he said.

They all took their places in the canoes and shoved off from shore, then started the small outboard engines. Eric advanced the throttle to about a third and swung the bow away from shore to find the channel. While still in the wider part of the creek, he deliberately maneuvered the canoe from side to side, seeming to be avoiding obstructions. He glanced over his shoulder and saw with satisfaction that the second craft was tracking him as if on rails.

Nearing the mouth of the canyon, he advanced the throttle to about two-thirds. As the walls closed in on both sides, white water churned along the shoreline. Abruptly the canoe slowed as it encountered the swift current coursing through the narrowest confines of the canyon. It buffeted the bow, but the heavily loaded boat rode low in the water and tracked easily down the channel. Water sprayed over the gunwales and dampened their shirts. He pushed the throttle almost to the maximum.

Laurel maintained a short but adequate distance between the two canoes, and stayed well within his wake. In the bow, Walt crouched low to allow her a clear field of vision ahead. Sara sat on the bottom in the middle, down low in front of the seat and clinging to both gunwales. She looked apprehensive.

As they neared the first S-curve, Eric looked back and waved, capturing Laurel's attention. He gestured toward the canyon wall, indicating the tops of rocks that were just visible through the cascading water. He waggled his hand in the air, first left and then right, to show her the path he would take, and she nodded. Then he entered the bend.

The surface of the water was too disturbed to show a consistent wake, and Laurel had to estimate the path of the first canoe by its position relative to the shore. Walt scanned the channel unnecessarily for rocks, as she steered smoothly and evenly in an almost exact replica of Eric's route. They came through safely with room to spare. *That's the first hurdle*, Eric thought, *and Walt wasn't kidding. The kid is good!*

The next two bends went as smoothly as the first, and the canyon widened out briefly as they neared the mouth of the lagoon. Taking advantage of the broader channel, Eric throttled back, maintaining just enough way to counteract the current. He waved Laurel on and waited until she pulled alongside, then gestured ahead to where white water spilled into the canyon. There seemed to be no channel.

Holding onto the other canoe's gunwale, Eric called out to Laurel over the sound of the water and the outboards. "It looks shallow, but there's enough water under the boat right *there*, on the edge of the whirlpool!" He pointed to a spot just off the left hand wall, slightly to the right of a jumbled pile of boulders. "The current sweeps around in a circle. See the whirlpool? If you keep your bow aimed right at the rocks, it'll carry you past them!"

"Got it!" she answered.

Faced with the churning water, Eric suddenly regretted agreeing to let her run the other canoe. *She's only twelve, and even if she's a good sailor, a canoe is different from a yacht, and pretty skittish.* He looked at Walt, but his friend just smiled at him, a relaxed look on his face. *Okay*, Eric thought, *but I hope we won't be fishing all of you out of the drink.*

He throttled up, and the small outboard whined thinly as the blades bit into the current. He released the other craft's gunwale and pulled ahead, then checked over his shoulder to be sure Laurel was in control. She eased over directly behind him, letting some space develop between the canoes.

Eric turned his attention to the water ahead. Underwater shelves at each end of the canyon kept the depth constant all year, with considerable turbulence over the spillway from the lake. He had traversed the passage many times, and always safely, but he never took anything for granted, and gave it his entire concentration.

Drawing abreast of the whirlpool, he eased the bow around its circumference. He let the current pull the canoe into position, parallel to the rocks that guarded the left side of the spillway. A narrow band of clear water marked the channel, and he pointed the canoe toward the rocks at the spot where the current changed direction.

Eric suddenly realized how wrong the approach looked from that angle. The round-bottomed craft seemed headed for a certain pileup on the rocks. But at the last second, as he knew it would, the rapid flow shoved the hull broadside just enough to keep it clear. The little outboard labored against the current. *Will she see it? I never should have let her try it.* At the very lip of the spillway, his canoe came almost to a standstill, then fought its way through the passage and shot forward into the more placid lake.

Eric swung away from the turbulent flow and brought the canoe about, giving himself a clear view of the canyon's entrance. The second canoe was just entering the narrow gap, nicely lined up and following nearly the same line Eric had taken. But as it approached, he thought that Laurel seemed indecisive. Instead of heading straight toward the rocks, she was aiming slightly high, on a bearing that would allow the swirling current to strike the opposite side of the canoe and swamp it.

He shouted a warning, but the rushing water and the high-pitched wail of the outboard swallowed up his voice. As he watched anxiously, Laurel levered herself part way up off the seat and strained to study the surface of the water over her father's shoulder. She scanned the crests and eddies, and at the last possible second she swung the tiller so the bow cut into the current less than a dozen yards from the spillway. The canoe spun like a top on its axis, the bow came up, and it barreled through the pass at twice the speed Eric had managed.

My God, he thought, *she's better at this than I am! And on her first try, too!* Laurel throttled back and turned the tiller to head toward the first canoe, her face alight with the pure joy of her accomplishment. Walt lazed in the bow, the picture of unconcern, but with obvious pride in his daughter's skill. *Told you so.*

Eric half rose off the stern seat and gave her a smart salute. She grinned back at him, trying hard not to look too smug. "Let's do it again!"

"Not on your life!" Eric retorted. "You're not getting another chance to show me up."

Now out of the canyon, they found themselves at the southern end of the most peaceful, broad, placid lake the MacKenzies had ever seen. It was bordered on three sides by dense forest, and a narrow beach of fine white sand lined the western shore. Beyond the sand was a grassy meadow. Eric headed in that direction, shutting off the outboard a few dozen yards from shore and tilting it forward so the shaft came out of the water. Their momentum carried the canoe smoothly up onto the sandy shelf. Laurel followed his example and brought her craft in cleanly.

They quickly unloaded the canoes and set up the tents, two lightweight umbrella pop-ups for the adults and Walt's ancient military-style pup tent for the girls. Lunch was a quick affair of sandwiches and fruit drinks, after which Laurel and Sara explored the beach and nearby woods while their stomachs began the digestion process. The adults cleared away the remains of the meal, and then lounged on the grassy verge of the shore.

Eric was lavish in his praise of Laurel's boatmanship. "Damnedest thing I ever saw a kid do," he said. "I thought you were going to tip over for sure. Where did she learn how to read the water like that?"

"She was five when we bought *Mayflower*," Walt said, referring to his thirty-foot yacht. "Right from the beginning, she wanted to learn how to sail. It was like she was born on deck. I've always considered myself pretty good with a sailboat, started when I was nine, but it's like she's an integral part of the boat. I taught her the basics, but I soon discovered she was sensing the wind and water better than I could. She seems to feel what's going to happen before it does."

"If it's genetic," Fran put in, "she gets it from you. I haven't yet figured out how a boat can go *forward* when the wind is coming at you from in front."

Walt laughed. "You could if you'd come sailing with us a little more often."

"No thanks. Two or three times a year is enough for me, and not beyond the harbor, thank you very much. You two can have your own brand of father-daughter bonding. I'll teach her how to cook!"

That comment made them all laugh. "You should have seen her at about seven or eight, though, standing at the wheel," Fran continued. "She was the tiniest little thing, a little sailor's cap on her head, the rest of her practically hidden under her life jacket, looking like she owned the world. Used to boss her father around something fierce, telling him to pull in the sail, haul in the sheet, whatever that is, and her favorite, 'Coming about!' at the top of her lungs when she was going to turn."

"Even back then she hated that life jacket," Walt added, remembering. "Still does, wants to stand the helm in her bikini like a film star or something, but she's never learned to swim. *Mayflower's* really quite stable, but if the water's even a little bit rough, I make her wear the vest."

"Can't swim?" Deanna was puzzled. "That's hard to believe, the way she seems to love the water."

"I've tried to teach her," Walt said. "We both have. As far as I know, it's the only thing she's really afraid of. Hates water up her nose, and panics if her head goes under. We even paid for private lessons with the instructors at the Y, but they couldn't get her to relax enough to learn. When Sara decided to go out for the swim team last year, Laurel gave it one more try, but it didn't work. I think she's given up for good now, resigned herself to never learning how."

"And yet she loves boating, and knows the water like an expert," Eric mused. "Strange..."

"I know. Go figure."

The children arrived back from their hike and changed into their swimsuits, and by one-thirty they were enjoying the surprisingly warm water. Sara practiced the various strokes she had learned in swim class, and Laurel searched for minnows in the shallows, scooping them up in a clear plastic sandwich container. Periodically she brought her catches ashore for them to admire, then turned them loose again.

"This is the way life should be," Walt exclaimed, watching them from the shore. "How did you ever find this place?"

"This tract used to be part of a logging claim," Eric said. "Deanna's family acquired the whole thing when the company closed out operations, and we built the cabin when our girls were small. I'm somewhat of a hermit, I guess. Deanna humors me by coming with me a couple of times each summer, but most of the time I come out here alone, or sometimes with Paul. It recharges my batteries after the winter term at the university. I used to teach summer school, but no more. Remember what Travis McGee advocated?" Eric asked, referring to John D. MacDonald's fictional hero. "Like him, I take small parts of my retirement right now, while I'm fit and well enough to enjoy it.

"Anyway, as soon I got the cabin livable, I started exploring the acreage. I found that canyon toward the beginning of our third season here. It was late spring, and we'd had a big runoff that year. The water was fast and really rough, and I took it as a personal challenge to beat it. Nearly smashed the canoe on my first try, but I finally made it through, and that's when I found this lagoon.

"Where the creek enters, up there to the north, it drops off suddenly to a depth of about fifty feet. There's a natural rock face under water, just like a sheer cliff, then a gravel bottom that gradually slopes upward toward the south. The way it widens out, just before the canyon, it keeps the current moving slowly. The whole thing is spring fed, and it's full like this all year, always the same depth.

"Where it enters the canyon, the bottom rises to within a couple of feet of the surface, then forms the spillway we came over. The water moves fast through that bottleneck, but up here it's always calm, and it stays fairly warm until well into the autumn."

"It seems like paradise to me," Fran said, "and I can't tell you how kind it was of you to invite us. Laurel has talked all summer about how you promised to show this place to her, but we never expected it to happen."

"Our pleasure," Deanna said.

"But we already owe you so much." She turned toward Eric. "If you hadn't been at the cabin when Laurel was kidnapped, I don't know how she would ever have found her way out. And with that terrible person still chasing after her..."

"Don't kid yourself," Eric said. "She was well on the way to safety when she found me. For a twelve-year-old, she used remarkably good judgment. And when we were coming out, she did her share and then some."

"But with that man after her, she wouldn't have made it without you," Fran said, "and we're very grateful."

"Forget it. I'm just glad it all turned out okay. I'm ready for a swim. Anyone else?"

"Count me in," Walt said, rising to his feet. Deanna and Fran stayed put. "Looks like these two old ladies aren't up to it, though," he teased.

"We just have better sense," Deanna said, "than to thrash about among all those leeches. Don't come complaining to us when they latch onto your scrawny hides and suck your veins dry."

"No leeches here," Eric laughed. "Nothing worse than a few man-eating trout. Ever seen a man eating trout, Fran?"

"Old joke, Eric. Go! Play in the water. Recapture your adolescence."

Eric and Walt stripped to their shorts and entered the water. Eric set off in his strong crawl toward the center of the lagoon, and soon outdistanced his friend. Although a capable swimmer, Walt realized he was no match for the older man, and contented himself with slow and steady laps, back and forth along the shoreline.

Eric Kelman swam at least three times a week in the university pool, all through the academic term. It served as a good substitute for outdoor exercise when the winter weather set in. Having barely reached the age of twelve when he lost his father, Eric was determined to maintain his own health to the best of his ability. Alistaire Kelman had been a devoted, hard-working and loving father, but his lack of concern for his physical condition had cost him his life. Seriously overweight, a heavy smoker and addicted to long hours in a sedentary job, he had suffered a series of debilitating cerebral hemorrhages. A massive heart attack took him at age forty-four.

Several hundred yards out, Eric rolled over and switched to a backstroke. He suddenly became aware of another swimmer, swiftly approaching from the side. Using a seemingly ungainly but nevertheless efficient breaststroke, Sara Hancock was overtaking him.

Eric waited until she caught up. "Pretty good moves for a kid," he said to her.

"Thanks, Dr. Kelman. I take lessons every Saturday. I'm going to join the swim team when I get to high school. I can already do the butterfly and the crawl, too."

"Looks like you'll have a good head start on the others. Keep it up."

Sara appraised him confidently. "You're pretty good yourself, considering."

"Considering what?" Eric feigned indignation. "Pretty good for an old guy, I suppose!"

Sara was embarrassed. "I didn't mean that," she stammered, although that was exactly what she had meant.

Eric splashed ineffectively at the surface in a crude dog paddle, sputtering and pretending to sink. Then he affected an old geezer's voice. "All right, ya young squirt, we'll just see what you're made of. Wanna race? How about ten times around the lake?"

Sara was still embarrassed at her gaffe, but she laughed at his antics. "I'm sure you can beat me."

Eric bristled, hamming it up outrageously. "Don't patronize me, you rotten kid! Now that *really* makes me mad. How about flat out from here to shore, free style, loser has to wash the dishes for the rest of the trip. Put up or shut up."

Sara entered into the fun of the game. "You're on, *old man*. How much head start do you need? A hundred yards? Two hundred?"

"We'll see who needs a head start. Just say when, and you'll be eating my wake."

"When!" she shouted, and porpoised toward the shore, her slim young arms cutting the water with barely a splash. Eric took off in pursuit. He was in excellent condition, but soon realized that the two months of convalescence and the weakness in his healing leg were a definite handicap. Sara was gradually pulling away.

He lowered his head, streamlined his body, and settled into an efficient crawl, letting his arms do most of the work. After a hundred yards he looked up to see Sara still in the lead, but not widening the gap. He redoubled his efforts, amused at his own competitiveness. *What are you doing, you old fool? She's just a kid, and you should let her win anyway. Assuming you can even beat her, that is, and it looks like maybe you can't.*

Another hundred yards, and the gap had narrowed. Sara still stroked strongly, but her slighter frame and shorter reach, not to mention the determination of her adversary, put her at a disadvantage. As they neared the shallows they were almost side by side, and suddenly they could touch the bottom and were on their feet, racing for the beach. They collapsed on the sand, both panting too hard to speak in complete sentences.

"I won!"

"No way!"

"Did so!"

"Prove it! Let's do it again!"

When he had caught his breath, Eric laughed at their foolishness, and Sara joined in. "I give up. Truce! You're the best…"

"You, too," Eric agreed.

Sara couldn't resist: "...for an *old guy!*"

Their caper had attracted everyone's attention, and Laurel and Walt left the water and flopped down on the beach.

"Anyone else want to challenge the champion?" Eric asked.

"He means me, of course!" Sara teased.

"How about you, Laurel? Wanna race?"

Laurel gave him a half smile. "No thanks."

Walt started talking, rather suddenly, Eric thought, about what they should do with the rest of the afternoon, in a transparent attempt to cover Laurel's embarrassment over not being a swimmer. He didn't realize that Eric's jibe had been intentional, his opening salvo in a battle to overcome the child's fear of the water.

Walt suggested a game of catch *(Dad, really!)*, and then a safari into the woods. This appealed to the girls, but Eric said he'd sit this one out. The three of them pulled on T-shirts and found their sneakers, then crossed the sand and passed through the line of evergreens bordering the meadow.

Eric rose and walked back to where Deanna and Fran were relaxing at the edge of the grass. Still somewhat out of breath, he lowered himself gingerly beside them. "I'll bet there's a dolphin somewhere in Sara's gene pool," he said, then turned his attention toward Fran. He was thinking of Walt's quick intervention when he challenged Laurel to a race. "Walt's somewhat protective of Laurel when it comes to her not swimming, isn't he?"

"Not really," Fran answered. "Well, maybe. It's just that he knows it embarrasses her, and so he tries to avoid the subject. He used to push her pretty hard to learn, and it backfired. It really upset their relationship for a while."

"That's a shame," Deanna said. "She's missing out on some real fun. And every kid should know how, for their own safety."

"I know, and we've tried. Maybe we started too late. Or maybe it's because a neighbor child drowned a few years back."

"She told me about that last June," Eric put in, "but I didn't realize how much it had affected her."

"Anyway," Fran went on, "please don't say anything to her. We hope someday she'll overcome her fear, but for right now, any mention of learning to swim makes her very unhappy."

For the next hour the three of them talked about a variety of subjects, and got to know each other better, but Eric's subconscious mind was chewing on this new problem. Such an irrational fear didn't seem consistent with the rest of Laurel's personality, especially in view of the courage she had displayed during their escape two months back. Despite Fran's request that he ignore the subject, he began formulating a plan.

Three

The three friends' conversation was interrupted by the sudden and noisy arrival of the girls as they burst out of the woods and came running across the sand. Walt followed some paces behind, under the burden of a red canvas backpack that he hadn't had when they left.

"Look what we found!" Sara called out. "Somebody must've lost their backpack. Some kid, a boy probably." They reached the three adults, then turned and waited impatiently for Walt to catch up.

"Found a treasure, did you?" Deanna commented. As Walt came closer and dropped his load, she realized that the backpack looked almost new, not, as she had expected, old or faded from being left out in the woods for any length of time. "Anything special in it?"

"It's a bit of a mystery," Walt said, setting it down carefully and squatting beside it. "There's some clothes, about right for a boy their age," he gestured toward the girls, "and some of those Pokemon cards, soap and toothbrush and stuff, too." He paused for effect. "And a Harry Potter novel and a Nintendo Game Boy."

"Not likely a kid would lose something like that," Eric commented. "And more important, what would a boy that age be doing up here anyway? Not very many people know about this place, and there are no paths to it. The only ways in are by water or a really long trek through the forest, with no clear trail to follow."

"Sometimes there are camping groups that go exploring out of the national park," Deanna said.

"It's a pretty rough hike through uncleared forest, though, especially for kids. It's too far for a day trip." He turned to the girls. "Did you see any sign of a camp site?"

"Nope. Just the backpack, sitting half in plain sight under a bush."

"There were some marks in the grass, sort of flattened out," Walt said. "It almost looked like someone had dragged it. Or an animal, maybe."

"Did you see anything else?" Eric asked.

"I didn't take time to look. These two were too excited to get back here and show you."

Eric was troubled. An obviously new backpack, abandoned in an almost inaccessible part of the forest, could mean another lost child. He rose stiffly and retrieved his cell phone from the tent.

"Who are you going to call?" Deanna asked.

"Jim Carmichael, I think." Carmichael was their town's police chief, as well as a good friend. "If there's been a report of a lost kid, he'll probably know about it." Eric punched the numbers and got the town hall voice mail. He waited for the recorded instructions, then pressed "3" to get the police desk. He asked the duty sergeant for Carmichael, and presently the chief came on the line.

"Jim, Eric Kelman here. We've got a puzzle for you." He relayed details of their find, and waited while Carmichael checked the reports on his desk.

"Nothing about any lost kid here, Eric," Jim came back on the line. "Everything's been pretty quiet, and a missing person, especially a child, would raise some serious alarms. Did you try the ranger station at the park?"

"Not yet. Figured I'd check with you first."

"Okay, sit tight and I'll look into it for you. What's your number there?"

Eric gave him the number of his cell phone, and they exchanged pleasantries for another minute before hanging up. He turned to the others. "Jim said he'd call the park, and get back to us if there's anything to report. And right now I want some supper. My tremendous victory in the water against overwhelming odds made me really hungry."

"*Your* victory!" Sara blurted. "I don't remember you beating anybody!"

"You're not under the mistaken impression that you beat *me*, are you?" Eric teased her. They argued their way good-naturedly back toward the tents, followed by the others, and soon all were busily putting together a typical camp meal of hot dogs and beans.

Jim Carmichael called back while they were eating. According to the park rangers, no one had reported any missing kids. Aside from individual families, there were three organized groups using the park that weekend: a mixed-gender scout campout, an Airstream trailer rally, and a day camp for pre-schoolers. The rangers had checked with the leaders of all three, and none had shown any concern over missing charges.

"Anyone report a missing backpack?" Eric asked him.

"I asked them specifically," Jim replied. "No luck. How long do you figure it's been out there?"

"Couldn't have been long," Eric replied. "It's bright red and new looking, and there's no sign it's been rained on. It can't have been out here much more than a few days."

"I'll try the ranger station again in the morning. Just hang on to it, will you? If they've had any missing person or property reports by then, I'll tell them to take a look at what you've found."

"Thanks, Jim. We'll be heading home in a couple of days. You can get me at the house after that." Eric disconnected and folded up the phone. "Guess that's that," he said. "We'll take the backpack with us when we leave, and drop it off with the rangers when we pass the park gate." But he was still uneasy, and decided that the next day, he would get Walt to show him where they had found the backpack, and then check out the surrounding area.

Hastily they cleaned up after the meal, accompanied by another noisy argument between Sara and Eric over who was responsible for washing the dishes. There was still plenty of daylight left when they finished. They all tossed a ball around, and a frisbee, and then decided to take to the water again.

This time Fran and Deanna decided to join in, and they all quickly changed to swimsuits and plunged into the lake. The water seemed especially warm, in contrast to the cool evening air. Only Laurel remained aloof, staying timidly in the shallows by herself.

Eric watched with deep affection as his wife entered the water. In her maturity, Deanna remained a beautiful and charming woman, thanks in part to good genes and a healthy respect for proper nutrition, but due mostly to her strength of character. Radiant intelligence lighted her eyes, and her warm smile invited friendship and trust. In every respect she was, to use an old-fashioned expression, a *good person*.

At barely five-foot-four, Fran MacKenzie was slight and almost fragile in appearance, much like her daughter. At barely a hundred pounds, only her softly rounded limbs saved her from scrawniness. Her triangular face made her appear much younger than thirty-three, as did the frilly, feminine two-piece swimsuit she wore, size three.

Despite his mostly desk-bound profession, Walt was an avid weekend athlete, adept at most sports. He played in a local softball league, and enjoyed both squash and racquetball with his coworkers. His trim hips and muscular shoulders suggested a careful attention to conditioning, a concern he shared with Eric.

By contrast, Laurel seemed destined to be a carbon copy of her mother, inheriting little of her physique from her tall, robust father. Her blue and white checked swimsuit was conservatively cut. With small ruffles around the legs and a little lace between her small breasts, it seemed styled for a much younger child. Only her very tiny waist, and the way it accentuated the developing feminine flare of her gently rounded hips, hinted that she was entering adolescence.

Eric stood quietly for a couple of minutes and glanced back and forth between Laurel and Sara, contemplating the contrast between the two children and marveling at their continuing friendship. Physically they were worlds apart, but seemed to be a perfect fit emotionally. Although only a few months older than her friend, Sara had matured much more quickly. Her hormones had kicked in at age ten, and she was now almost inappropriately voluptuous. Her competition tank suit molded a surprisingly full figure, somehow out of context with the innocence of her open, child-like face.

Sara and the others were boisterously engaged in a game of frisbee keep-away, churning the water and splitting the evening air with their shouts and squeals. Eric turned from his thoughts and joined in with enthusiasm.

Sara was completely at home in the water, just as Laurel was on top of it. As Walt caught the spinning disk, Sara leaped out of the water and tore it from his grasp, and he grabbed her around the waist and plunged her head first under the surface and dropped her. She executed a neat underwater back flip and yanked his feet out from under him, then came up laughing, the frisbee grasped triumphantly in her hand.

Walt surfaced sputtering, and took off after her, but she sailed the frisbee to Deanna and dove out of sight, neatly avoiding his grasp. As he looked around for her, she surfaced directly behind him and jumped on his back, overbalancing him and ducking him again.

Eric glanced behind him at Laurel, sitting somewhat disconsolately near the shore. It wasn't hard to guess the source of her depression. Although not exactly jealous of her friend's aquatic expertise, she felt sorely left out, especially when excluded from games with her beloved dad.

After about fifteen minutes, Eric left the fun and joined her near the beach, feigning fatigue. "You've got the right idea, runt. They play too rough for me."

"Yeah, right." Laurel didn't bother to try to cover up her listlessness, not even rising to the bait of the annoying nickname.

Eric sat quietly in the shallows for a couple of minutes. Then, ignoring Walt's request that he avoid the topic of swimming, he decided to stir up a little trouble if he could. "Do you want to see a trick?" he asked.

Laurel turned a gloomy face toward him. "I guess so. What is it?"

He got up out of the water and walked over to the tents, then returned with a clear plastic straw. "Watch."

He dipped the straw vertically into the lake, nearly covering it, then put his finger over the end. He drew it out completely and held it up in front of her face. "What do you see?"

"Duh! A straw full of water. So what?" In her present unhappy mood, she was not inclined to be patronized.

"So how come the water doesn't run out?"

"Air pressure or something. You've got your finger over the end, so no air can get in the top, and that makes a vacuum when the water tries to run out, so it can't. Magic, huh?" she said sarcastically, immune to what she saw as his attempt to cheer her up.

"Wow! Smart kid!" Eric teased. Laurel regarded him with a barely tolerant expression. "Now watch this."

He released his finger and the straw emptied in a rush. Then he covered the end again and stuck the straw back into the water. "What do you see now?"

Laurel was becoming curious in spite of herself. She knew Eric well enough to know that he really was going somewhere with all of this. She peered at the straw through the clear water. "A straw full of air. And before you ask me, it's because of air pressure again. The air in the straw keeps the water from coming in the bottom. That's third grade stuff. So what's the trick?"

"Your straws work the same way."

"My what?" Now she was plainly puzzled and intrigued. "I don't have any straws."

"Sure you do, two in fact. We all do." He touched the tip of her nose.

Laurel wrinkled her nose and laughed. "So I suppose you want me to suck water up my nose? That's gross! Besides, it feels really awful."

"Is that why you haven't learned to swim? Hate to get water up your nose?"

Laurel stiffened and looked away from him. She stared down into the water and began sifting pebbles through her fingers, ignoring him.

Eric spoke very softly. "Nothing to be ashamed of, Laurel. I didn't learn how until I was almost thirty-five."

She flared. "That's a lie! You swim like a fish."

"Now, maybe. Not then, until somebody showed me the trick. Then I learned how, really fast."

"I don't care. I can't swim, and I don't ever want to learn." She turned her attention back to the sand and pebbles.

Eric kept his mouth shut. He lay down on his back and skidded outward through the shallows until the water was deep enough to cover his prone form. Then he turned over to stare at her, only his eyes and the top of his head visible. He waited patiently, blowing bubbles noisily out through his nose.

Laurel steadfastly ignored him as long as she could, then began to giggle uncontrollably. "You look like a frog!"

Eric scissored his arms and legs, and propelled himself forward in a frog kick, provoking more giggles. Then he exaggerated the bubbles, making a racket with each exhalation. Finally he stuck his nose up out of the water and pointed to it. "See? Straws! As long as I keep the air pressure in them, no water can get in."

Her face fell again. "I can't do that."

"No, I suppose you can't. Out of six billion people in the world, Laurel MacKenzie is the only one who can't blow out through her nose."

"Stop it! I just don't *want* to, okay?" she shouted. "I know what you're trying to do, and it won't work, so please just leave me alone."

Her eyes flashed and she glared at him. Eric pulled himself upright, favoring his injured leg slightly, and moved a dozen yards downstream, where he sat down once again in the shallows and gazed out over the lake.

Four

Laurel continued sifting listlessly through the sand, occasionally sneaking a look at Eric out of the corner of her eye. Finally she sighed, stood up, and waded over to him. She plopped down next to him, as close as she could get without touching him.

"I'm sorry I yelled at you." Her softest, tiniest voice.

Eric turned and smiled at her. "I'm sorry, too. I guess I pushed you a little too hard." They sat silently for a while, good friends in spite of the friction between them. They watched the raucous game still in progress out in the lake. Then he continued, "Know why I did it?"

"I guess so. You're like my dad. He always says, 'You're missing out on all the fun.' But I wish he'd just leave me alone."

"He only does it because he loves you, and wants you to get everything out of life that you can. And he especially doesn't like to see you afraid of anything." Eric paused. "And neither do I."

"I can't help it. I tried. I really did. I'm just a coward, I guess."

"Sure you are! And I'm a three-toed bullfrog!"

A small half smile crossed her face as she stared down into the water, remembering his absurd bubble-blowing a few minutes before.

"You and I came through a lot last June, runt," he continued seriously. "And whatever else you were then, you definitely were *not* a coward."

"I'm not a runt, either. And swimming's different."

"How come?"

She looked him straight in the eye. "The water hurts when it goes up my nose, and I can't seem to keep from getting scared, and that makes it worse, and I can't seem to think. Dad says I thrash around like a hooked fish."

Eric drew himself up importantly, adopting a stately, professorial bearing. "'The only thing we have to fear is fear itself!'" he quoted.

"Hah! F.D.R., right? During some war, or was it the Depression?"

"You've got it. And you know about the Depression, do you? I thought the schools weren't teaching kids much any more."

"I didn't learn that in school. I *told* you I read a lot. It's all in a book Dad gave me about history and stuff. I like learning about the way things were in the old days."

"Hey! Watch that! I was born in those 'old days' of yours."

She stared at him in amazement. Like most twelve-year-olds, she had only a superficial concept of the passage of time, and the placement of events in history. "Were you really alive back then?"

"Darn right I was. In fact, I was alive when they invented dirt."

"You're teasing me again."

"Okay, the last part was a slight exaggeration. But I really have been around for a lot of years, since Franklin Roosevelt was President, in fact. And he was right about fear. That's what you're really afraid of, not the water."

"Wow! You *are* old!" She was teasing, but also partly serious.

Eric fell silent in amusement, letting her contemplate his immense age. Finally he spoke in a quiet and measured voice, seemingly changing the subject.

"Remember last June, when you found my cabin, and then ran off when you saw me coming?" Laurel remained silent. "Can't say I blame you. I hadn't shaved in days, and I guess I looked pretty rough. After what you went through, you were right not to trust me at first." He paused, but she still didn't respond.

"Then later, when the storm hit and we both ended up in the cabin, you figured out all by yourself how to tell whether it was safe to be there with me. Remember?"

"Yeah. So what?"

"So then you decided to trust me. And now we're friends ever since, right?"

She turned her small face toward him, looking solemn. "Uh huh."

"A few minutes ago, I told you I didn't learn to swim until I was an adult. What I didn't tell you is that up to then, I had always been afraid of the water. But I'm telling you now."

She looked concerned. "I didn't think you were ever afraid of anything."

"Everyone is afraid of something, sometimes. And the thing they're most often afraid of is telling someone else that they're afraid. But that's the sort of thing you can always tell a good friend, just like I told you."

"I'm not really afraid of the water. I just don't like it."

Eric smiled at her and said nothing. She wouldn't meet his eyes. Finally she said, in her smallest voice, "Well, maybe I'm afraid of it just a little."

"No, you're right. Just like Roosevelt said, you're sort of afraid of being afraid. It isn't really the water that gets to you. It's the way you don't feel in control of things when you try to swim. Right?"

"I guess." She thought about it a moment. "Yeah. That's really it, isn't it?"

"What were you afraid of last June, when you found my cabin?"

"That was different. That Richard guy was *after* me." Laurel's kidnapper had tied her and beaten her before she escaped from him, and then he had gone after both of them as they made their way through miles of forest back toward the main road.

"So what did you do when Richard knocked me out?" Laurel hadn't run away. With courage beyond her years, she had stayed hidden nearby until she could help Eric outwit their tormentor.

Laurel sighed. "I couldn't just leave you there."

"Well, I'll be darned!" Eric postured. "Faced your fear and beat it, did you? Imagine that. Pretty good for a little runt."

Laurel grimaced, and then caught sight of his kind smile. She sighed again. "Okay, I get it. Another one of your object lessons. But that was still different from being scared of the water."

"It's no fun being afraid, is it?"

"Nope."

"And we're still friends, aren't we?"

Laurel shrugged and bumped her small shoulder shyly against his arm.

"And you still trust me, don't you? Enough to see if my straw trick really works, maybe?"

She sat quietly. Eric didn't say a word, just waited. Finally she stirred, rolled over on her stomach and pushed backward into slightly deeper water. "Show me what to do."

"Just breathe out through your nose."

"But I'm afraid to put my face under water. It feels really gross."

"Try this. Pinch your nostrils shut." Laurel did so. "Now try to blow out through your nose."

She tried, turning red in the face with effort, her eyes crossing slightly. Eric laughed at her, and she joined in.

"Now think about it. The air couldn't get out past your fingers, in spite of all that pressure inside. Your fingers kept it in, and that works both ways. How the heck can any water get *in* if you're forcing all that air *out*? Think about the straw. I wasn't even blowing through it, just keeping my finger over the end, but no water got in because of the air inside. Watch."

He pinched his nose shut and put his face in the water. Then he lifted his head, removed his fingers, and lowered his face again while blowing out. Bubbles streamed past his cheeks.

He raised his head. "See? Same result, fingers or no fingers. As you said so eloquently, the magic of air pressure." He waited again.

Tentatively Laurel lowered her face toward the water, letting it cover her mouth. She closed her eyes, snorted in an exaggerated manner through her nose, and plunged below the surface for a couple of seconds, and came right out again. She looked surprised.

"Any water up your nose?"

"Nope."

"Told you so."

She tried it again, staying down a bit longer, but this time she panicked and inhaled slightly as she lifted her head. She sputtered, shaking her head. "Ugh!"

"Not so good that time," Eric said. "So I suppose you're going to give up now." Laurel glared at him. "No? Okay, this time, don't breathe out so fast. It only takes a little bit of air to keep the water out, and you can stay down as long as you have any air left. Just breathe out real slow, and be sure you don't breathe in until you get your face all the way back out."

Determinedly, Laurel took a deep breath and began exhaling slowly, then lowered her face again, her eyes squeezed tightly shut. After ten seconds she showed no sign of coming back up. Eric saw the tension drain out of her small body. Then she began waving her arms behind her back. *Look! Look what I'm doing!*

Eric laughed as she shot back up out of the water. "I can *do* it! I was down for *hours* and I didn't get any water up my nose at all!" She gasped and plunged her face back down again, came up for air, then did it again. "Wow! That's not so hard."

"Oh, yeah? That's only the first step. Now that you've got control of your nose, you have to get your arms and legs coordinated, and learn how to float, and..."

"I can *do* all that! Show me! Show me!"

For the next hour, until the sun had set and the others had abandoned the lake for the warmth of a camp fire, Eric patiently guided Laurel through the basics of swimming, "pseudo piscine propulsion," he told her, and was rewarded by her silvery laughter. Even at twelve, lack of vocabulary wasn't one of her problems.

Laurel's slight frame had little buoyancy in the clear fresh water, and her tension worked against her. At first Eric held her firmly to give her confidence, until she grasped the concept of keeping afloat by holding air in her lungs. Gradually reassured by his strong support, and trusting him completely, she began to relax. Finally she accepted the fact that with her lungs full of air, she couldn't sink.

He moved around in front of her and supported her lightly at the points of her shoulders. He showed her how to breathe through her mouth by tilting her head sideways out of the water. Then they moved on to kicking her feet, keeping her knees nearly straight. With only his lightest touch beneath her shoulders to give her confidence, she found she was actually able to move forward.

Next he showed her a simple overhand stroke with her arms. She caught on quickly and was soon making progress, awkwardly at first but with growing assurance. At her insistence, they moved out to deeper water, up to Eric's neck and over Laurel's head. A couple of times she failed to clear the water when she tilted her head to breathe, and inhaled a mouthful. Eric was quick to catch her as she began to flail her arms. The second time it happened, he lifted her upright and held her vertically so her head was above the surface, letting her rest.

"The next time that happens, I'm not going to catch you," he said, "but I'll be right here beside you. You have to learn to recover by yourself. Just remember that you can't sink, because there's still some air in your lungs, and that will keep you up until you get control again. Don't wave your arms around. Do the stroke thing, and it will lift your face right out of the water."

She looked at him uncertainly. "But what if I *do* sink?"

"Then I'll just stand here and watch you," he pretended seriousness, "as you go down for the third time. I wonder how I'll explain it to your mother and father, though, if I let you drown? Oh, well, I'll think of something..."

She giggled and squirmed in his grip. "Let me go! I can *do* this!"

He lifted her halfway out of the water and placed her prone again, not letting go until she was kicking and stroking. For a couple of minutes she coordinated everything perfectly, then missed her timing and tried to lift her head at the same time as her opposite arm broke the surface. She started to thrash, and he reached out and tapped her shoulder lightly to let her know he was still right there.

Laurel regained control. She kicked strongly and dug her arms in deeply, lifting her head high. She sputtered and spit, then inhaled a great lungful of air, took three more strokes and breathed successfully again. Her momentum carried her several yards away from Eric. She managed to turn and thrashed her way back to him, catching him around the neck. "How's that? How's that?" she laughed excitedly, spraying water in his face.

"Pretty good. But I think I'm sinking. Quick, save yourself!"

Eric bent his knees and settled lower in the water. As it closed over the top of his head, she released her hold on his neck and stroked away on her own. He surfaced behind her and watched as she managed to coordinate everything well enough to get closer to shore, until she could stand up on her own. Then she turned and splashed her way back into the deeper water, eager for more lessons.

She delighted in each new success, laughed at her setbacks, and had to be dragged from the water when it became too dark to see. Seated by the campfire and wrapped warmly in a blanket, she bored everyone immensely, especially Sara, as she chattered endlessly about how *easy* it was to learn to swim.

Eric sat quietly and listened to her childish enthusiasm, as proud of her accomplishment as she was. *A small victory, to take the fear out of the next challenge. Well done, runt.*

As the air cooled, they drew in closer to the fire. "I had a pretty creepy experience once, when I was learning to swim," Walt said.

"What happened, Dad?"

He leaned forward confidentially. "I was just about your age when I went to scout camp for a week one July. We stayed in tents, and the second night we were there, we had this great big campfire, and we all sat around it like we're doing here, and the counselors told us some ghost stories. Then, when the fire was burning down low, one of the counselors, I'll never forget him, his name was Joshua, and he had almost black eyes and these big dark eyebrows, and when he used to look at you, cold shivers ran down your back... Anyway, Joshua said he had a *true* story to tell us."

Walt hunched forward and dropped his voice to a low, conspiratorial murmur. The others leaned in to hear him better. "It seems that the summer before, one of the scouts had disappeared from his tent on the very first night. They organized a search party in the morning, and they looked all over for him, but the only thing they found was his sneakers, right at the edge of the lake."

Sara was clinging to every word. "Did he drown?"

Walt continued, lowering his voice even more. "They never found out for sure, Joshua said." Laurel and Sara squirmed excitedly and edged over closer to him. "Anyway, the second night, when we were all in our tents and supposed to be asleep, we heard somebody crying, out near the lake. I was too scared to go out and look, but two of the other guys did. They woke up the counselors, and they all went down and looked around the lake, but by then the crying had stopped. I got over being scared and went out, too. We looked everywhere, but we couldn't find anybody. After about a half hour, they made us all go back to our tents."

"So what happened?" Sara's eyes were huge and round in the flickering light from the fire.

"That's when the really *creepy* stuff started."

"What, Dad?" Laurel was quivering with excitement.

"Well, we all tried to go back to sleep, and I guess almost everybody else did, because it got real quiet, but I was still awake, and I heard this *voice...*"

"What voice? What did it say?"

"It came from outside the tent, down by the lake, and it just kept saying the same thing, over and over." Walt added a light, singsong quality to his voice. "'Come on in, the water's fine... Come on in, the water's fine.'"

"Wow! What did you do?"

"Nothing! I buried my head in my sleeping bag and covered up my ears, but I could still hear that voice, over and over. 'Come on in, the water's fine,' over and over again. The next morning, I thought I had been dreaming, but when we all got up and started to make breakfast, somebody noticed that one of the scouts was missing.

"We organized another search, and we spent the whole morning going all around the lake, and in the woods, and everything, but we couldn't find him. The only trace of him was a pair of sneakers, right beside the lake, right where Joshua said they found the first pair the summer before. And that night, after everyone was asleep, I heard that voice again. 'Come on in, the water's fine.'"

Laurel was wiggling nervously by Walt's side. "You didn't go out there, did you?"

"Not *me*," Walt replied. "But I heard some of the others get out of their tents and go down by the lake to see what was happening. I just squeezed my eyes shut and covered my ears, and finally I went back to sleep.

"The next morning, three more scouts and a counselor were gone! And down by the lake, there were *four pairs* of sneakers, all lined up in a row. The rest of us didn't stay around there any longer. We packed up our tents and gear and got out of there, *fast*. The next week they closed the lake and put a big chain-link fence all around it, and nobody's been back there since."

"Did they ever find the missing scouts?"

"Not even one of them," Walt said in a hoarse whisper. "But the next summer, in another lake in the same county, some campers reported hearing that voice again: 'Come on in…' They'd heard about the scouts, of course, and they got out of there real fast. And ever since then, there have been reports from one lake after another, all from people hearing the same voice, over and over, 'Come on in, the water's fine…'"

Laurel was finally becoming skeptical. "This is an urban legend, right? Like the escaped convict with the hook instead of a hand, that got caught in the door handle of the car when the teenagers drove away? It didn't really happen, right?"

Walt raised his eyebrows knowingly. "Believe what you want. But remember, I was *there*..."

Sara looked apprehensively at her friend. "He's kidding us, isn't he?"

"Sure he is," Laurel said confidently. But Eric noticed that several times over the next half hour, both girls glanced uneasily over their shoulders at the dark forest beyond the clearing.

By eleven the girls' endurance failed, and they squirmed into their tent. The adults listened to their giggles and chatter grow gradually fainter, until they fell completely silent, exhausted after a very full day.

"All right," Walt said finally. "How did you do it?"

"Do what?" Eric pretended ignorance; he knew exactly what his friend meant.

"I've paid the best teachers I could find, and they spent *weeks* trying to teach her what you accomplished in one evening. How?"

"Maybe they were teaching her the wrong things."

Walt and Fran looked at him with puzzled expressions, although Deanna smiled. She knew his techniques well, the same ones that had earned him a solid reputation for quality teaching at the university. Eric possessed keen insight, and the ability to see beneath the surface of a problem to the underlying, often hidden causes.

"It wasn't really the water she was afraid of, not exactly," he continued, "although I think that the two-year-old that drowned a while back disturbed her even more than she herself realized. Then she had a few setbacks when she first started to learn, and she decided she couldn't do it, no matter what. She set herself up for failure, and made it come true. Self-fulfilling prophecy, and all that..."

"Assuming that's right," Fran asked, "how did you get her past it?"

"*I* didn't do anything; *she* did. I just helped her to see what was really bothering her. Oh, and I reminded her of what she was capable of. I gave her another challenge, that's all, and once she faced up to it, the rest was easy. Then I showed her the basic principles, and she caught on quickly."

"But how did you know it would work?" Walt asked.

"I didn't, for sure. But her fear just didn't seem consistent with the courage I saw in her last June, or the competence that she showed today out in the canoe."

"There's something else," Fran added. "She obviously trusts you completely."

"Well," Eric answered, "most kids pay more attention to other people than they do to their own parents. I know our two sure did."

The conversation turned gradually to other topics, and it was long after midnight before they retired to their tents. Eric and Deanna slipped into their sleeping bags, and as he reached to turn down the lantern, she whispered to him, "Swallowed a big canary, didn't you?"

"Huh?"

"Don't play dumb with me. You've got yellow feathers and a smug grin a mile wide on that handsome mouth of yours. You did what nobody else could do, and your ego is as big as a barn right now."

Eric laughed softly, keeping his voice low so the MacKenzies couldn't hear him in the adjacent tent. "It didn't show, did it?"

"No, at least not much. As usual, you managed just the right blend of dignity and humility. That big red 'S' on your chest did stick out a little, though."

He smiled at how well his wife knew him. "Small victories, my sweet, and small satisfactions. At my age, I have to take them however they come." They kissed warmly and closed their eyes.

Eric was dozing lightly when a piercing scream echoed off the lake, immediately followed by several more. Almost instantly he was out of the tent, followed closely by Deanna. Laurel and Sara were hopping up and down in front of their pup tent, arms clasped about each other. They were screaming and pointing at several objects on the ground. Fran hurried toward them, fright and concern masking her face. Only Walt seemed disinterested, squatting beside his own tent with a half smile on his face.

Lined up in front of the girls' tent, a dozen yards from the flap, were two pairs of old sneakers, soaking wet and covered with seaweed. Sara was babbling incoherently, and Laurel was only slightly more understandable.

"We heard it! We heard *the voice!*"

"It was right outside the tent, and it kept saying, 'Come on in... Come on in... The water's fine...'" They squealed and clung to each other.

Fran glared at Walt. In the light from the dying campfire, his face resembled a smug Buddha. "Stop it, girls! Settle down! It was only your father."

"It *wasn't*, Mom!" Laurel protested. "It was this real creepy, high voice, and it made me want to go out to the lake! Honest! And what about those sneakers?"

Walt could no longer contain himself. "Was it like this?" He raised the pitch of his voice and crooned, *'Come on in… The water's fiiiine.'*

"Dad!" Laurel hated being tricked. She stamped her bare foot and glowered at him, while Sara still trembled uncertainly beside her.

Fran shook her head, laughing in spite of herself. "Get back to bed. There are no voices, and your dad probably got those sneakers from the Good Will store. And he and I are going to have a *long* discussion about this, scaring the wits out of all of us like that in the middle of the night!"

Walt couldn't resist. *"Come on in, Fran… The water's fine…"*

"That'll be quite enough. Now scram, you two, into the tent."

Laurel and Sara reluctantly disappeared through the tent flap. Walt was unsuccessfully trying to stifle his laughter, almost in tears, and it quickly became infectious. Soon all four adults were laughing uncontrollably.

Laurel stuck her head out of the tent. "Big joke! I suppose you were all in on it, right?" She flounced back inside and let the flap fall shut.

Fran recovered first. "And just how long have you been planning this?" she asked her husband.

"Long enough to have smuggled those old sneakers into my duffel bag before we left home."

"And just who's going to deal with those two when they have nightmares for the next six months?"

"Why, you are, my sweet, you and Sara's mom. That's what mothers are for."

Five

Troubled anew by the pain in his weakened leg, due no doubt to his exertions in the water the day before, Eric was up and out of the tent before sunrise. He exercised his sore muscles with a couple of circuits around the shore of the lake, and had the camp stove warmed up and the coffee brewing by the time the others woke up.

Deanna appeared next as the first rays of sunlight penetrated the lower branches off to the east. They were savoring their first cups of coffee when Fran and Walt emerged, and they all gathered around the camp stove, enjoying its heat in the brisk morning air.

"That water looks inviting," Walt said, looking out over the lake. "I'm amazed at how warm it felt last night."

"You might not think so if you went in right now," Eric said. "Everything's relative. In contrast to the night air, and especially after all that exercise we were getting, it felt good. But it's a different story after a night in a warm tent."

Fran was mixing pancake batter when Laurel and Sara burst out of the pup tent together, already in their swimsuits, and headed for the lake.

"Hey," Deanna called, "how about some breakfast?"

"In a minute," Laurel called back. "I have to see if I can still do it!" She and Sara started to run.

"You'll be sorry," Eric shouted after her as they plunged into the water.

They came up sputtering and gasping. "Cold! Holy cow!"

"Kids think they know everything," Eric complained, and Deanna just laughed at him. He turned his attention to the stove, and soon had heaps of pure cholesterol sizzling in the pan: scrambled eggs, sausages and bacon to go with Fran's pancakes. *When it comes to diets or health, camp food doesn't count,* he thought.

There was soon more food ready than any of them ever ate at home, but Eric knew they'd clean most of it up in short order. Fran called the girls as she flipped the last of the pancakes, and they came reluctantly out of the water.

Sara seemed almost as excited as Laurel over her friend's new prowess in the water. It was one more thing they could share. She bubbled over with suggestions, all the neat strokes she could show Laurel how to do, almost too excited to eat. They wolfed down everything that was on their plates, and then begged to go back in the water. Fearing cramps, Fran tried to make them wait, but after ten minutes of hearing their complaints, she relented.

Sara enthusiastically assumed the role of Laurel's swimming coach, much to Eric's relief. The four adults watched them for a short time as they finished their meal. Laurel took her lessons seriously, copying Sara's example carefully.

She made rapid progress. Every so often her coordination failed her, and she inhaled a mouthful of water. Instead of panicking, however, she always came up laughing. Eric noted with satisfaction that she was progressing beyond the basic crawl he had shown her the previous evening. Her head bobbed up and down in a comical parody of a graceless breaststroke, but he could tell she was rapidly getting the hang of it.

He turned to Walt. "Feel like a walk?"

"I'm not sure I can even get up, much less move around after all that food. What's on your mind?"

Eric gazed back toward the forest. "I'd like to take a look at the place where you found that backpack."

"What do you expect to find?" Walt asked.

"I'm not sure. Maybe nothing. Or maybe some hint as to who might have left it. Anyway, it kept me awake last night thinking about it. No kid that age would be likely to forget where he left his Game Boy."

Walt patted his stomach and got to his feet. "Okay, let's take a look. But it's probably a fool's errand." He turned to his wife. "Don't let those two get too far from shore. Our little water baby might be getting a trifle too overconfident."

"I'll keep her close," Fran answered.

The two men crossed the meadow and entered the woods. Walt had no trouble retracing the path he had blazed for the girls the day before. The area adjacent to the lake was mostly forested by conifers, and their acid kept the underbrush to a minimum, so the going was easy. Within fifteen minutes they reached a thick grove of alders and white birches, which then gave way to dense underbrush and a natural clearing beyond. As they came out into the open, Walt pointed to an area of flattened grass.

"That's where we found it. Sara spotted it first. You can see how it looks like it was dragged from somewhere."

Eric squatted and examined the grass, tracing the area of bent fronds backward into a thicket. He pushed the weeds and bushes aside.

"Here's where it was tossed, I think," he said. "Looks like claw marks in the dirt, too. My guess is some animal dragged it out, a raccoon maybe, even a bear, looking for something to eat." He stood up again. "Maybe the kid just lost it, but how come it ended up under the weeds in the first place?"

Eric considered the problem. "It's almost as if someone tried to hide it, isn't it?"

"Some kid playing a trick on one of his buddies?"

"Maybe." Eric feared the reason might be somewhat less innocent, and he stood with his hands on his hips, trying vainly to penetrate the dense ground cover with his eyes. "What do you say we beat the bushes a little, and see if anything else turns up?"

He and Walt began a more systematic examination of the clearing. They ranged out in a rough grid pattern, and on the third pass they noticed a broad area of flattened grass near the trees on the far side. Stooping to examine the ground more closely, Walt spotted some small holes that had been driven into the ground.

"There's part of the answer. Tents," he suggested. "You can see where they hammered in the pegs. "Somebody was camping here, and not very long ago." He walked the perimeter of the trampled zone, stopping occasionally to brush aside the tops of the weeds and grass. "Four tents, probably pop-ups."

Eric joined him. "Seems normal," he mused. "So maybe the backpack was simply lost, after all. Jim said there was some kind of scout troop camping in the park. Could have done an overnighter here, I suppose."

They continued on around the edge of the clearing and found no other areas of disturbance, but Eric discovered a rough trail blazed through the underbrush on the eastern side, leading off in the direction of the national park. "This looks like where they came from."

He knelt to look for footprints, and could make out scuffed traces of athletic shoes. "Sort of small feet," he went on, "smaller than ours, anyway." He rose again and looked back toward where the tents had been. The site was very clean, with no garbage or campfire remains. Once the grass recovered in another day or two, there would be little evidence of anyone's presence.

"Neat campers," Eric observed. "Nothing left behind. That suggests scouts, again, doesn't it? They teach them to look after the woods."

"I guess that solves the mystery," Walt agreed. "Somehow the kid just forgot the pack when they broke camp."

But Eric still felt uneasy, and stood looking left and right around the clearing. "It just doesn't make sense somehow. If this was one of the groups from the park, and somebody lost a backpack with something valuable inside, they would certainly have reported it to the ranger station. And then somebody would have come back looking for it. But Jim Carmichael said the rangers had no information about anything being reported missing."

"What other explanation could there be?"

"I don't know." Eric scuffed his feet at the spot where one of the tents had recently stood. Then he looked up. "Let's give the perimeter of the clearing a really close look, especially the underbrush. Maybe something else got left behind. I'll go the other way, and meet you back where we came out of the woods." They set off in opposite directions, and after about fifteen minutes of cursory searching, they reached the opposite side of the clearing.

"One more circuit," Eric suggested. "Let's go a little deeper into the woods this time, and really beat the bushes." Again they separated, and after just a couple of minutes, Walt shouted to his friend. Eric doubled back and came up to him.

Walt pointed to a wide, dense growth of low-growing yews, spread out about two dozen yards from the edge of the clearing. Barely visible, sticking out from under one of the prickly branches, they could see a buckle on the end of a canvas strap. Eric bent and pushed the branch aside, revealing a blue backpack of a design similar to the one they had found the day before.

He started to reach for it, planning to pull it out into the open, but then paused, thinking better of it. Instead he thrust his arms deeper into the yews, ignoring the scratchy growth, and widened the gap between the branches. Behind the blue backpack were several more, piled haphazardly together out of sight of any casual observer. Instead of being flat, they all appeared to be fairly full.

"Something has happened here," he said. "There's no way a bunch of scouts, or anybody else, would go off and leave all their stuff behind like this."

Walt peered over his shoulder. "Looks like five or six of them in there. Should we pull them out?"

Eric rocked back on his heels, considering. "I don't think so. We'd better get some official help up here. These things were deliberately hidden by someone, and there has to be a reason. If we disturb them, it might make it harder for the police to piece together what happened."

"You're right. We'd better let the rangers know about this, and let them sort it out."

Eric stood upright and let the yew branches fall back into place. "I wish I'd brought the cell phone with me. Let's get back and call in."

Walking quickly, it took them less than ten minutes to get back to the lake. As they came out of the woods, Deanna caught sight of them and hurried to meet them.

"Jim Carmichael called," she said, handing Eric the cell phone. "He wants you to call him right back. Something about some overdue campers out of the park."

"Thanks, dear," Eric replied. He snapped the phone open and started punching numbers, and Carmichael came on the line quickly. "What's up, Jim?"

"Thanks for calling back, Eric. I got hold of the rangers again, and there's been a development. Seems part of the scout group went on a two-night hike, and were supposed to be back by last night. As of this morning, there's been no sign of them."

"How many are missing?" Eric asked him.

"Three boys and three girls, plus two counselors. Nobody's too excited yet, but they are concerned. The scout leaders are out looking for them now. According to the leader, they were planning on camping somewhere to the north of your cabin."

"I think I know where." Eric told Jim about the clearing, the evidence of tents, and the cache of backpacks. "We left everything alone. I figured you'd want the experts to get first crack at whatever there is to find, so we didn't touch anything."

"You did the right thing. I'll get right on it," the police chief said. "Is there somewhere the rangers can meet you? They'll need you to show them where to look."

"It's north and west of our cabin. Tell them it's not far from the lagoon near the head of Shrewsbury Creek. They'll know where I mean. But it'll take them some time to get here." Eric thought for a minute. "Tell them there's room to land a copter. That's the fastest way. There's an open meadow on the west side where we're camped."

"Okay, Eric, stay put. It shouldn't take them too long to get a team in the air." Carmichael hung up, and Eric walked back to the tent. The others looked at him questioningly, and he relayed his conversation with the police chief.

"Nothing to do now but wait for them," he said. He gestured toward the lake, where Sara was showing Laurel the basic principles of the butterfly. "Not that we're likely to be going anywhere soon, anyway. At least not until those two seals get their fill of swimming."

They settled down near the shore to watch the girls at their play.

Six

Shortly before eleven, the slap of rotors approached from the southeast, and presently a forest service helicopter rose over the tree line and descended toward the meadow. The pilot skillfully avoided their tents and camping gear and set down a dozen yards from the shore. The campers were forced to shield their faces from the sand and dirt that swirled in the backwash from the blades.

As the copter's engine dropped to an idle, three rangers emerged. Eric recognized Al Kennedy from the aftermath of his and Laurel's June adventure. Kennedy introduced himself to the others, and then identified his companions. "This is Brent Scarsi, Eric. He's in charge of our station. And this is our pilot, Don Vidito."

"Nice to know you." They shook hands all around. As Kennedy turned, he caught sight of Laurel, trailing Sara out of the water.

"Hey, champ!" He called to her. "You up here to get the old professor out of trouble again?"

Laurel ran up to him excitedly, her expression a question mark. "What are you doing here?"

"Your dad and the Doc called us. It's about that backpack you two found in the woods."

"You'd better not call him Doc," she laughed, "or he'll bite your head off. I'll get it for you." Laurel and Sara ran to the tent, and came back with the red backpack. They dumped it at Kennedy's feet.

The rangers examined the exterior carefully, noting its almost-new appearance. There were no identifying marks or labels on the outside. Gingerly, Brent Scarsi opened the top flap. "Have any of you looked inside?" he asked.

"We all did, I'm afraid," Eric said. "We didn't have any reason to think it was anything but a lost pack. We handled everything."

"No need for gloves, then." Scarsi extracted the contents, one item at a time, and spread them out on the ground.

Everything was consistent with a young male camper's possessions. Each item of clothing carried a set of identifying initials in indelible ink on the label. There were basic toilet articles and a scout handbook. Otherwise the pack contained mostly treasures that would interest a young boy: trading cards, a yo-yo and, most puzzling of all, the expensive portable Nintendo Game Boy.

After making a list of the contents, Kennedy returned them to the backpack, and Don Vidito carried it over to the copter and put it inside.

Kennedy addressed Walt and Eric. "Where did you find the rest of them?"

"What rest?" Laurel was listening to them avidly.

Eric laughed uneasily. "These two have been in the water almost since sunup. They don't know about our little expedition." He turned to the girls. "Your dad and I went back into the woods this morning and looked around where you were yesterday. There are some more backpacks hidden away under some bushes out there, and signs that somebody was having a campout."

"We'd better get going," Kennedy said. "How far is it?"

"Ten or twelve minute walk."

"Wait for us!" Laurel and Sara shouted together, and ran to get their sneakers.

"They'd better stay here," Kennedy said to Eric. "We don't know what we'll find."

"As near as I can tell, there's no danger out there. The place is deserted now. I think they're entitled to come along, since they found the first backpack. Unless it's against some regulation, that is."

"I guess it's okay," Scarsi spoke up. "Just as long as they stay out of the way."

Laurel and Sara came running up, sneakers on but still in their swimsuits. "Hold on, you two," Fran cautioned them. "You'd better cover up some. You'll get scratched up pretty bad out in the bush."

"Oh, Mom!" The girls were bouncing on their toes in their eagerness to get going.

"We'll wait for you," Kennedy laughed, "but make it quick."

Five minutes later, Eric led them single file through the woods, followed directly by Al Kennedy. The other two rangers brought up the rear, with the girls sandwiched in the middle, now dressed in shorts and T-shirts. Walt remained at the camp this time.

With the trail now clearly defined and trampled down, they lost no time in reaching the clearing. They examined the area where the tents had been pitched, and identified the spot where the trail led off through the woods toward the parklands. Then Eric led them to the plot of yew bushes where the remainder of the backpacks had been secreted.

Scarsi and Kennedy put on gloves and carefully extracted the backpacks from the underbrush. One by one they examined them externally, just as they had done with the first one back by the lake. There appeared to be nothing unusual about any of them, although one was somewhat larger than the others. There were six in all.

Next they carefully laid out the contents, one at a time. The packs held an assortment of clothing, a handful of electronic games, various types of kid toys and collectibles, and the kind of personal items one would expect for an overnight hike. Like the red one back at Eric's camp, each of the backpacks held a scout handbook. All but the larger one were obviously the property of young campers, two boys and three girls, judging by the clothing.

The sixth backpack was somewhat different, aside from its greater volume. The clothing was appropriate to an older girl or young woman: adult size shorts, tops and underwear. In addition to the scout handbook, there was also a field guide, a compass, a fire-making kit, a manual of edible plants, and a handwritten list. Scarsi examined the list, which contained eight names.

"These names match the missing campers," he said, "six kids and two leaders, both older teenagers. But along with the backpack you found yesterday, there are only seven accounted for."

"Which one is missing?" Kennedy asked his superior.

"Looks to me like the other counselor's, the boy. Name's Stu Piersol, according to the list." Scarsi stood up and scanned the clearing. Then he turned his attention to the girls. "Where did you two find the other backpack?"

"Show you," Sara said, turning back the way they had come. With Laurel close behind, she led them to the spot where they had first entered the clearing, and pointed to the underbrush and the drag marks in the dirt and grass. The rangers bent to examine the spot, then retraced their steps to where the tents had been pitched.

After a slow, careful walk around the clearing, the rangers moved out of earshot of Eric and the girls. It was obvious to Eric that they had found something he and Walt had missed. After a few minutes, Kennedy called him over, but motioned for the girls to stay where they were. Laurel and Sara looked at each other questioningly, and then up at Eric. He squeezed Laurel's shoulder and tousled Sara's hair, then walked away from them and joined the waiting rangers.

"Something else, Al?" he asked as he neared the group.

Kennedy kept his voice low. "About a hundred yards to the east," he told Eric, "just beyond where you found the backpacks, there's some more disturbed dirt and grass. Looks like someone was messing around, maybe fighting. And there are drag marks, like heel prints from a pair of running shoes, going off into the bushes. We don't want the kids following us in there."

"No problem," Eric said. "I'll keep them busy." He made his way back as the rangers set off eastward toward the target area.

"What's up, Doc?" Laurel assailed him with her favorite tease.

"You will be. Upside down with your head in the lake if you don't stop calling me that."

"That doesn't scare me," she laughed. "I've always got my straws with me now."

Eric smiled at her. "Come on, brats. Let's see if we can find anything else the campers left behind." He led them northwest to a far corner of the clearing, making a show of looking through the tall reeds that circled a somewhat swampy area on the northern rim. All the while he kept track of the rangers, watching the spot where they had entered the woods.

Scarsi and Kennedy returned to the site of the disturbed dirt and grass, and had no trouble finding footprints leading further into the trees. The undergrowth thickened about fifty yards from the clearing, and they could see where someone had forced a pathway through some dense bushes. Keeping their eyes on the ground, they followed suit, and Kennedy soon spotted a pile of loose pine branches, out of place among the shrubs. Then he caught sight of a bit of khaki-colored cloth and some bare skin, just visible at the far edge of the pile.

A girl's body lay face down on the ground, almost completely covered by loose branches. Her medium brown hair was disheveled and lay across her partially exposed left cheek. The two men carefully lifted the concealing branches and held them aside.

Scarsi quickly ascertained that she was dead. There was some evidence of interference with the body, probably by some scavenging animals. He made a cursory visual inspection, noting the deep red welts on her neck, just above her collar, and the unnatural angle of her head. Her arms were bruised and filthy.

Kennedy squatted beside the body. "God, I hate this!" he exclaimed. "What was she, sixteen or seventeen? The missing counselor, I suppose. Sex thing?"

"I doubt it," Scarsi replied. "No sign of her clothes being disturbed, shorts still on, blouse tucked in." He could see the outline of her bra beneath her top, and panty lines clearly defined where the shorts were stretched over her buttocks. "Not likely somebody'd rape her, then put all her clothes back on just to kill her anyway. Looks like a struggle, though, and probably strangulation." He debated turning the girl over, then decided against it. "Better leave it for the lab boys. The less we mess around, the easier it will be for them to tell what and when, maybe even who."

They stood and surveyed the scene sadly, looking for any other sign of what might have happened. Finding nothing physical, they turned their attention to the footprints and other marks in the soil and foliage. They retraced their steps and came out into the clearing once more, paying additional attention to the ground as they walked.

Eric saw them emerge and head back in the direction of their makeshift trail. He could tell from their expressions that the news was not good. Sara and Laurel could also see that something was wrong, and they looked at the rangers expectantly.

"We need to speak with you privately," Scarsi told Eric. The girls looked back and forth between the two of them.

"Whatever it is, these two will hear about it eventually," Eric said. "I think it's better if they hear it now."

Scarsi looked at Kennedy, who nodded briefly, then smiled wanly at Laurel and Sara. The head ranger turned back to Eric. "We've found one of the teenage counselors, I'm afraid. We believe she's been dead for at least twenty-four hours."

The girls looked wide-eyed and solemn. Eric digested the news, and then asked, "Can you tell what happened?"

"Not for sure. She might have been strangled. It doesn't look like she's been…" He paused, looking toward the children. "She was fully dressed. There's some sign of a struggle. We won't know anything more until we get a team up here."

"Any sign of anyone else? How about the scouts?"

"From the way it looks, they've been taken somewhere," Al Kennedy replied. "We can tell that there were some others here at one time. Adults, I mean, not kids. There are some pretty big footprints, at least two different sets, along with the kid-sized sneaker tracks."

"The girl's body was hidden under some heavy undergrowth," Scarsi said, "with extra branches piled on top. We didn't find anything else. It looks like whoever was here went back toward the national park. Their footprints just keep on going, so we'll need a larger team to check it out, and some dogs too, probably. From the way the weeds are mashed down, quite a few people went out that way. I'd say at least two adults, maybe three, and they took the kids out with them."

Laurel and Sara were staring fixedly at the rangers, fear etching their features and reflected in their eyes. To the men, they seemed small and very, very young. "Are you sure they should be hearing this?" Scarsi asked.

Eric turned to the girls and smiled at them sadly, his eyes troubled but calm. He kept his voice steady, soft and measured. "This is a bad thing, kids, but it's over. There isn't any danger now. What we have to do is find out what happened here, and maybe you can help us. Think you're up to it?"

Silently they nodded at him, their eyes still wide. He gave them both a quick hug, then addressed the officers again. "They'll be fine, and maybe they'll catch something we've missed."

Kennedy added his own reassurance. "I'm proud of you both. You're really grown up." He sounded patronizing, but the girls were too upset to notice or take offense.

Brent Scarsi radioed a report back to the park outpost, requesting an investigation and forensic team. They agreed that Al Kennedy would remain behind at the scene, and the rest of them headed back to the Kelmans' campsite. All of them were silent as they trudged back through the woods, each lost in thought.

Seven

As the morning wore on, Don Vidito made several trips by helicopter to bring in reinforcements. Shortly before noon, a team of police investigators established a base of operations at the site of the scouts' disappearance, and a secondary base in the meadow by the lagoon. Deanna kept the coffee brewing, and offered lunch to those who were working the scene. Several accepted gratefully.

At close to one o'clock, after having examined the physical evidence in the red backpack yet another time, two officers interviewed the Kelmans and MacKenzies and both girls exhaustively. The campers had little additional information to offer. One of the officers prepared written statements from their notes, then asked all six to read them over carefully and add anything they thought might be important.

As Eric and the others were signing their statements, two plainclothes detectives, a man and a woman, arrived on the scene by helicopter. They conferred with the uniformed officers who were directing search operations, then asked to speak with Eric and Walt in private. They moved fifty yards away from the campsite and stood near to the shore.

Identifying themselves to the men as part of a special task force on child sex crimes, the investigators consulted their statements and reviewed all of their observations in painstaking detail. Eric was curious about the direction the investigation was taking, and wondered why it involved a sex crimes unit, but his questions were ignored. Finally at about three-thirty, the authorities took their addresses and telephone numbers, and asked that they make themselves available in case any other questions should arise. Then they asked that the campers leave the site. Despite their polite manner, Eric realized that the request was really an order.

They collapsed and folded their tents, gathered up all of their gear, and loaded the canoes. The official activity continued as they shoved off from shore, their departure all but ignored by the investigators.

The trip back through the canyon held none of the excitement and adventure of the previous day's passage. Eric again led the way, with Deanna and Sara as his passengers. This time Walt piloted the second canoe, with Fran and Laurel aboard. The child sat morosely in the bow, still shocked and disturbed by the day's events. Usually eager to take command of any watercraft, Laurel showed no interest in the helm or even in her surroundings.

Not having to fight the current when heading downstream, they found the return trip through the canyon relatively fast and uneventful. Everyone was solemn and nearly silent. Walt tried some lighthearted banter to raise their spirits, but his efforts fell flat and he gave it up. When they left the tributary and entered the calmer water of Shrewsbury Creek, Laurel moved to the middle seat and clung close to her mother for the rest of the journey, barely responding even when addressed directly.

In the lead canoe, Deanna tried similarly to comfort Sara, but with little success. When they finally arrived at the cabin, the skies were overcast and daylight was fading. Everyone turned to the task of unloading their equipment, and took it inside against the possibility of rain that the overcast sky seemed to threaten. Walt and Eric stored the outboard engines under the eaves at the back of the cabin, and they turned the canoes over to keep the insides dry.

No one felt hungry, but Eric built a fire in the wood stove and made coffee, while Deanna and Fran set out the makings for sandwiches. They all picked listlessly at their food, then sat morosely around the cabin, lost in their individual thoughts. By nine-thirty they had turned down the oil lamps, and all were in their sleeping bags.

Eric was slow to fall asleep, and found himself awake again before midnight, roused by the sound of rain on the roof. Gradually he became aware of a soft sound from one of the upper bunks, a gentle sobbing. He squirmed out of the sleeping bag and followed the sound to Sara's bunk. The child lay rigidly on her back, staring at the rough log ceiling. Her breath caught repeatedly in her throat as she tried to hide her misery. When Eric's head appeared over the side of the bunk, she turned toward him. Tears streamed from her eyes.

Eric glanced around the cabin. In the dim light from the single oil lamp, it appeared to him that everyone else was asleep. This didn't surprise him; their rest had been disturbed the night before by Walt's ghost story prank, and the day had been an exhausting one for everyone. He turned back toward Sara and motioned for her to sit up. She swung her legs over the side of the bunk, and he gathered her up in his arms and lifted her down.

Sara was trembling as if cold, although the cabin was warmed by the glow from the fire. Eric set her down gently on a chair next to the stove, and retrieved a blanket from the shelves between the bunks. He wrapped it around her shoulders, then pulled another chair for himself over next to hers and drew her in close against his side.

As they sat there in the dim light, her trembling gradually subsided, along with the gentle sobs. Gradually her tension eased, and she nestled in against him, but her eyes remained wide and staring.

Finally she tilted her head back and looked up at him. "Do you think she's still out there?" she whispered.

Eric knew she meant the dead counselor. "I don't think so. I'm sure they're taking good care of her."

"I wish my dad was here."

Eric smiled secretly. "I guess you're just stuck with me, at least until we get home tomorrow."

She snuggled in more tightly against him. "You took care of Laurel when she was lost out here, right?"

"Uh huh."

Sara was quiet for a few minutes. She sighed deeply, then turned again so she could look up into his face. "It's so sad. She was all alone out there when we found the backpack, and we didn't even know it."

"There wasn't anything we could have done for her."

"I know. But... Maybe she was still alive then."

"I don't think so." Eric tried to shift his weight. The chair offered little support for his back, and he was tiring rapidly from the strain of supporting the child, but still she clung tightly to him. "It has nothing to do with you, you know. Whatever happened out there is in the past, and you're here with us *now*, in the present. And I promise that nothing will happen to you."

"I just keep thinking about her, out there all by herself."

"Sara, she isn't suffering. She isn't really there any more, and nothing can hurt her again."

Although he wasn't sure she understood what he was trying to say, the child seemed to accept his words, and lay quietly against his side. Then she asked, "What do you think happened to all those kids?"

"I don't know. The police told me that the trail they found led all the way back to a campsite near the edge of the park. They found a bunch of tire tracks, but nothing much else. I think that probably means the kids are okay." *Whatever "okay" means*, he thought. He was still troubled by the involvement of the sex crimes investigators. *Maybe not dead, at least, but maybe there are worse things than that.*

"Ready to go back in your bunk now?" he asked her.

"Can't I stay here a little longer?"

"Okay, just for a little while." Eric stroked her hair gently and rhythmically, and within a few minutes he felt her lapse into sleep. He knew he couldn't get her back into the upper bunk without rousing her, and was contemplating giving up his own sleeping bag for her. Glancing around the cabin for any other alternative, he spotted a pair of round eyes watching him from the other upper bunk.

"Hi, Doc." A tiny whisper.

"Hi, yourself. How long have you been awake?"

Laurel scrambled noiselessly over the side and dropped lightly to the floor of the cabin. "Ever since you got Sara up. Didn't hurt your back, did you, old Doc?"

"My back's just fine, thank you." He spoke very softly, pretending an insulted tone. Then he looked down at Sara. Her weight was beginning to take its toll. "My arm's gone sound asleep, though."

Laurel turned serious. "She's pretty upset, huh?"

"I guess we all are. How about helping me move your friend here? I'm going to try to put her in my sleeping bag without waking her up, and then I'll use her bunk. Want to open it up some for me?"

"'Kay." Laurel unzipped the bag, folded it open, and flattened it out across the floor. Eric lifted the sleeping girl and carried her gently across the room. As he tried to lower her down, Sara half wakened and clung to his neck. He eased himself down on the bag and braced his back against the cabin wall. She burrowed in again and fell completely asleep once more. "Looks like you're stuck with her." Laurel flopped down on his opposite side and smiled up at him again. "Here we are again, Doc," she whispered, remembering the time in June when he had held her close in the middle of the night, as he now did for Sara, pushing back her fear.

"Let's not make a habit of this, shall we? Could you grab one of those blankets for me?" He gestured toward a shelf on the wall next to the left hand bunk. Laurel moved over to it and took down a puffy cotton coverlet. She carried it back to him, and he wadded it up and stuffed it between his head and shoulders and the wall, managing to get more comfortable.

Laurel scrunched down next to him on top of the sleeping bag. "Where is she now?"

Eric was puzzled. "Who? Sara?"

"No, the girl in the woods. You told Sara she isn't suffering because she isn't really there any more."

"The police have taken her out by now, back to town."

"That isn't what you meant. I could tell."

He collected his thoughts. "Where are you, Laurel?"

She frowned at him. "Right here with you."

"No, I mean, where is the real you? Are you just your body, or is the real you *in* your body? Or are you in your brain, inside your head? Where is the real Laurel?"

"I don't know what you mean."

"I can see you, just like you can see me. Is what you see all there is to me, or am I something more than that? And how about you? Are you more than just what we can see and touch here? Fingernails and hair and your old knobby knees?"

She grinned at his insult, then thought for a moment. "I'm not sure. It *feels* like there's more to me than that. I'm in here somewhere, but I'm not just inside my hands and my feet and my head. I'm *somewhere else*, too."

"So where are you?"

"It feels like I'm in here behind my eyes. That's our brains, right? And we can't see them."

"Sure we can. Although we have to take them out to see them."

"Gross!"

"But you've seen pictures of brains, haven't you?"

"I guess so. Yeah."

"So is that the real Laurel? That wrinkled gray thing?"

She was beginning to catch on. "It feels like a lot more than that. Like there's a part of us that's more than just our bodies. Right? A spirit or something?"

"I don't know."

Laurel became exasperated. "Sure you do! Why have you been asking me all this stuff if you don't have the answer to give me?"

"No one has that answer. Some people say they do, like all the different religions, but they have all kinds of *different* answers."

"So they can't all be right?"

"What do you think?"

Laurel took a deep breath, puffed out her cheeks, and blew out sharply. "More questions! You drive me nuts sometimes. So what's this got to do with the dead girl in the woods?"

"Where is she?"

"The police took her away, I guess, like you said."

Eric pressed on. "So is that her? Her body? Is that the real person?"

Laurel turned her head and looked at him closely in the dim light. "Maybe not. I don't know."

"Neither do I. But I feel like there's more to me than just this bunch of skin and bones I live in, and I'd prefer to think that there's more to her, too. That's what I meant when I told Sara she wasn't really there any more, and that nothing could hurt her now."

Laurel stared deeply into his eyes. Then she smiled. "When am I going to understand all this stuff?"

Eric laughed softly. "Maybe never. But don't you *dare* ever stop trying."

She laid her head against his shoulder. "I feel better now. And I think Sara does, too."

Eric looked down at the sleeping child. "Things won't seem so bad to her in the morning. Pretty soon she'll be strong too, like you are."

She smiled at him again, and cuddled in against him. Soon her breathing slowed, and Eric found himself trapped between their two small bodies, giving them comfort but strangely drawing comfort of his own from their presence and trust. He rested his head back against the makeshift cushion, and soon fell into a deep sleep of his own. For the first time in months, he slept straight through until morning.

Eight

About an hour after sunrise, when he was sure the police chief would be at work, Eric called Jim Carmichael on the cell phone again. He listened for a few minutes, then disconnected and sat down at the table, where the others were having breakfast.

"Nothing much new," he said. "After we left they brought in some tracking dogs. They searched all along both sides of the trail between the clearing and the park, and found the tents and other camping stuff dumped in a shallow ravine. Other than that, all they found were a couple of candy wrappers and a kid's ball cap."

"Does that mean all those kids are all right?" Sara asked with genuine concern.

Eric turned toward her, thinking that in this case, *all right* was a highly subjective and relative term. "The police chief says he thinks they were loaded into a truck or van and taken away. The tire tracks they found were too big for a car."

"Why would someone do such a thing?" Fran exclaimed, although she had a pretty good idea. Walt had told her about the involvement of the child sex crimes unit of the police force.

"That's what they're trying to find out," Eric answered "Whoever's responsible apparently took the other counselor with them, the boy, what was his name?"

"Stu Piersol," Walt answered.

"Right. According to the scout leader, he was a new recruit, but he had a lot of camping experience. And he was older, eighteen or nineteen or so. They're trying to trace him now."

"The parents must be frantic," Fran said, "the way we felt when Laurel was taken last June." This memory silenced them all for a bit. Then she tried to lighten the moment, hoping to ease everyone's concern. "But that turned out all right. I bet they'll find this bunch of kids, too."

They began clearing up the remains of their meal, and Eric suggested they get an early start for home. All the joy of the trip had drained away. The rain had stopped, but the day was overcast and somewhat cool, and the cabin no longer seemed so inviting. Walt and Eric went outside to right the canoes and mount the outboards, while the others straightened up the cabin.

By ten-thirty they had the canoes loaded and ready to go. Laurel had regained a small measure of enthusiasm and asked to steer the second canoe, and Eric suggested she lead the way. Walt relaxed in the bow, keeping watch for any unexpected obstructions in the channel, and Laurel let Sara share the task of maneuvering the outboard. The trip down the creek was uneventful.

They stopped at Paul VanOostrum's general store to return the borrowed canoe, and to stow Eric's own craft in Paul's barn. They transferred their gear to Eric's Pathfinder and Walt's big Volvo 940 station wagon. Paul helped them service the outboards, and they carried them to the rack inside the barn and padlocked them securely. When all that was accomplished, they entered the store for a late lunch before starting for home.

Paul's wife Marge greeted them as they entered, but without her customary cheerful enthusiasm. Concern for her friends showed in her kind eyes. The morning news reports had dramatized the murder, and had fueled sensational speculation over the fate of the missing children. Although the announcer hadn't mentioned the Kelmans by name, Marge knew by the radio's description of the murder's locale that they might have been involved.

Marge led them all into the small and nearly deserted dining room behind the retail counter, and produced menus. As they were ordering, Paul entered and pulled up a chair between Eric and Walt.

"We had cops all over the place last night," he said. "They wouldn't tell us much, and what we heard on the radio this morning is long on conjecture and short on facts. Where'd it all happen? Were you anywhere near?"

"We were up at the lagoon," Eric answered. "The kids found a backpack in the woods, and when Walt and I went back to look around, we found six more of them. We called the rangers, and they discovered the girl's body."

"My God!" Paul exclaimed. "I had no idea you were so closely involved." He looked sympathetically toward Laurel and Sara, who were sitting somberly, waiting for their food.

"Not our idea of a fun trip, that's for sure," Deanna put in. Then she tried to lighten the tone. "But we had a good time before that, didn't we, kids? Laurel even learned to swim."

"You did? That's great!" Paul managed to coax a small smile from her with his praise. Then he turned back to Eric. "Have they got a line on what happened to the scouts?"

"Not that I know of. I talked to Jim Carmichael this morning, and..."

Marge interrupted, bringing them their lunches, and Paul got up from the table. "Terrible thing. Folks can't even let their kids go camping any more..." Fran and Deanna cut him off with their icy stares. "Uh, oh. My big mouth again. Sorry." He turned to the children to find them staring at him, eyes wide and frightened. "I didn't mean you kids. Your folks wouldn't ever let anything like that happen to you. I mean, if you were ever..."

"Okay, Paul," Eric cut in. "They're okay with all this."

"Yeah, well... Anyway, you go ahead and have your lunch." He backed out, embarrassed by his faux pas, and returned to the front part of the store. In the two months since first meeting the MacKenzies, he had become quite fond of them all, especially Laurel, and felt badly that he might have inadvertently frightened the children with his thoughtless outburst.

"Well, that really helped!" Deanna stated when he was gone.

"He means well," Eric said. "He just didn't think before he spoke." He turned to the girls, who were visibly upset. "Shake it off, you guys. Nothing's going to happen to you." They returned to their sandwiches, but to Deanna and Fran, they didn't seem reassured.

After lunch, Paul drew Eric aside. "I'm really sorry I shot my mouth off that way. I didn't think about how it might scare the girls."

"Forget it, Paul. They'll get over it once everything blows over. By the way, this is probably the last time I'll be out here until after the fall term starts. I've got to finish my course outlines. I hate to ask you, since you've been looking after the cabin since June, but would you mind checking on it occasionally? Until this leg heals some more, anyway."

"Glad to. The leg still giving you trouble?"

"Keeps me awake some. The swimming seemed to help, though. I'm going to try to make it down here before September's out. Feel free to use the cabin yourself, any time you like."

"I'll do that, thanks." Paul looked over Eric's shoulder and out the door toward the parking lot. Fran, Laurel and Sara were seated in the Volvo, and Walt was standing next to the passenger door of the Pathfinder, talking to Deanna. "Looks like your gang is getting a little impatient."

"Time to hit the road," Eric said as he opened the door and stepped out. "Thanks again for everything. I owe you."

"Forget it. See you next month."

Eric waved goodbye and walked over to the Volvo. He shook hands with Walt and nodded to Fran and the girls, then climbed behind the wheel of the Nissan and started the engine. But before he could pull out of the parking lot, Walt got out of the other vehicle again and walked over to him. "You two got any spare time before you go back to teaching?" he asked.

"Not for the next week or so," Eric answered. "Becky and her husband are bringing the two kids for a visit. Deanna hasn't seen them since June, and it's been longer than that for me."

"How about over Labor Day? We're going to take *Mayflower* up the coast, and we'd love to have you come along. Laurel wants to show off her sailing ability. If you think you can put up with her and Sara in such close quarters, that is."

"Where do you sail?"

"You know the chain of offshore islands that stretches up the coast as far as the Capital? We like to explore the channels between them. It's really beautiful out there, but you have to sail some distance to see the best ones. We usually make a three-day excursion out of it."

"Thanks for the offer," Eric replied. "We'd like that." Neither he nor Walt saw the slight grimace that crossed Deanna's face. Sailing was not her idea of a good time. Anticipating a long conversation between the men, she got out of the car and walked over to talk with Fran.

For the next ten minutes, Walt enthused over the joys of sailing, and described his daughter's love for the sea. "She'll have even more fun now, since you've taught her to swim."

"Don't let her get too reckless," Eric cautioned. "She still has a lot to learn."

"Think it'll be safe to let her out of the life jacket some? She really hates wearing it."

"Has she ever gone overboard?"

"No," Walt answered. "She has good sea legs, and a healthy respect for the way the boat moves."

"I'd say use the vest any time it gets rough, then. Otherwise she should be okay. She doesn't panic any more when her head goes under, and she'll bob like a cork in the salt water."

They talked a while longer, until Deanna returned to the car, restless and anxious to get on the road. As she got in beside Eric, Walt leaned back from the window and said, "Can we count you in, then?"

"Can we let you know after Becky's bunch goes home?"

"Sure. I'll call you." Walt returned to his car, and the two vehicles pulled away from the general store. They headed east along the border of the national park, toward the limited access highway that would take them home.

Deanna was silent for the first fifteen minutes, conscious of Eric's preoccupation with the weekend's events. Finally she said, "Do you think what Paul said upset them a lot?"

Eric knew she was referring to Laurel and Sara. "More than I would have liked. But they'll bounce back. School starts soon, and they'll have lots to look forward to, going to the new middle school and all. What do you think about accepting that boat trip over the Labor Day weekend?"

"You know me and boats," she replied. "I get seasick in anything larger than your canoe. In fact, I get seasick just *looking* at anything larger than a canoe. How big is it?"

"A thirty-foot sailboat of some kind."

"Thirty feet long? That's practically a ship!"

Eric laughed. "Not quite, but from the way he described it, it's pretty nice. Enough berths to sleep six, a complete galley... All the comforts of home."

"Not *my* home." Deanna was clearly apprehensive. Although she humored Eric by accompanying him occasionally to the cabin, she really preferred ready access to all her creature comforts. She exaggerated her tendency toward seasickness, but she knew that the oscillating motion of a big boat on the open sea would keep her constantly queasy. And she admitted to herself some uneasiness at being too far from dry land. "Would they be really insulted if I were to beg off?"

"I guess not. I think he'll be a bit hurt if at least one of us doesn't accept the invitation, though," Eric answered. "Ever since Laurel's escapade last June, he's been anxious to repay me somehow, and I think this invitation is his way of trying to do it. To tell the truth, it embarrasses me a little. I don't want them to feel indebted to us. But I really enjoy his company, and Fran's, too."

"I like them too, all of them. But I'm not so sure about this sailing thing. What if the weather gets rough? With my touchy stomach, you might have an invalid on your hands for three days. Do they camp on the islands or sleep on the boat?"

The sign for the limited access highway loomed on the right, and Eric flipped on his turn signal, preparing to drive up the ramp. "My guess is they use the boat. It would only be for two nights."

"Don't take this the wrong way, my dear, but all that togetherness in a thirty-foot boat is pretty close quarters for me. Is Fran really going?"

"I get the feeling she's not too keen on sailing, either, but Walt's been trying to convert her. She usually goes along to please him. Walt says she mostly sits in the cockpit and knits." He laughed at the image that brought to mind. "Laurel's the one who really loves it. He says she wants to run the boat herself most of the time. They usually take Sara along, too, and what the two of them really like best is to stretch out in the sun on the deck in their bikinis, pretending to be Britney Spears or somebody."

"Whoa! Sara in a bikini? That boggles the mind," Deanna said. Sara Hancock was the Dolly Parton of twelve-year-olds, while Laurel's slowly developing curves were considerably less flashy. "And there's no way Laurel would ever wear a bikini with you around. She blushes anytime she thinks anybody's looking at her sideways. You, especially."

"You've got a point," he laughed. Laurel's exaggerated sense of modesty was a private joke among the adults.

"Why don't you go without me?" Deanna went on. "Play pirate, do some male bonding or something. I can't imagine Fran wants to be cooped up like that for three days, especially with those two little dervishes aboard. Maybe I can haul her off for some serious shopping instead."

Eric smiled fondly at his wife. "Let's wait and see. If the holiday weekend looks nice, you just might enjoy yourself." They drove on in companionable silence. His mind soon turned to the courses he would be teaching at the university in the fall, and to how much he had to accomplish before the students arrived on campus. Foremost in his thoughts was the much-anticipated visit with his daughter's family. The tragedy near his lagoon was already beginning to fade from his immediate consciousness.

Nine

For a few days the news was dominated by the story of the murder and apparent abductions in the woods west of the national park. Despite a massive effort by law enforcement officials, however, little new evidence came to light, and the story quickly became a back page item, then disappeared entirely.

Shortly after noon on the Wednesday following their return from the cabin, Jim Carmichael called Eric, as he had promised, at his university office.

"We still don't know much," he said. "There's no trace of any of the scouts. We've put out bulletins with the Child Find agency, and a public appeal asking for any information from someone who might have seen a van in the area on the weekend. But since we don't have any description, or even know what make or color it was, there's not much hope. The tire tread marks matched common original equipment types on most Chrysler products, and a few others too."

"We heard the bulletin," Eric said. "How about the other counselor?"

"That's our only solid lead at present. It turns out Stu Piersol has a juvenile record, and somehow the scout leaders missed it. Otherwise they'd never have taken him on as a counselor."

"What was he charged with?"

"The usual. A couple of break-and-enters, drug use and suspicion of dealing. He got probation on all of them, and he seems to have kept his nose clean for the past few years, either that or he's gotten better at getting away with things. After the probationary period, the court ordered the records sealed, which is how he got past the scouts."

"Has he got a family?" Eric asked.

"Dysfunctional, apparently. The father's been unemployed for years, and the mother is an alcoholic. They claim they haven't seen the boy in months, but I don't believe them. They seemed evasive. In any case, there's no trace of him that we can find."

"What about the girl who was murdered?"

"That's a really sad situation," Jim said. "Her name was Naomi Eagles, sixteen years old, and highly respected for her volunteer work with kids, especially disadvantaged ones. Candy Striper at the hospital, taught Sunday School classes; a real nice kid. She was an only child, too."

"Damn shame. So what's next?"

"We're running out of ideas. We've done air reconnaissance, and they've taken the dogs over the whole area, but it's a dead end at the park. Right now we're hoping someone may come forward with some information."

"How about motive?"

"That's not hard to guess, I'm sorry to say. It's almost certainly the child sex trade again. The pimps are getting bolder all the time. We've had a couple of cases of kids being taken right out of school yards."

"In this country?" Eric was amazed. "I've heard of it in the Far East, Thailand and so forth, but *here*?"

"Used to be they'd stake out bus stations in big cities, and make a play for obvious runaways when they got off the bus. A whole lot of small town girls, boys too, for the gay trade, get caught up that way and end up practically slaves. Big market, especially for young teenagers, and now the pedophiles are getting bolder, too. Not too many runaways in the pre-teen set, so they're snatching them off the streets."

"How the hell do they get away with it, Jim?"

"Money talks. It's getting to be big business, I'm afraid. There's apparently a growing market for little kids in some European countries now. The pimps break them in here, physical and psychological abuse, mostly, until they're easy to handle. The sex comes later. They get top dollar for virgins overseas, girls and boys both, and the younger the better. Gives them more shelf life."

"Jesus Christ!" Eric was sickened and astounded. "Damned perverts! Sometimes I wonder what's wrong with our species."

"It's all economics to the organizers," Jim continued. "Years ago, certain travel agents discovered they could make a bundle out of setting up sex tours in the Far East for rich western pedophiles. These sick bastards are willing to pay a fortune for the first crack at guaranteed virgin Oriental kids. Soon we began to see poor families in third world countries actually selling their children into that kind of slavery. Now the infection's spread right back to us."

"Can't anyone stop it?"

"We're trying. But you wouldn't believe how organized these creeps are. There's a world-wide network, and it's been growing exponentially over the internet. Every time the feds manage to close one operation, half a dozen more open up somewhere else. We've made a little progress on an individual basis by exposing some of the customers publicly, stories in the press and so forth. And there have been some prosecutions of the tour companies. But when there's a lot of money to be made, morals go out the window."

"I still can't believe it goes on right here," Eric said.

"Believe it! Up until the past few years, the international trade in kids has been mostly a foreign problem, but we've got domestic rings showing up in a lot of major cities now. Snatching kids here and selling them overseas is relatively new, and so far we've had no luck tracking down the organizers. Up to now we can't seem to get a handle on just exactly how they operate, or who's behind it."

"How do they get the children out of the country?" Eric asked.

"We're not entirely sure. It could be over the border, but more likely it's by boat. It's easier to elude the Coast Guard than to smuggle kids past Customs and Immigration. We just keep hoping for a break, a tip about a shipment, or maybe a boat stopped for some other reason and caught in the act."

Jim and Eric chewed on the subject for a few minutes longer, then promised to keep in touch and disconnected. Eric returned to writing his courses of study, but the problem of the missing kids ate at him. Unable to concentrate, he decided to call Walt MacKenzie and fill him in on what Jim had said.

He tried to reach Walt at his office, the successful architectural firm that bore his name, but was told he was out at the site of their most recent project. Walt had outbid the competition to design a new medical services building adjacent to the university campus. Eric decided to walk across the common and see if his friend could spare a few minutes for coffee.

The late August afternoon was warm and pleasant, the humidity low. A gentle breeze carried a trace of salt overland from the not too distant ocean. Eric found Walt consulting with the on-site engineers.

He waited as they completed their discussion, then offered his friend a coffee break at the Faculty Club. Walt gratefully accepted.

As they walked down University Avenue toward the Club, Eric's mood contrasted greatly with the perfection of the afternoon. His disgust showed plainly in his voice as he relayed the essence of his conversation with the police chief. Walt was nearly incredulous. As a relatively young father with a somewhat limited knowledge of the world, he found it hard to believe that such perversion could touch so close to home. Fears for his own child arose threateningly in his mind.

They entered the Faculty Club and sat down with their coffee. "The sad thing," Eric said, "is that it's so hard to pin down the slime who sponsor this stuff, the so-called customers. Most of them are supposedly respected members of the community, and they've got pretty deep pockets, too. They could even be our neighbors, family men, professionals, and we'd never know it."

"How can people who are parents themselves do things like that to other kids?"

"They don't see them as people, I guess. Just objects they can use to satisfy themselves."

"Hasn't anyone got any idea where those scouts ended up? What about this Piersol kid?" Walt asked.

"Jim says he's either a victim himself, or he's involved in the operation and gone to ground. No one's seen him since he and the Eagles girl took the kids into the woods for their camp-out last week. If he *is* involved, and they're almost certain he is, he couldn't very well show up now. He must know everyone would be looking for him, once they discovered he has juvenile record."

"My God! You mean the scouts had a young criminal working with them?"

"It wasn't really their fault. You know how it is with juvenile records. They erase them when the kids grow up, hoping they'll straighten out. Otherwise any kid with a record would never be able to get a decent job later on."

"But Jesus, Eric! Don't we have a right to know who's walking around loose out there? How do we know who's being entrusted with our kids? It makes me want to go and build a fence around Laurel, lock her up somewhere."

"I know. But all you can really do with them is monitor where they go and who they see as best you can, and arm them with knowledge. And that isn't easy to do without frightening them."

"But those kids were on a scout camping trip! You'd expect them to be safe there, if anywhere."

"I know they try to screen their counselors pretty carefully, but someone messed up this time. Piersol must have had some recommendations from somewhere, and since his court records weren't made public, they probably didn't think it was necessary to check any further. It's a flaw in the system, that's for sure."

"Those poor kids. They could be anywhere by now. I wish we could help somehow." He paused, deep in thought. "Was the world this screwed up when we were kids? I don't remember my parents watching my every move, or being scared to let me go out alone."

"We were careful with our two," Eric said, "but we tried not to let them know it. And we made sure they were street smart."

"I guess my folks did, too. I knew not to go off with strangers, and so forth. But I don't remember taking it very seriously. With Laurel, we were a lot more direct, and probably scared her more than we wanted to. But if it works…"

"When I was a kid, in the forties," Eric mused, "we were free as the wind. In the summer, we were out of the house early in the morning, and we practically lived in the woods. We rode our bikes all over, and explored, and invented our own games. Stretched our minds and imaginations, too. That all changed, sometime around the nineteen-sixties, I think. Now we regiment our kids, enroll them in every kind of organized sports, give them lessons in this and that… Sometimes it seems that every minute of their time has to be filled, maybe so we know where they are all the time. Safety in numbers, or something."

They rose from their chairs, dropped their cups off at the bar and left the Club. Walt headed back to the building site and Eric returned to his office. Having unburdened himself somewhat to Walt, he found he was once again able to concentrate on his work. Gradually his course outlines began to take shape.

On Thursday, the Kelman household was turned upside down. Eric drove to the airport at noon and picked up their daughter Becky, her husband, Douglas Campbell, and their two children. Although they could only stay for a week, the visit was a real treat for Eric and Deanna, whose home was over a thousand miles away from their offspring and her young family.

For the next six days, Eric's hours were full. He started his day at the university before sunrise, and completed his work by the early afternoon in order to spend more time with the children. Three-year-old Daniel was fascinated by Eric's hobby, the model railroad empire that occupied over half of the basement. From the time Eric entered the house, Danny was his ever-present shadow, and the two of them spent many hours guiding heavy freights and speedy streamliners through meticulously detailed villages and towns in Eric's private miniature world.

Danny was the ideal first child. He quickly acquired his father's love of sports, and could actually sit through an entire major league baseball game without losing interest. At age two, he had been able to recite from memory the names of an astonishingly large number of hockey players, cued by nothing more than their pictures on Doug's extensive collection of trading cards.

But the child's personality was not one-sided. His mechanical aptitude showed itself early. With understandable impatience, Eric had given his grandson an electric train set at the too-early age of two, but the boy wasted no time in mastering the speed control. Before long he was assembling the track without help. Now, at age three, he understood the basics of Eric's master control panel, and could throw the switches that governed the various routes over which the trains passed. The child showed strong signs of possessing his parents' intellectual capacity, too. He was quickly developing a love for the printed word, enthralled by the books that Deanna read to him every evening before bedtime.

The baby, Melody, was just four months old, and was only now becoming really interesting. Eric and Deanna delighted in her, and he admitted to being absolutely smitten. Much to Becky's amusement, she caught him sneaking into their spare room to watch the baby sleeping in the crib, and more than once his presence woke her too early from her nap. Whenever she cried, Eric was the first to pick her up. When her teething caused her pain, he walked for miles throughout the house with her nestled on his shoulder, softly singing to her. Often he just sat with her lying on his lap, making faces at her to make her laugh.

The week's visit flew by, and the following Wednesday Eric and Deanna drove them to the airport with great reluctance, sending Becky and her family back to their separate, far-too-distant lives.

Ten

In addition to the excitement of Becky's family's visit, the preceding days had been filled with departmental meetings and committee deliberations. Eric had his hands full, preparing for the largest enrollment in the Music Department's history. While the problem of the missing children remained ever-present in the back of his mind, it was crowded to a far corner by his preparations for the fall term.

On the Wednesday before the Labor Day weekend, shortly after Eric returned from taking the Campbell family to the airport, Walt called him to remind him of their planned boat trip. Eric had nearly forgotten the invitation. When he mentioned it to Deanna later in the day, she was again resistant to going, unwilling to give up the entire long weekend's holiday for what she expected to be a boring period of captivity in a not-too-stable floating environment.

Eric sighed and called Walt back to break the news. "I guess we won't be able to make it after all."

Walt was far from obtuse. "Deanna's not too keen on the idea, I suppose. Listen, I think we're the victims of a conspiracy. She's been talking to Fran about it, and they've cooked up some alternate plans. Believe me, she won't care if you go without her."

"I hate to leave her alone the whole weekend," Eric said.

"Alone? I've got news for you. She's going to be glad to get rid of you. The four of them, that's Deanna and Fran and their credit cards, are planning an assault on the mall on Saturday, and who knows what on Sunday and Monday. I expect they'll greatly enjoy our absence, so let's not disappoint them."

"Hang on." Eric lowered the handset and called to his wife over his shoulder. "Deanna, Walt says you and Fran are willing to forego a thrilling sea adventure for the sake of a boring shopping trip. Any truth to that? Can you really do without me for the weekend?"

"Somehow I'll manage to bear it," Deanna called out sarcastically. Eric turned back to the phone.

"I guess you're right," he said to Walt, "so count me in. But remember, I'm no sailor. Take away my canoe and outboard, and I'm likely to be totally helpless. You'll have to give me lessons if you want me to help you run the boat."

"No need. My first mate's coming, and bringing her best friend. Laurel considers running the boat to be her primary responsibility. She loves being in charge. Sara's beginning to catch on, too, and between the three of us, we've got the chores covered. You can just lay back, relax, and enjoy the scenery."

"You mean those two kids don't want to get in on the shopping? They're not sick, are they?"

Walt laughed. "It was a toss-up, but the boat won out. Besides, Fran practically told Laurel she wasn't welcome. Apparently she and Deanna are planning long, leisurely lunches in some chic cafes, a matinee, and who knows what else. To quote my daughter, *'Boring!'* So we're stuck with the kids."

"No need to twist my arm, then. If I don't have to work, I'm in. Where do we meet and when?"

"I've got *Mayflower* moored at the Stillwater Basin Marina," Walt answered. "We always try to get an early start. Travel light. The weather is supposed to be good, so figure on clothes for three warm days. The nights will probably be cool, though. We don't bother with any bedding for the bunks, so bring your sleeping bag."

"What else can I bring? Food? Drinks?"

"I thought you'd never ask. All contributions gratefully received. The kids are bottomless pits, by the way."

Eric laughed. "I'll bring plenty. How are you fixed for cooking?"

"You've got a choice. There's a two-burner propane stove in the galley, and a covered barbecue that we sling over the aft rail."

"Okay. Suppose I bring chicken and corn-on-the-cob? I'll ask Deanna for a carload of her famous potato salad, too. And we've got plenty of soft drinks to contribute."

"Good stuff. The kids go for hot dogs and burgers, too, so I'll bring those and the rolls. And chips and stuff, of course. You'll be amazed at how hungry you'll be out on the water."

"When should I be there?"

"Is seven too early?"

They talked over the details of the trip for another five minutes.

After he hung up, Eric reconsidered the work he still had to accomplish before the first day of classes. *Two full days in the office should do it,* he thought. It was a small price to pay for the prospect of three relaxing days on the water, away from the demands of his job. His spirits lifted, and he could almost feel his cares flying away. Briefly he visualized them as feathery dandelion seeds on the wind, then laughed at the foolish romantic imagery. *More like bats escaping from my dusty cranial attic.*

On Thursday morning, his clock radio clicked on at six and brought him rudely back to reality. The lead story on the news concerned the disappearance of two more children, a brother and sister named Benji and Emily Carter. Details were sketchy, but apparently they had failed to come home from a trip to the playground, just around the corner from their home.

Later that morning, Eric called Jim Carmichael. "I heard about the two missing kids. Have they been found yet?"

"Not a sign of them," the police chief said. "According to some other kids at the playground, they were there for about an hour, then left to go home for lunch. It was less than a block to their house, in broad daylight and with other people around, but they never made it home."

"Any connection to the missing scouts?"

"God, I hope not. The little girl is only eight. The boy is eleven, and the parents claim he's very responsible, takes good care of his sister when they're out, and keeps careful track of the time when he's supposed to go home. Wears his own watch and everything. We questioned everyone we could find who might have seen or heard something unusual, someone talking to the kids, or an unfamiliar car or van. Nothing."

"How about the girl's murder, or the other missing counselor? Have you made any progress solving that one?"

"We're up against a stone wall, Eric," Jim said. "The Piersol kid is either gone for good, or if someone knows where he is, they aren't talking. Whether he's involved in the kidnappings or was murdered himself and dumped somewhere we haven't found yet, I don't know. They've had tracking dogs out covering the whole park, and crawling all over most of your land, too."

"I know," Eric said. "Deanna got a call last week, asking her for permission to conduct the search. She got the impression it was just a courtesy call, and that they were probably already out there with the dogs. Is there anything else I can do to help?"

"I wish there was."

After hanging up, Eric turned again to the pile of books and references required for his courses, and forced the problem of the missing children to the back of his mind. The day was filled with interruptions, and by suppertime he had completed only one of his course outlines. He called Deanna and told her to go ahead and eat without him.

By six the music building was virtually deserted, and he accomplished more during the next three hours than in the morning and afternoon combined. His concentration began to fail, and he determined that he would be able to complete everything the next day. Shortly before nine-thirty he arrived home exhausted, and found the dining table set for two and delicious odors drifting on the air.

Deanna appeared in the kitchen door. "Surprise! Dinner is served."

"You, my dear, are the *best*!" He dropped his briefcase and sat thankfully at the table. Deanna served the meal, and for the next half hour they talked animatedly about pleasant inconsequentials as they ate. At ten-thirty he fell into bed, but his dreams were troubled, haunted by the unknown fate of eight innocent children, and by his inability to help them.

On Friday morning, he was out of the house by six, and completed his third course outline while the building was still quiet. Knowing that the department's lone secretary was swamped with requests from the twenty-four full- and part-time members of the music faculty, he ran off sufficient copies for his classes himself.

Next he updated his opening day lectures and checked with the bookstore to be sure his texts had all arrived. Not bothering to stop for lunch, he completed his work just in time to attend the general faculty meeting in Convocation Hall, in his opinion a bureaucratic waste of everyone's time. At four-twenty, no more enlightened about anything than at the start of the meeting, he filed out with his colleagues, located his car, and headed for the mall downtown.

Eric quickly found the food items he needed for the boat trip, including potatoes for the salad Deanna promised to make that evening. His last stop was to pick up ice for his cooler, and as he got back in the car for the short drive home, the five o'clock news was just coming on the radio. After five minutes of national and international headlines, the announcer turned to a more detailed reading of local news.

He pulled into his driveway before the newscast was over, and sat in the car listening carefully. There was no mention of the two missing children. With no new leads or discoveries, the item was no longer worth even a few seconds of airtime. *And that's all those young lives are worth to some people, I guess*, Eric thought disgustedly. *Yesterday's news.*

After listening to the weather forecast (*sunny, warm, light winds for most of the next three days; perfect for being on the water*), he climbed out and went into the house, determined to jolly himself into a more positive mood by morning. *Who knows, I might even help Deanna make the potato salad.*

Eleven

Eric packed his duffel on Friday night and left it by the back door. He tumbled out of bed at five-thirty the next morning, wolfed down a quick breakfast, and transferred his food purchases and ice from the freezer to the cooler. He loaded it and the duffel, along with his binoculars and sleeping bag, in the back of the Pathfinder. He returned to the house, looked in on his still-sleeping wife, and then headed out for the drive to the marina.

Despite the early hour, there was already considerable activity in the boat yard. He spotted Walt's empty Volvo in the parking lot, and inquired at the office for the location of *Mayflower*. The attendant directed him to the far end of the northernmost T-shaped dock, and he slung the duffel over his shoulder and walked out under an almost cloudless sky.

The tide was low and just beginning to turn. He reached the end of the dock without spotting his friend, then discovered a gangway leading down steeply to an empty floating platform where a half dozen boat tenders were tied up. He looked out over the harbor among the colorful yachts, swinging with the tide on their buoys, and read the name *Mayflower* on the stern of a graceful white and blue craft about a hundred and fifty yards straight out. He could see Walt standing behind the wheel, and heard the gentle throb of an auxiliary diesel.

The boat was truly beautiful, glistening in the early morning sunlight. The gleaming white hull tapered gracefully from bowsprit to stern, its streamlined and portholed cabin in perfect proportion and its mast towering majestically. The sails still lay inside their royal blue covers, and a colorful flag hung over the stern, limp in the still air.

Eric spotted Laurel getting out of the tender, which was now tied to the buoy. She climbed up the stern ladder into the cockpit, slender in a long T-shirt and ball cap, sunglasses perched on her tiny upturned nose. He saw no sign of Sara. As he watched, *Mayflower* came about and headed toward shore. Walt guided the yacht slowly and expertly toward the dock, and Laurel waved cheerfully as it came alongside.

She tossed Eric the bow rope. He hitched it to the stanchion, and Walt shut off the engine and climbed over the rail. Laurel jumped down gracefully onto the floating platform and secured the stern line.

"Avast, matey!" Walt greeted him with a piratical parody. "Stow your gear and let's weigh anchor!"

"Got to make another trip to the parking lot," Eric replied. "There's still some stuff back up in the truck."

"I'll help," Laurel said, bouncing up to him.

"Where's your buddy, runt? I'm looking forward to a couple of good swimming races with her."

Laurel looked disgusted. "She's got the measles!"

"What? You're kidding!"

"Nope. She was fine until yesterday morning. Now her mom says she's got a million spots. And she's mad, too, 'cause she says she feels fine and really wanted to come."

"So your dad and I are stuck with just you, huh?"

"Hey! Without me you wouldn't get anywhere. I'm the only one who really knows how this boat works."

Walt laughed at her confidence. "We'll see, big shot. Help Eric get the cooler and let's be off."

"Come on, Doc!" She raced off up the gangway.

"I'm warning you, Walt. If she keeps calling me Doc, I'm going to keelhaul her."

"And if you keep calling her runt, you'll find snails and leeches in your sleeping bag."

Eric laughed and started up the ramp onto the dock, then trotted after Laurel toward the parking lot. He found her waiting impatiently at the Pathfinder, sitting on the lowered tailgate and swinging her legs. "What took you so long? Getting old?"

"Now listen! That's entirely enough abuse. Show a little respect, or I'll toss you to the sharks."

Laurel was delighted to get him going, paying him back for his own frequent teasing. "Sorry, won't work. You taught me to swim, remember? And now I'm faster than any old shark." She hopped down off the tailgate and slid the cooler toward the edge. "I'll take the heavy end."

"What did your dad call you? Big shot? You can just carry the whole thing yourself!"

Laurel loved the banter, and they both dissolved in laughter. They each grabbed a handle of the cooler and lifted it down to the ground. Eric located his binoculars and slung the strap around her neck. Then he hoisted the sleeping bag to his shoulder, closed and locked the tailgate, and checked the doors. He picked up his end of the cooler again, and they headed back to the dock.

Walt was checking the anchor lines when he saw them coming. Laurel scrambled over the rail, and Eric boosted the cooler up to her. She balanced it while he got aboard, then helped him carry it below. They began transferring the contents into the ship's large icebox.

"Where's the safest place to stow my binoculars?" Eric asked. "I don't want them falling when we're out on the bounding main."

"How about the cubby over the sink?" Laurel suggested, lifting the strap of the case over her head and handing it to him. "It's got a wide rail in front to keep stuff inside."

Eric stowed the case and was storing his empty cooler in a locker when they heard Walt call out, "All hands on deck!"

"Dad really likes playing Captain," Laurel confided. "Better go along with him. And I'm First Mate."

"Aye, aye, sir," Eric replied. "Do I get a rank?"

"Swabbie!" Laurel laughed and started up the ladder. He followed her up through the hatch into the cockpit. She jumped to the dock and cast off the stern line, then scampered up to the bow. Eric watched her with admiration. "She really loves this, doesn't she?" he said to Walt.

"A natural-born sailor," he replied as he started the engine. "And she knows the ropes, too, literally and figuratively. Wait until you see her handle the helm."

As Walt advanced the throttle, Laurel swung back aboard, and he eased *Mayflower* away from the dock. "Haul in the fenders, swabbie!" she ordered delightedly.

Eric looked at her with mock surprise. "Hey, Walt, whatever happened to, 'You can just lay back, relax, and enjoy the scenery.'"

"Sorry, buddy. That was when we had Sara for Second Mate. Without her here, you get all the scut work."

"And suppose I refuse?"

"Mutiny," Walt pronounced authoritatively, "is punishable by walking the plank."

Eric laughed. "I surrender. What the heck is a fender?"

Laurel reached over the rail and hauled up a white, sausage-shaped float. "These things. They protect the side of the boat from rubbing on the dock. You have to untie them and stow them in the deck locker, like this." She dropped the float on the floor of the cockpit, untied its line, and shoved it into the storage area under the port seat.

Eric walked forward and began to untie the next fender.

"Hold it, swabbie!" Walt ordered.

"Now what?" Eric said, feigning exasperation.

"If you untie it before you haul it in, you might drop it overboard, and we'll have to go back for it."

Eric had to admit the logic of the procedure, and was slightly embarrassed not to have thought of it himself. He hoisted the fender to the deck and untied it, then went forward and collected the remaining three. When they were all safely stowed, he snapped to attention and saluted Walt smartly. "What next, my Captain? Paint the hull? Overhaul the engine? Maybe build a bigger cabin for you?"

"Nah, we've tortured you enough. Relax." Eric sank gratefully onto the starboard seat.

Laurel asked to take *Mayflower* out of the harbor, and Walt relinquished the wheel. Eric was surprised to see that Walt was paying little attention to her, apparently fully confident of her ability to handle the craft. He lounged back and took a good look at his surroundings.

Mayflower was a CS 30, Canadian-built and fitted with a small but sturdy Volvo diesel engine. A large blue canvas dodger protected the front of the cockpit, fitted with clear plastic panels for side and forward visibility. As Laurel moved out into the channel, Walt hoisted a makeshift canopy overhead at the rear of the cockpit, just below and extending aft of the boom, to give them some extra protection against the strengthening morning sun when sitting in the stern.

Eric spotted a number of ropes that entered the cockpit from the mast area and forward deck, but had no clue as to their function. Although he was a skilled canoeist and familiar with speedboats, his experience with sailboats was nonexistent. He noted the two heavy winches that flanked the hatch, with thick ropes wound twice around each one. A gimbaled compass floated in the top of the console at the back of the cockpit, behind which Laurel stood under the canopy, manipulating the wheel and engine controls.

He looked over the side and spotted a green buoy passing to starboard. "Hey, First Mate, you seem to be pretty good at this. How do you know where to steer?"

Laurel rewarded him with a big smile in appreciation for his praise, and said to her father, "Dad, how about we teach Eric to be a sailor?" Eric smiled at her use of his name, instead of teasing him with "Doc." Although her parents had tried to insist that she call him Dr. Kelman, the closeness that had developed between them during their narrow escape in June made first names more natural, despite the wide gulf between their ages. Eric wouldn't have had it any other way.

"Only if he wants to," Walt answered her. "He's our guest, remember?"

"I'm game," Eric said.

"Okay, first lesson. When you go out of the harbor, you have to keep the green buoys on the starboard side. When we come back in, they're on the port side. And you have to be sure to stay between the green ones and the red ones. That's where the channel is."

Eric played dumb. "What's a channel?"

"The deep water," she answered. "We have to have at least six feet to clear the keel." She thought for a moment, then caught on. "Hey, you knew that! You're teasing me again!"

"Sorry. But I still don't see how you remember which buoy goes on which side of the boat."

"Alliteration, professor," Walt put in. "Tell him, First Mate."

"'*Red right returning*,'" she sang out. "You keep the red ones on the right, starboard, when you come back in to the harbor. So they're on the port side when you're heading out."

For the next twenty minutes Laurel lectured him, delighted to know more about something than a university professor did. He learned that sheets and halyards were ropes, that a tickler was a little string threaded through the mainsail about halfway up, and half a dozen other nautical terms. By the time they reached the mouth of the harbor, a warm offshore breeze bathed them, steady off the port bow.

Walt stood up and assumed a commanding posture. "Engines full stop, crew! Sails aloft!"

"Aye, Captain," Laurel responded with a salute. "Permission to relinquish the helm, sir?"

Eric was amused by their exaggerated dramatics. Walt took the wheel, and Laurel ducked out from under the canopy and stepped over the rail onto the walkway. "Come on, Eric. We have to uncover the mainsail." She pronounced it "mains'l" in true nautical fashion.

He followed her up onto the top of the cabin, and she showed him the ties that held the blue canvas cover around the sail. After they loosened them, she showed him how to fold it back neatly, and raised the front hatch so he could drop it down below. Then she attached the main halyard to the eyelet in the top of the sail and checked a few other lines. Satisfied, she led Eric back to the cockpit.

"The next job is all yours," she said to him. "See the winch handle in that pocket next to the hatch?"

"This First Mate of yours is a real slave driver," Eric complained good-naturedly to Walt. He attached the handle to the port winch and turned to Laurel. "Now what?"

She flopped down on the port locker cover. "Crank away."

Walt kept the bow pointed into the wind, and Eric wrapped the halyard around the body of the winch and began to turn the handle strongly. The sail climbed the mast, and Laurel stopped him when he had achieved the proper tension. "Now we have to lock it off, and take it off the winch," she told him, pointing under the dodger to a series of clamps through which the lines passed. She reached in and slapped one home, securing the main halyard, then released the line from the winch.

"Now check the traveler," she ordered.

"The *what?*"

She pointed beneath the dodger, above the cabin hatch. "See that crossbar with the lines attached to the ends? It goes back and forth from side to side. Travels, traveler, get it? It changes the position of the sail." She checked the wind. "It needs to be right in the middle for the heading we're on." She was momentarily uncertain, and turned to her father. "Right, Dad?"

"Right, *who?*"

"Right, *Captain*, sir?"

"Aye, Mate. Good job."

Pleased, she turned back to Eric. "Now the jib," she commanded, pointing to another line. It had a few colored strands woven into it to distinguish it from the main halyard, and it led forward all the way up to the bow area. "Pull on it hard and fast until the other sail pops out."

Eric turned to Walt again. "Now I see why I was invited on this cruise. All this work is supposed to be done by the First Mate, isn't it? And she's sloughing it off on me."

"Quiet, swabbie," Walt laughed. "I warned you what happens to mutineers aboard my vessel."

Pretending to grumble under his breath, Eric hauled on the jib sheet. The forward sail spun off the roller furling, and when it was completely free, he wound the line on the winch and began cranking. Again Laurel specified the tension she wanted on the sheet, but on their present heading, the sails flapped ineffectually in the wind.

Laurel was all business. "There's another jib sheet on the port side. You'll need it when we tack. And put the handle back in its pocket, right there," she pointed, "so you'll be able to find it when you need it."

Eric was entranced by his pint-sized boss. He followed her directions and awaited her approval, but instead she turned to Walt. "Did we get it all right, Dad?"

"Great job, sweetheart. You want the helm again?"

"Sure! Are we going north through the islands?"

"Uh huh, same as last time." Laurel replaced him at the wheel, and he gave her the range of compass headings she could use. Expertly she caught the wind, and the sails billowed and began driving the boat forward. *Mayflower* dipped her rail toward the sea. The needle on the electronic knot meter wavered between four and four-and-a-half.

She gazed at the big sail, analyzing the flow of wind around the ticklers, and explained to Eric how to trim the sails by moving the traveler back and forth. He followed her instructions carefully. Finally satisfied, she assumed a nautical stance, her ball cap turned at a jaunty angle, the sunglasses giving her a professional air. All her attention was focused on the boat and the sea. Eric hid his broad smile and sat down next to Walt.

"This part of the coast is lined with islands," his friend explained, "most of them uninhabited. There's no fresh water, except on a few of the largest ones. We can sail between some of them, although we draw six feet of water, and in some places the channels aren't that deep. Mostly we just enjoy their beauty from the boat, but there are a few places where we can anchor and go ashore in the Zodiac." He leaned out around the dodger and pointed to the small rubberized raft that sat inflated on the forward deck.

"Any cell phones or faxes?" Eric joked.

Walt laughed. "Not a chance. We've got the radio, and there's the ship-to-shore operator if there's an emergency, but other than that, nobody can get at us. We're *free!* For three whole days!"

"Paradise!"

"Part of the way we have to head out into the open ocean. These islands are really just the tops of some sunken hills, and we draw too much water to go between them all."

Eric gazed out at the receding mainland, then ahead to some vague smudges on the horizon, the first of the islands they would encounter after lunch. He glanced back at Laurel, and found her enmeshed in a world of her own, capably playing the freshening wind to keep them moving at better than five knots. He lay back against the cabin wall, thoroughly relaxed, and he and Walt engaged in pleasant conversation, none of it about Walt's architectural business or about the university.

Twelve

As the morning wore on, Eric became more and more fascinated with the workings of the sails. By careful observation he worked out how the wind drove the boat, somewhat like the lift of an aircraft's wing. They were blessed with a favorable wind direction, and after the initial setup, Laurel had little to do but steer to the compass heading.

"Hey, runt," he asked finally, "what do you do if the wind is coming directly at you over the bow?"

"Show me a little more respect, and maybe I'll teach you," she replied with exaggerated dignity.

"I beg your pardon, *First Mate, Sir*. Would you be so good as to answer this poor swabbie's question?"

Laurel giggled delightedly. "Can I show him how to tack, Dad?"

"Sure," Walt replied, "if he really wants to learn. There's lots of deep water to experiment in. But does he know how much work is involved?"

"I knew there'd be a catch to it," Eric complained.

"Come on, Doc, it's easy. All you have to do is man the jib. I'll do the rest."

"Explain it to me first, professor."

"Okay, it works like this," Laurel began, then drew herself erect and assumed what she thought would be a professorial tone. "The basic scientific principle behind sailing is to manage the force and direction of the wind, with respect to the position of the various sails, keeping in mind…"

Eric burst out laughing. "If you're going to try to imitate me, this lesson will be a bust. Besides, I don't sound like that when I teach."

"I hope not. Okay, this is what you have to do." Patiently she explained how the sails form an airfoil shape when the angle of the wind isn't too acute, and demonstrated. Eric interrupted a couple of times with questions, and was surprised at how clearly the child could express herself.

"Okay," Laurel said again, her favorite word. *At least she doesn't constantly say "like" or "you know,"* Eric thought. "If you try to point up too close to the wind..."

"Point up?"

Laurel pretended exasperation with her slow student. "Turn too much into the wind, Eric. Pay attention!"

"Sorry." He tried to look penitent, but couldn't quite hide his growing amusement. "I'll concentrate."

"Okay, if you point up too far, that's called pinching, and the sails will flap and stop pushing the boat forward, and that's called..."

"Wait a minute, are you going to pinch me?"

"Stop it! Be *serious!* I think you know more than you're letting on, and I don't appreciate being teased! Do you want to learn, or not?"

Eric realized that his kidding was bordering on condescension, and was genuinely contrite. "All right. So you point up too close to the wind, and the sails... what?"

"Luff!"

"Luff, right. But suppose you want to go in *that* direction." He pointed directly into the wind. "What then?" Eric understood the concept of tacking, but he wanted to hear her explanation. And he was truly interested in the finer points of how the sails were managed.

"You can't sail straight into the wind, so you have to tack. That's like going first to the right, then to the left, like about... What, Dad?"

"Something like forty-five degrees off the wind, a little more, each way," her father put in. He was proud of her practical knowledge and skill, and let her continue on her own.

"Yeah, like that, and you just sort of zigzag back and forth. It takes longer to get there that way, because you aren't going in a straight line, but the only other way to do it is with the engine, and no *real* sailor does that if there's any wind, and..."

"Whoa! I've got all that. What I want to know is *how*?"

"You have to put the sails on the side of the boat that can catch the wind. See how it looks now? Both the mainsail and the jib are puffed out to starboard, so that means the wind is coming from the port side. If we turn to port ninety or a hundred degrees, the wind will be coming from starboard, so we have to swing the mainsail over to the other side. Get it?"

"Seems pretty simple to me," Eric answered.

"That part is. But you've got to get the jib over, too. Remember how you left the jib sheet on the winch when we started out?" She pointed to the rope that was held fast on the starboard winch. "That's what's keeping the jib in the right place. Now look at the other winch."

She pointed to port, and Eric spotted another rope, loosely looped around the winch on the opposite side of the cockpit.

"When we come about to tack in the other direction, you have to take the starboard sheet off the winch. Just let it go, and haul like mad on the port sheet. That yanks the jib to the other side. If you're really good at it, you can set the jib just as the mainsail comes across, and you won't lose much speed." She turned to her father, a look of pride on her face, mixed with just a bit of apprehension in case she had left out a step. "Did I get it all right, Dad?"

"You sure did, sweetheart."

"It all makes sense to me," Eric added. "Now show me."

"Nope," Laurel answered. "I'm steering. You have to do it."

Eric sighed. "I knew it. The catch."

Laurel showed him how to release the starboard winch, then told him he'd have to step across the cockpit, haul on the port jib sheet, and wind it around the winch and pull it tight. "Oh, yeah, and keep your head down, or the boom'll knock you overboard when it comes across."

Eric ignored her broad smile as she gave him the warning. "How do I know when to do all this?"

"When I yell 'Coming about!' and spin the wheel, you have to time it so the jib catches the wind at just the right second. Think you can do it?"

"No, but let's try it anyway."

"Coming about!" she shouted gleefully, and spun the wheel sharply to port. Eric jumped for the winch, fumbled with the release, then lost his footing and sprawled on the cockpit floor. Scrambling up, he reached for the port sheet.

"Boom!" Walt yelled, and Eric ducked his head just in time as the big mainsail crashed across above them. He started pulling on the rope, hand over hand, and finally managed to get it on the winch. Then he couldn't find the handle. The port side pocket was empty.

"Over there!" Laurel cried happily, pointing to the starboard pocket.

"Quick, crank it in tight." He fumbled with the handle and finally managed to trim the sail to her satisfaction.

"Almost two minutes," Walt said as Eric collapsed on the port side locker. "Not too bad for a first time swabbie."

"Not too bad?" Laurel said. "That was terrible! You have to practice, practice, *practice!* And get up. You have to sit on the high side after we come about to help keep us balanced."

"Who was your ancestor, anyway, Sir Francis Drake? Blackbeard the Pirate?" Eric dropped the winch handle into the pocket and moved to the opposite side of the cockpit, pretending exhaustion.

"Coming about!" Laurel whipped the wheel right, and *Mayflower* obeyed the helm almost instantly. Although caught by surprise, Eric gained the port winch without falling and released the rope. With surprising agility he seized the starboard sheet and hauled it in with long, powerful hand-over-hand tugs. He reached for the winch handle, remembering where he had left it this time, and quickly tensioned the jib. The big boat plunged on, barely slowing.

"All *right!*" Laurel crowed. "That was *awesome!* You learn really fast!"

"Lots of practice, runt. Learning, I mean, not sailing." He was slightly winded, and sat down again, remembering to move to the high side.

"Coming about!"

Five more times Laurel tacked, running Eric ragged. Walt finally took pity on his friend and called a halt, but by that time Eric had the maneuver down pat, acting almost by instinct. He took a silent but certain pride in his developing seamanship. *Old dog, no new tricks? Who says?*

Walt took the wheel as Laurel announced the next lesson. Eric groaned and followed her below, and she instructed him in the fine points of managing a propane stove at sea. He was amazed at the way the gimbals kept it level, in spite of the motion of the boat, and soon they had coffee, soup and sandwiches ready. Laurel got a can of cola for herself, and they carried everything up on deck.

Walt turned the wheel, lessening the sails' angle of attack, and *Mayflower* slowed and came almost fully upright, her forward progress slowed by more than half. He set the self-steering gear and sat down on the port hatch, eager for the meal. They ate in companionable relaxation, accompanied by the child's almost constant, happy chatter.

As they passed one of the smaller islands, Walt pointed to where a narrow cove penetrated the mainland. "See the buoys in that channel? That's the Coast Guard station in there. It's partly hidden by that point of land, but you can just see the end of their dock when we get a little further along."

Eric strained his eyes, and presently he could make out the horizontal lines of a substantial dock, and a couple of small sheds. He assumed there was more to the complex, shielded from their view by a low hill and trees.

"That's our last view of civilization," Walt said. "The coast gets really rocky from this point on, and there are no communities along the water until you get almost to the Capital."

Eric shifted his gaze out over the bow. The mainland stretched ahead, apparently barren of any human habitation. The islands that he could see were similarly deserted, and covered thickly with trees and dense underbrush.

After they cleaned up the remains of lunch, Laurel again took the helm. She and Walt discussed their course, and she brought the boat about almost ninety degrees, pointing it out to sea. With the gentle wind at a less efficient angle, their speed barely approached four knots. Eric asked why they didn't head directly toward the islands, which now loomed in stark detail ahead.

"See the big island directly off the port bow, at about eleven o'clock?" Walt asked. "Most of it is under water. There's a long shelf that extends for more than a mile in this direction, and it's close to four miles wide off shore. The depth varies from less than a fathom, six feet to you landlubbers, to only about twice that, and there are too many rocks. Even though the tide's in now, we don't want to risk it, so we'll head out to sea and go around."

"How do you know where the deep water is?"

"When we first started coming out here, Laurel and I studied the charts and plotted our course by the book. This is the third year we've come this way, and we know where all the danger spots are pretty well by now. Hey, look!"

Laurel was shouting and pointing, jumping up and down at the rail.

103

Eric followed her gesture. Off to starboard, a pair of dolphins kept pace with them, scribing graceful arcs above the waves.

"They're racing us, Dad!" she cried. Eric stared in fascination as the mammals narrowed the gap until they were less than ten yards from the boat. Despite Laurel's excited shouts, they seemed completely unafraid. For more than five minutes they shepherded *Mayflower* along, then veered off and disappeared beneath the waves.

"That was *amazing!* Why do they do that, Dad?"

"Probably as curious about us as we are about them," Walt answered her. "Some people think they're as smart as we are, maybe even smarter. They even seem to have their own language, clicks and squeals and such."

"I wish they'd come back."

"If we saw them all the time," Eric said, "pretty soon they wouldn't seem so wonderful."

"I guess..."

Laurel returned her attention to their course, and presently they cleared the tip of the shoal and turned back into more favorable wind. They heeled over and began to drive forward at nearly six knots. Five minutes later Laurel eased the wheel a quarter turn, and *Mayflower* fell off the wind slightly and slowed. She turned to her father. "Want to take the helm so I can get some sun?"

"Let Eric do it," Walt replied. "All he has to do is keep it on a straight heading." He gestured for his friend to take the wheel, and Eric replaced her at the console. "Half an hour's enough for you, though. It's pretty hot. And don't forget the sun block."

"Right!" She padded over to the cabin hatch, grasped the handrails and stepped over the sill. Briefly she looked over her shoulder at Eric, as if considering something, then walked back next to her father. She stretched up on tiptoe and whispered in his ear. Walt whispered something back, and she turned and disappeared down the gangway, the tail of her overly long T-shirt flapping against her legs, halfway to her knees.

"What was that all about?" Eric asked.

Walt sighed. "We had a major wardrobe crisis last night. Usually when we're out on the boat, Laurel practically lives in a bikini, at least when it's just Fran and I, and maybe Sara or one of her other girlfriends aboard. About a week ago, Fran took her shopping for a new one. I haven't seen it yet, but Fran says its really rather daring, given how conservative Laurel usually is."

"So what's the problem?"

"You are."

"Me!" Eric pretended amazement. "What did I do?" Then he laughed. "To tell the truth, Deanna predicted something like this would happen."

Walt smiled at his friend. "That's a smart lady you're married to. Even Fran didn't see this coming. In case you haven't noticed, Laurel has you on some sort of pedestal. First you rescued her last June, then you taught her to do the one thing she wanted to do more than anything else in the world, but thought she'd never learn: swim. In spite of the way you two insult each other, she's always just a little bit in awe of you."

"I still don't get it. What's that got to do with her choice of swimwear?"

"She's self-conscious around you, that's all. She's very concerned that you think well of her. Last night when she was packing her duffel, Fran noticed that the only suit she was taking was her checked one, the old one-piece thing you saw out at the lake. She's had it since she was ten. It turns out she didn't want to wear anything skimpier when you're around."

Eric laughed. "After what we went through last June, she shouldn't be shy around me."

"That's exactly the problem. She still feels embarrassed by the condition she was in when you found her. And later on I guess you teased her a little. Called her 'sexy,' she said."

"That was just to help her get over her fear. I didn't realize it bothered her."

"She's just insecure, I guess. Having voluptuous Sara for a friend intimidates her a little, anyway, and she's always afraid someone might be making comments about how she looks. According to Fran, she's afraid you'll think she's showing off, or that you'll think she's trying to look too old, or something. I don't really understand it either, but then I'm just a poor male. What do I know?"

Eric smiled. "I remember our two at that age. They were sure they were being stared at all the time, too. Amy was the worst. She inherited Deanna's ample bust line, and hated it. Deanna bought her several very expensive, flattering swimsuits, but from the time she was eleven, she wouldn't go out on a public beach, or even in the water, without a T-shirt on over top. That lasted until she was sixteen."

He sighed. "So how am I supposed to act, then? Put on blinders, maybe? Stare out to sea like the Ancient Mariner?"

Walt laughed. "Just don't look her over too closely. Whatever you do, don't make any comments about her suit, even a compliment. Just be natural."

Eric thought for a moment. "I'm not sure that's the best strategy. She's used to me teasing her, and if I ignore her, I think it will just make her even more uneasy. She'll know I'm *deliberately* ignoring her, and be twice as self-conscious."

"Maybe. But I'll bet if you say anything, you'll scare her right back into that ridiculous oversized T-shirt."

"How much are you willing to bet?"

"Oh, no. Forget I mentioned it. But I still think this time I'm right."

They turned the conversation to other matters. A few minutes later, Laurel's face appeared in the companionway. Slowly she levered herself up on deck, a fragile, pale golden doll. Her bright red two-piece suit looked to Eric to be quite modest on her slim body, more than covering the essentials and flattering her taut young frame. Wide straps on the bra top crisscrossed behind her narrow shoulders, and the ample bottom hardly qualified as a bikini. Although the legs were cut somewhat high, the waistband rode only an inch or two below her navel. Nevertheless she stood nervously in the hatchway, fingering the towel that she clutched loosely in front of her.

"Did you remember the sun block?" Walt asked.

"Of *course*, Dad!"

Not usually a fearful man, Walt was abnormally haunted by the specter of cancer. His father had succumbed to a fast-growing liver tumor fifteen years earlier, and his mother had fought a courageous and agonizing six-year battle against breast cancer. She had died when Laurel was only five. Fran's parents were also gone, killed on the highway the same year she was married, which deprived Laurel of the joy of having grandparents.

Laurel seemed reluctant to step out from beneath the dodger, twisting the towel and casting sidelong glances in Eric's direction. After a casual glance at her and a smile, he decided to ignore Walt's advice and tackle the problem head on. "Hey, runt, do you ever look beautiful! New swimsuit?"

Walt groaned softly, anticipating her reaction and expecting her to bolt down the ladder again, but she stood her ground. However, she blushed furiously and didn't answer, looking down at her feet. When she raised her eyes, expecting to be the center of his attention, Eric was instead studying the sails, and making minor unnecessary adjustments with the wheel.

Walt tried to ease the tension. "Remember, only half an hour out there, now."

"I *know*, Dad." Exasperated, and with none of the confidence she normally exhibited, she paced stiffly along the gunwale toward the bow, consciously restricting the movement of her slim hips and shoulders. Ducking under the mainsail, she spread the towel on the forward roof of the cabin, adjusted her sunglasses, and stretched out on her stomach.

Once she had turned her face away from them, Eric and Walt watched her with melancholy amusement, admiring the smooth, strong limbs and the perfect skin of her youth. Still boyishly slender, she was at the same time heartbreakingly feminine in the gentle curves of her small waist and bottom. She would never be more beautiful, Eric knew, nor more vulnerable.

"Well," Walt said, "at least she didn't run for cover. But it was a near thing."

"Just watch. The worst is over. She'll be okay when she gets back to running the boat, and she'll take my presence for granted."

"I hope you're right, but I doubt it." Walt paused, then commented quietly, "She scares me to death sometimes. One minute she's happy to be a little kid, and the next she's desperate to be taken for an adult. I feel like I ought to hide her away somewhere until she's thirty."

"I know just what you mean," Eric answered. "We went through the same thing with our two. Deanna was better with them than I was, more relaxed. Mothers seem to take it in stride, while fathers tend to panic. Both of our kids turned out pretty sensible, though, and Laurel's just as levelheaded as they were. It's obvious you're doing a good job with her. She's already got good values."

"I'm glad you think so," Walt said. "It's just that there's so much that could happen to her, things I can't always foresee. But I know that if we're always protecting her from everything, we'll smother her. Worse, she might rebel and go wild."

"She'll make mistakes," Eric said, "but she's incredibly resourceful. Trust me. Outside of you and Fran, no one knows that better than I do. I saw her under the worst possible conditions last June, and she came through like a winner."

Eric sounded more confident than he felt. He was overcome with memories of his own two, Becky and Amy, at that age. They had seemed so incredibly defenseless in the face of the world's evil, yet they had survived and prospered. He would like to have thought it was because of his wisdom and his guidance. He feared instead that it was only in spite of him.

And now this golden child, still relatively innocent and possessed of an allure that could make her a tempting target, seemed similarly vulnerable. She had only her own common sense, and her parents' limited protection, to safeguard her while growing up. It didn't seem like enough.

Walt took a deep breath, shook off the apprehension over his daughter's coming maturity, and joined Eric at the wheel to give him some lessons in helmsmanship: steering to a compass heading, recognizing when they were pinching (*sailing too close into the wind*, Eric reminded himself), and how to estimate the proper tension of the sails.

Eric was eager to learn how to adjust the sails for maximum speed. Despite Walt's careful instructions, he let the boom slam across the cockpit on his first try, and *Mayflower* heeled over hard, prompting a shriek from Laurel as she struggled to maintain her perch. The next two tries were more successful, and Eric quickly grasped the basics of making the wind work for him.

After half an hour, almost to the minute, Laurel made her way back to the cockpit. She stepped shyly down under the dodger and sat on her towel on the leeward side, watching Eric out of the corner of her eye, as far away from him as she could get. She soon realized he was paying no attention to her. He was concentrating on the ticklers, keeping them flying while trying to coax the last tenth of a knot out of the hull. Walt corrected him several times, but the boat began to wallow as the sails refused to fill. Their speed dropped.

After watching for a few minutes, Laurel got up and moved toward the wheel, forgetting her towel. "You're confusing him, Dad." She pushed Walt aside playfully. "Let me show him how."

"Ah, the master mariner has all the answers, as usual." Smiling, he retired to the rail.

"Do it this way," Laurel said, taking the wheel from Eric's grasp. "Hold it really light, and watch the ticklers." She spun the wheel a half turn, and the brightly colored strings stood out from the sail and fluttered loosely.

"Now we bring her back into the wind, gradually. The trick is to try to anticipate when the ticklers are going to flatten out against the sail. You have to guess when, and just before they touch, bring the wheel back just a little. That catches them at the last possible second. See?" She pointed *Mayflower* up into the wind, and Eric saw the strings approach the sail, just as they had when he was steering. But with unfailing instinct, she eased off at the last instant. The ticklers kept flying, *Mayflower* dug in a little deeper, and the meter jumped a half-knot.

Eric's admiration was genuine. Although Walt was obviously a fine sailor, Laurel had a more instinctive, natural touch. For the next ten minutes she issued orders, and the two men adjusted the traveler, tightened the mainsail and brought the jib in close. Walt didn't say a word, but just did whatever she asked for. And when they were finished, *Mayflower* was making an honest six knots.

"You're amazing!" Eric told her.

She beamed under his praise, then let the big boat fall off the wind again. "Now you try it."

Eric took the wheel once more, and had better luck predicting the condition of the sails. He couldn't maintain quite the speed she had achieved. Still, her patient instruction was much more successful than Walt's, and her father complimented them both warmly.

As Eric smiled down with affection, Laurel's embarrassment returned in a rush. Standing so closely to him, she was suddenly acutely aware of her bare middle, and the way the swimsuit bottom rode up slightly on her buttocks. She tugged it down in back self-consciously. She felt her face flush, and looked up to see if he had noticed, but he seemed to be concentrating on the sails, and was paying no attention to her.

Eric was painfully aware of her discomfort, however. At first he ignored her, following Walt's advice, but as the unnatural silence continued to grow between them, he changed his mind. He leaned down slightly and spoke very quietly, too softly for Walt to hear from his seat on the opposite side of the cockpit.

"You're not going to get all shy on me again, are you?"

Laurel looked up at him in wonder. "How did you know?"

"Oh, just a hunch I had. That, and those pretty red spots on your cheeks, and the way you won't look me in the eye."

"I'm sorry. It's just... I don't know..."

"Relax, squirt. I wasn't kidding before when I said you looked beautiful. If we had a cell phone aboard this barge, there'd be six Hollywood producers on the line right now. And you're covered up in all the important places, so what's the big deal?"

She blushed furiously, looking down at the deck. Then she summoned her courage. "If I ask you a question, will you promise not to tease me?"

"Nope."

"Eric! I'm serious!"

"Me, too," he said. "Ask your question, and be prepared to face the consequences."

"Is it okay?"

"Is *what* okay?"

"You know. Do I look too flashy, or anything? When Sara..."

"Whoa, hold it! Sara's Sara, and you're you. You have to be yourself, and make the most of what you are. Above all, you have to be *comfortable* with who you are, and not make comparisons."

"But Sara's... You know how she is, and she's sort of showing off all the time, and the boys are always hanging around her and stuff, and they make these comments about her, you know, boobs, but she seems to like it when they do. It makes me feel all kind of crawly inside. I still like her and everything, she's my best friend, but I don't really want to be like that."

"Are you sure?"

"What do you mean?"

"Look, I think you've got yourself all tied up in a knot because you want to look a little bit grown up. And in that swimsuit you really do, I might add. But you don't really want anyone to look at you, right?"

"I guess…"

"Okay, here's how I see it. You're going to become what you are, no matter what you try to do about it. Just like Sara did, only she grew up a little too big and a little too fast, and hasn't learned how to handle it yet. And you'll never be like her, anyway, because you have your mother's genes."

"Thank goodness!"

"Right. Now I don't know from experience, but I've heard from very reliable sources, a wife and two daughters, that being female can be great fun. You're going to become a lovely young woman before long, in fact you already are, and you *should* enjoy looking the part. It's nothing to be ashamed of."

Her voice was so soft that Eric could barely hear her. "So you really think I look all right?"

"Nah. You're pretty ugly. In fact, that's your new nickname. Hi, ugly."

"Eric!"

"Okay, I think you look fantastic, the prettiest twelve-year-old I've ever seen, at least since my own two girls were that age. And your new swimsuit is definitely *not* too flashy." Despite Walt's warning, he decided to take a chance on his own judgment, and risked a gentle tease. "A little bit sexy, maybe…"

Still red with embarrassment, she stuck her tongue out at him. She searched his face and saw only approval in his smile. She grinned back at him. "This isn't even my new one," she said. "Mom helped me pick one out last week, a really pretty yellow one."

"How come you didn't put that one on?"

"It's too bare…"

"Then why did you buy it?"

She hesitated a long moment, and finally said, "I guess I just didn't think about you… I mean… Nuts, now I'm *really* embarrassed."

"There's no need to be. After our adventure last June, we know each other pretty well, don't we?" She nodded shyly, and he continued in a soft and serious tone. "I guess I tease you a lot, but that's because we're good friends, and you give *me* a pretty hard time, too. But it would make me sad to think I ever said anything to make you feel uncomfortable."

She shrugged and bumped his arm with her shoulder, her patented show of affection for her older friend.

"And I can't wait to see your new swimsuit," he went on. "But you know, it's what's inside your head that's really important. The outside is just decoration."

"Come *on!* You sound just like Dad!"

"I'll take that as a compliment, thank you very much. Anyway," he continued, "you'd better stay dressed for the water, because if you keep on calling me Doc, I'm going to toss you to the sharks."

"Oh, *really?* Well just remember, you'll make a bigger meal for the sharks than I ever could. You try to throw me in, and I'll take you with me, *Doc.*"

"We'll see about that, *runt.* Now how about showing me some more about how to sail this thing?"

Laurel squeezed over next to him behind the console, and took the wheel again. She still moved a bit stiffly and self-consciously, but over the next few minutes her tension eased. Gradually she relaxed into the easy, unconstrained familiarity she enjoyed when just her family was aboard. Eric finally felt completely accepted.

Their voices had risen, and Walt had been listening to them discretely. He admired the psychology behind Eric's words. He had thought he knew his daughter well, and was surprised and pleased at how well the tactic had worked. He had underestimated the degree of trust that had grown up between the child and this senior professor who had saved her life the previous June. Walt suddenly realized that Eric had become a substitute for the grandfather Laurel had never had. And a welcome substitute, at that.

Thirteen

As the sun dropped toward the horizon, they anchored *Mayflower* fore and aft in the lee of a cliff-bound island. Eric and Laurel furled the jib and lowered and covered the mainsail, while Walt fired up the barbecue and set out the ingredients for a substantial evening meal. All three downed large amounts of chicken, corn and Deanna's potato salad. After clearing away the remains, they sat lazily in the cockpit, enjoying the cool evening air until a squadron of mosquitoes found them and drove them below decks.

By the time they had cleaned up the dishes and stowed them away, it was almost full dark. They switched on the battery-powered cabin lamps, and Laurel curled up in the roomy forward bunk with a book. Eric and Walt sat comfortably at the folding table with mugs of fresh coffee. The wind had vanished along with the light, and the boat lay almost motionless in the calm waters that were protected by the island.

They were discussing the next day's agenda when, at about ten o'clock, Laurel wandered sleepily back into the main part of the cabin. She kissed her father and gave Eric a hug, then ducked into the after berth beside the engine compartment and squirmed into her sleeping bag. Turning on a small flashlight, she resumed her reading, but after only a minute or two the light wavered and dropped from her hand.

Walt slipped over quietly and turned it off, closed her book, and tucked her arms into the sleeping bag. He returned to the table and sat down again, speaking softly. "She had a big day."

"I'm amazed at how well she sails," Eric commented. "She seems so grown up behind the wheel."

"She's a strange kid in some ways. She has lots of friends at school, but she doesn't go in for most of the typical pre-teen nonsense, clothes fads and mooning over rock stars and such. She gives it lip service when her friends are around, but you can tell she doesn't take it seriously."

"Kids have a lot of pressures on them. The old biological imperative to belong, I guess. The ones with something upstairs see through all the phoniness, but even so, it takes a rare one to go it alone without alienating the rest of the herd."

"Her head works, all right, overtime in fact. She reads, she writes poetry, and she takes her music lessons very seriously. In fact, I've been meaning to talk with you about that. Her band director at the elementary school says she has the potential for a substantial career in music."

"Does she seem really serious about it?" Eric asked.

"I'd say so. But who knows what she'll eventually want to do with her life. I changed *my* mind a dozen times when I was a teenager. But if she has the talent, and if it's what she wants to do, we want to be sure she gets the right background training."

"There are some signs to look for. For example, do you have to nag her to practice?"

"We never even mention it. She's off to her room with her clarinet every evening, and twice as much on weekends. Fran often has to make her quit and chase her to bed. She never misses a day, even in the summer, except when we're on an outing like this. She loves to play alone, too, not just in the band. And there's another thing."

"What's that?"

"She's taught herself to play the piano. Not just picking out tunes like some kids do, but both hands together. I don't know much about it, but she seems to be able to find the right chords to go with whatever song she wants to play."

"Does she read from sheet music?"

"That's just it," Walt answered. "She doesn't seem to need music at all. She hears a song on the radio or someplace, and she can go to the piano and play it, harmony and everything, right off. Not that it sounds really professional or anything, but she seems to get most of the right notes the first time. Can a lot of people do that?"

Eric laughed. "Sure. Mozart, Mendelssohn, Yehudi Menuhin… People like that. But your average kid? Not one in a hundred thousand." Eric thought for a minute, then smiled broadly. "And MacKenzie… Maybe having a last name that starts with 'M' has something to do with it."

"Yeah, right, 'M' for music, I suppose. Seriously though, how does she do it?"

"We don't know how the mechanism works, exactly, but people with that gift seem to be able to hear and grasp the pattern of chord sounds by instinct. At the piano, their hands just naturally find the keys that produce the sounds they hear in their heads. I assume it's genetically linked somehow. Are you and Fran musical?"

"Not me. Oh, I like it, especially show tunes, but I never learned to play anything. Fran had lessons when she was a kid. That's why we still have a piano, but she never did much with it, and she only plays occasionally now. So we're not sure what to do about Laurel."

Eric pondered the problem for a few moments. "Kids like that, the ones that don't have to be forced to practice, just need the proper guidance to channel their natural talent, someone to make sure they don't acquire any bad habits, steer them to good repertoire, help them develop taste… Then, when they're ready, to polish their technique. I might know just the right person."

"Who's that?"

"His name is Alexander Knowlton, a professional clarinetist. He lives in the Capital. He's retired now, but he held a succession of major first chair appointments: Philadelphia, the Montreal Symphony, and two posts in Europe. I think I might be able to persuade him to give Laurel an audition."

"Audition for what?"

"He accepts only a handful of students these days," Eric said. "He's almost eighty. But he has a special interest in encouraging young people with unusual talent, those who seem to have the proper dedication. We could take her to play for him. If he likes what he hears, she's in."

"What kind of a person is he?" Walt asked.

"You'll like him. He has no affectations, no phony accent or dramatic mannerisms. In fact, if you sat next to him in a coffee shop, you'd hardly notice him. But put a clarinet in his hands, and he's magic. He also gets along great with kids; he has half a dozen grandchildren himself. He seems to be able to give them just the right blend of praise and criticism to keep them working. But he *does* make them work, and if they slack off, he drops them fast."

"Do you think he'd really consider teaching her?"

"All we can do is ask. He's a good friend, so I'm sure he'll be willing to listen to her play, as a favor to me. But from then on, it's up to her. If she's got the goods, he'll take her on, but if he doesn't think she has potential, it won't matter who asks him. And she has to want to do it, herself. Suppose I ask her if she's interested?"

"Fair enough," Walt said. "I really appreciate it, Eric. We want to encourage her, but we just didn't know how to go about it."

"She has to understand that it will be a big commitment in time. It'll cut into her social life, for sure."

"There won't likely be any problem there, not with anything she's really interested in. As you can see, given the choice of hanging out with her friends or being on the boat, she chooses the boat every time."

"She's certainly very independent. Fran tells me she's good at just about everything in school, too."

"It all seems to come so easily to her, I'm almost jealous," Walt said. "She devours books, and not just commercial stuff. Fran introduced her to the best children's literature long before she could read, and she can tell good authors from hacks every time. We're very proud of her."

"I can see why."

The conversation turned to Walt's architectural firm, then to the latest university politics. Shortly after eleven they turned in. Eric was given the comfort of the wide triangular forward berth. In the kitchen area of the cabin, Walt lowered the table to the level of the bench seats, and laid out cushions to make himself a roomy bunk.

Eric slept well, better than he had in months, partly due to the gentle motion of the boat, but mostly from being away from any responsibility. Even his recently healed leg fractures seemed less troublesome at sea. He awoke early the next morning with the first sign of light, feeling alert and refreshed.

The cabin was somewhat cold and damp, and looking out the porthole, he saw nothing but dense gray mist. He pulled on his jacket and padded quietly past Walt's bunk to light the propane stove. Once the coffee was under way, he popped the hatch and climbed the ladder up onto the deck.

The sea was flat and calm, and thick fog surrounded *Mayflower*, obscuring even the nearest island. He stood at the stern and tried to orient himself. The sun was barely over the horizon and hidden by the fog, but he could determine which way was east from its faint glow. The only sounds came from gentle ripples against the hull and the occasional tick of a line against the mast. He felt completely at peace.

He returned to the cabin to find it warming nicely from the heat of the stove, and filled with the rich odor of coffee. He poured himself a cup and was leaning against the doorframe enjoying it when Walt roused and climbed out of his sleeping bag.

"Got any food to go with that?" he asked.

"Just waiting for your order, Captain."

Walt poured some coffee and drank half a mug, then stowed the sleeping bag and cushions and set up the table. Eric opened the food locker. "Any requests?"

"I'll do it. You've done your share, making the coffee," Walt replied. "I've never been able to understand why I get so hungry out on the water. I'm up for some eggs and bacon. Damn the demon cholesterol!" He took them out of the icebox along with some butter, and soon had the fry pan sizzling.

"Deanna has a theory. She says calories don't count when you're out with friends. Maybe that goes for cholesterol, too."

"I hope so. The thought of dammed up arteries at my age isn't too inviting. Anyway, exercise is supposed to help keep them clean and clear, and I get plenty of that."

They sat down to eat, and were nearly finished when Laurel finally emerged, barely awake, and stumbled into the head. They heard the sound of running water. When she reappeared, sleep still clouded her eyes, and she slumped down next to her father, tucked her head in against his chest, and gazed unseeing across the cabin. He gathered her in close.

"This one is worthless in the morning," he laughed. "We can't get her up with dynamite at home. It takes her half an hour to become coherent, and if you try to rush her, she bites your head off."

"I do not!" Laurel glared up at him, then snuggled in closer.

"See what I mean?" Walt laughed.

"Does it help to feed her?" Eric asked. "Suppose we throw her a chunk of raw meat and see if she pounces." Laurel ignored him. "Hey, runt, I'm on kitchen duty. What can I fix for you?"

She stirred a bit. "Fruit Loops, please."

"Pure sugar! That should bring you around." He found the cereal and set out a bowl and some milk for her. He added a tall glass of orange juice. Laurel pried herself out from under her father's arm and began to eat, silent and still groggy.

After breakfast they cleaned up quickly. Eric and Walt both shaved, intent on maintaining some degree of civilization even when on holiday. The cabin was pleasantly warm, and they all dressed in shorts and T-shirts, but when Laurel went up on deck, she soon came back for a sweatshirt, as defense against the damp fog that still shrouded the boat. Eric and Walt followed suit.

With no wind, sailing was out of the question, so they prepared to motor their way north. Walt checked the Global Positioning System and determined their exact location. Since replacing his old Loran with the more accurate GPS, navigation had become much more precise, and the thickness of the fog did not worry him unduly. He and Laurel got out the charts and plotted a course to take them through the chain of small islets that lay half a mile off shore, where a deep channel promised safe passage.

Laurel turned on the ignition, pulled out the choke, and pushed the starter. The little Volvo engine coughed to life, and she checked over the stern to make certain the water pump was working. A reassuring stream of water cascaded from the exit tube. As soon as Walt hoisted the anchors, she put the transmission in gear, consulted the compass, and swung the wheel to take them around the high point of land that had shielded them from the open sea overnight.

"You ever get the feeling you and I aren't needed here?" Walt joked to Eric.

"Suits me," his friend answered. "I'm willing to defer to experts." Then in a louder voice: "She won't pile us up on the rocks, will she?"

He was rewarded by a disdainful wrinkling of Laurel's nose. She made a point of ignoring him, turning her attention back to the compass and adjusting the boat's heading. The two adults fell into easy conversation.

By about ten-thirty, the fog still lay thick overhead and toward the horizon, but visibility at sea level had improved somewhat. Nevertheless, the sun remained hidden, and the temperature of the air stayed chilly. *Mayflower* came abreast of the first small island in the chain, and Laurel expertly changed course to enter the unmarked channel. "Your turn, Dad. I don't know this part."

Walt got up and took the wheel, and sent her down to consult the GPS. She came back on deck with the appropriate chart, and for the next hour he pointed out reference points on the passing land masses. She eagerly compared them to the notations on the chart.

He showed her how the natural channel wove in and around the headlands, and explained how to spot submerged sandbars that formed in response to the flow of the tide and currents. Occasionally she found minor errors in the charts, places where shallows and sandbars had shifted since the surveys were done. They circled them in red.

Eric eavesdropped in silence. He tried to absorb their knowledge, and enjoyed watching the interplay between them more than the passing scenery. The fog dulled the variegated greens of the island foliage, and each piece of land tended to look like all the others.

He focused his attention on Walt's gentle teaching technique with approval, as his friend taught the child how to read the surface of the ocean. Patiently Walt first explained the concepts, then demonstrated them. Then he turned the wheel over to her so she could practice what she had learned. They explored first one side of the channel and then the other, noting subtle differences in the color of the water as it passed over shoals and sandbars. Eric found he was learning a lot just by watching them.

As the noon hour approached with no sign of the fog lifting, they found themselves deep within the island chain. They began searching for a place to stop for lunch. Eric spotted a narrow sand beach off the port bow, and pointed it out to the others.

Walt throttled back. Laurel ducked below to consult the GPS, and came back with the next chart. They determined that they could anchor safely within fifty yards of the beach, and Walt idled in neutral as Laurel showed Eric how to set the anchors. Then he shut down the engine and went forward to break out the Zodiac.

After launching the small boat and putting together a picnic lunch, they rowed to shore and had their meal. Laurel was eager to explore. Finding the undergrowth too thick for easy passage inland, they set off instead to circle the perimeter of the small island.

After they had spent about twenty minutes cautiously hiking along the sand and among the boulders that rimmed the island, the fog burned off abruptly. The temperature of the air rose several degrees within just a few minutes. Eric reckoned by the position of the sun that they were about halfway around. They stripped off their sweatshirts and continued onward, soon reaching the picnic site once more.

"Nuts!" Laurel exclaimed. "What a bust! No wild animals, no pirate treasure, not even a mysterious cave to get lost in. Some boring island we found!"

"Where's your spirit of adventure?" Walt countered. "For all you know, you might be a pioneer like Columbus, the first ever to set foot on this new world. Want to claim it for the king and queen? Maybe no one else has ever been here before."

"I can see why!" she said disgustedly. "Who'd want it?"

"Maybe they'll even let you name it," Eric put in. "How about 'Runt Island'?"

Walt laughed heartily as Laurel bristled and stamped over to the Zodiac. She started tossing their gear aboard. Greatly amused, Walt and Eric trailed along behind her, and shortly they were back aboard *Mayflower*, with the little inflatable securely hitched to the stern.

A moderately light breeze followed the lifting of the fog, and they set the sails and continued on into the channel. Even with the protection of the dodger and canopy, the cockpit soon became very warm. Leaving Laurel at the helm, Walt and Eric went below and changed into swim shorts. When they came back, Walt took the wheel from her, and she too disappeared below.

Five minutes later she emerged once more in a brief yellow swim suit, this one a true bikini. The bra was tied with tiny spaghetti straps, and was trimmed along the top with narrow and softly gathered ruffles, modestly flattering her newly developing breasts. The bottom was considerably more daring than the red one she had worn the day before. The sides were little more than strings, riding high on her hips. They supported a brief triangular diaper with stand-up ruffles at the leg openings in front, echoing the trim on the bra. Despite the limited coverage, the overall effect was cute rather than sensual, very feminine but still strangely childlike.

Eric couldn't resist a little taunt. As she passed by him, her walk somewhat constrained and stilted in her self-consciousness, he whispered softly, "Hi, ugly!"

She looked over her shoulder, blushing prettily, and stuck her tongue out at him. Turning away, she wiggled her hips in a saucy parody of sexiness, making Eric laugh aloud.

Walt was surprised and pleased, and he had to admit, a little bit disturbed, to see such an uncharacteristically confident and almost brazen reaction from his normally shy and reticent child. "Does that suit really have your mother's approval?" he teased her.

She looked him straight in the eye. "Nope. I'm practicing to be a stripper. You're going to be *so proud* of me."

That got the expected rise out of Walt, until he realized she was baiting him. Then he laughed and slapped her bottom. Laurel yelped and hip-checked him away from the console, grabbing hold of the wheel and taking over the helm with a huge grin on her face. But the appealing blush continued to play across her cheeks.

Looking out over the bow, Eric spotted what seemed to be the last of the islets. They were well off shore, and the open sea stretched beyond. "What now, O Captain?" he inquired.

Walt directed his attention toward the distant shoreline. "About three miles up the coast there's another string of islands, most of them bigger than these last ones. That's as far as we go. Otherwise we wouldn't be able to get back to the marina in one day's sail tomorrow."

"What's the attraction?"

"Several of them have sand beaches, and there's easier going in the woods. It's mostly pines, and not as much underbrush. They're Laurel's favorite spot for exploring, and she wants to practice her new swimming skills, too. There are several sheltered coves, and the water is usually clean and warm."

"So why aren't we heading straight toward them?" Eric asked.

"Shoals. See the color of the water, and the foam up ahead? Those breakers mean shallows and rocks. You can't see them too well when the tide is in, but they're deadly. With a keel as deep as ours, we don't dare chance it. We have to go off shore about a mile and then turn north again to skirt around them. The only alternative to the open sea is The Narrows."

"Narrows?"

"Look toward the mainland. See that long, high island, the one where the cliffs look really steep?" Eric followed his pointing finger, and could just make out the outline of a large and treeless land mass stretching well to the north. Its lower hillsides were cloaked sparsely in scrub foliage, but further up they seemed craggy and barren.

"There's a channel on the other side, deep enough but with almost no room to maneuver," Walt continued. "Tall, sheer cliffs come down almost straight, right to the edge of the water. The current moves through it pretty fast, and you have to watch for rocks every minute. Laurel and I went through it last year with a friend in a powerboat. Even with a shallow draft, it was scary, especially at the mouth on this end. The chart says there's enough depth, but I wouldn't want to try it in *Mayflower*."

"How come?"

"After you clear the headland, you have to bear left to avoid a series of sandbars. But if you turn too soon, you pile up on some nasty rocks. That's where the name comes from. It's the narrowest channel along this stretch of coast."

"I'll take your word for it. Let's go for the open sea."

Laurel had already started to come about, prior to taking the wind on the stern quarter. As the sail came across the cabin and filled, Eric hauled on the jib sheet. *Mayflower* dipped her bow slightly and began moving with the tide, although relatively slowly with the less favorable wind direction.

"Spinnaker, Dad?" Laurel pleaded. She loved the feel of the boat being driven by the big sail. "Please?"

Walt checked the wind, which was steady but still fairly light, and decided that conditions were right to use their balloon-shaped sail. Made of lightweight material, its greater surface could make the most of any gentle breeze that came from behind them. He went below and handed it out to Eric through the forward hatch.

Laurel furled the jib, and within minutes they had the spinnaker sheeted and cleated. A gust of wind caught it, and it billowed out with a satisfying snap. The boat responded at once, canted thirty degrees, and raced through the gentle sea.

"Yippee!" Laurel shouted. Eric clung to the low side as the boat dipped, and made his way carefully back along the gunwale to the cockpit. He crossed over to help balance the craft, and watched as

Walt adjusted the sheets and helped Laurel coax some extra speed out of the hull. The water ripped past the stern and sprayed them gently, cool against their exposed skin. He felt exhilarated, more so because of the delight in Laurel's eyes as she commanded the big, fast vessel.

Enjoying the rush of power, they gave *Mayflower* her head, and were well out to sea when Walt finally called a halt. They came about and took down the spinnaker, and Walt reset the jib. They set their sights on the nearest of the distant islands, trimmed the sails, and headed back toward shore, at a slower but still respectable speed with the wind diagonally off the port bow.

Almost immediately they spotted another craft lying low in the water, ahead and on the leeward side. A sleek planing hull, an eighteen-footer with a big four-cylinder outboard, drifted aimlessly without power. As they neared the vessel, they could see two men aboard. The engine cover was raised, and one of the figures appeared to be working on the mechanism.

As they came abeam of the smaller boat, Walt luffed the sail and hailed her. "Are you in trouble? Can we be of any assistance?"

The figure at the engine straightened and waved, nodding his head. Eric took the wheel and Laurel furled the jib as Walt lowered the mainsail, then started the engine. Once under power, he turned back and motored toward the disabled craft.

As they approached, they could see the two men more clearly. The younger of the two was dark haired and had a deep tan. He stood in the bow holding a line, preparing to throw it to the sailboat. When they were in range, he lofted it cleanly, and Eric caught the end so that the two craft would not drift apart.

The other man was in his mid-forties, and held a wrench in his grease-stained hands. He wiped his sleeve across his forehead and glared at the engine, looking disgusted.

Laurel leaned over the rail, eagerly surveying the disabled boat and its occupants. As Walt throttled back and drifted alongside, Eric became aware that the younger of the two men was staring intently at her. He moved to Walt's side and nudged his elbow, then gestured with a slight nod of his head.

Walt took in the situation quickly. He stepped away from the console over to Laurel's side. While still smiling at the men in the other boat, he spoke to her in an undertone. "Better cover up, sweetheart." She looked suddenly alarmed, and quickly backed away and ducked down the hatch.

Walt turned his full attention to the man beside the big outboard. "I'm Walter MacKenzie. What's the problem?"

"Chris Thibault, Mr. MacKenzie. Thanks for stopping," the older man replied. "We've got water or dirt in the fuel line, I think. It began to cough and then just died. The ignition seems okay, but it won't start. I know more about the electrical stuff than the fuel system. Haven't got the tools to fix it, even if I knew how."

Walt had little respect for boaters who couldn't do their own repairs, but as he looked on the man's open, friendly face and helpless expression, he knew he had to offer assistance. However, while well versed in the peculiarities of his own small two-cylinder diesel, he knew little about the massive outboards that speedboat enthusiasts favored.

"How can we help?" he asked.

"No sense trying to fix it out here," the man replied disgustedly.

"You want a tow in toward shore, then?"

"Can't put you to that trouble. I've got a buddy with a big ski tow that can come and drag us back in real quick. You got a ship-to-shore I can use?"

Walt silently debated whether to invite the stranger aboard his boat. His trouble appeared genuine, and there seemed to be no sense of threat from either of the men. The only thing that made Walt uneasy was the younger one's blatant interest in Laurel, who had now come back on deck with a T-shirt over her bikini. However, he was now sitting down in the bow, apparently paying little attention to the conversation or to anyone aboard the sailboat.

Judging it to be the quickest way to secure assistance for them, Walt hauled on their line and maneuvered their craft around next to the Zodiac. He tipped the stern ladder overboard and extended his hand to help Chris Thibault climb up into the cockpit.

Fourteen

As the man stepped into the cockpit, Eric spotted a handgun tucked into the waistband at the back of his shorts. Before he could react or shout a warning, the gun was out and leveled at Walt's chest.

"Sit!" the man ordered. Walt and Eric glanced at each other, and then eased themselves down side by side on the port locker cover. Laurel vanished down the hatch into the cabin. Their captor motioned over his shoulder, and the younger man scaled the stern ladder, a rifle cradled in the crook of his left arm.

"Get the kid back up here," the older man ordered. His companion started toward the cabin, but Walt called out Laurel's name sharply. He didn't want the man dragging her up. Her small frightened face appeared in the hatchway, and Walt told her to come out. She edged over to the port rail and sat, clinging to her father's arm, looking very small in her oversized T-shirt.

Eric considered the probabilities. They were hopelessly outgunned and almost certainly about to lose the boat, and possibly their lives. His greatest fear was for Laurel, however, and his mind raced, searching for any way to ensure her safety.

He was relieved to see that Walt remained calm, although he was obviously angry, as much at his own poor judgment as at the men behind the guns. He managed to catch his friend's eye, and they communicated silently their mutual determination to defend themselves, and especially the child in their care.

Thibault stood about five-eleven, and was dressed in jeans and a dark checked shirt. His friendly smile had vanished, replaced by a sneering complacency. The younger man deferred to him, and Eric could now see that he was probably not yet out of his teens. His demeanor was rugged and confident, however. He wore khaki shorts and a T-shirt a size too small, showing off the definition of powerful muscles in his arms and chest. If it came to a showdown, he would be the faster, tougher opponent, although probably not the smarter one.

Keeping their guns trained, the pair stood behind the console, whispering to each other. Then they moved to the center of the cockpit, assuming a wide-legged stance designed to intimidate. They looked their captives up and down, and their gaze lingered on Laurel, who shrank back against her father's side.

"What do you think, Stu?" Thibault asked. "She's just what they're looking for, isn't she?"

Eric's head snapped up. *Stu? Stu Piersol, maybe?*

"Oh, yeah," T-shirt answered, "big time." He grinned at Laurel obscenely. "A nice little piece like this'll bring us a fat, juicy bonus."

Blind, unreasoned anger clouded Walt's face, and he started to his feet, but Thibault stuck the gun under his chin and shoved him back down on the hatch cover.

Eric's heart pounded. Almost without volition he said the name aloud: "Stu Piersol?"

T-shirt's head snapped around. "What'd you call me?" Eric remained silent. "How'd you know my name?"

"You goddamn stupid kid!" his partner growled. "He didn't know for sure until you said that!"

"Jesus, Mike, he *knows* me from somewhere. I can tell!"

"Yeah, you jerk, and now he knows my real name, too."

"So what? They won't be telling anybody."

"Not now they won't, that's for sure. You've seen to that." The one called Mike grabbed Eric's arm and hauled him to his feet. He shoved him across the cockpit, and Eric stumbled against the starboard rail, feigning weakness in the hope of catching the man off guard.

"This one first. Do it!" he barked at Stu. The younger man whirled and took a single stride toward Eric, raised the rifle, and swung it at his head.

Eric saw the blow coming and managed to roll with it. The gunstock struck him on the ear and the side of his skull, but missed his temple where it had been aimed. Laurel screamed. The force of the impact knocked him backward over the rail, and he hit the water prone, then sank like a stone.

His head rang, but the shock of the cold water quickly cleared his mind, and instinct took over. He swam under the boat, the keel grazing his back painfully, then came up under the curve of the stern on the port side. Just the upper half of his head projected out of the water, allowing him to breathe.

He heard shouts from the boat, but could make out few words at first. He heard Laurel crying and Walt yelling, and the sound of another blow. Then he heard Piersol's voice more clearly, and realized the young man was leaning over the side, trying to spot him. Eric shrank back under the curve of the hull.

"He didn't come up on this side!" Stu shouted. Mike answered him from starboard, but Eric couldn't make out what he said. His left ear rang painfully from the force of the blow, and his vision remained clouded.

He was about to swim to the stern ladder to try to go aboard when he heard the diesel roar to life. The gears clashed, and *Mayflower* surged forward, hauling the tethered powerboat around in a narrow arc. Eric dodged the Zodiac, sucked in a huge breath, and dove out of sight, barely missing the spinning propeller blades. He managed to stay beneath the surface for almost two minutes, and when he finally came up, the boat was well under way. He could make out the two men standing near the console, but neither one was looking in his direction. There was no sign of Walt or Laurel.

As *Mayflower* grew smaller in the distance, traveling north, Eric assessed his situation. Saving himself was the first priority. He felt momentary panic for the safety of his friends, but quickly resigned himself to the fact that they were on their own, at least for now.

He rolled over on his back and breathed deeply to maintain maximum buoyancy. Lying low in the water, he was unable to see any land, which he knew to be at least several miles away. The distance wasn't his main concern, however. He had swum farther than that on many occasions, and was in good physical shape, except for his leg injury. His main problem was going to be the temperature of the water, which was not high enough so far off shore to prevent the onset of hypothermia. Wearing just a T-shirt and swim shorts, he needed to generate plenty of heat to keep himself warm.

He debated removing his shoes to make swimming easier and less tiring, but quickly discarded the idea. He would need some protection for his feet when he made it to land. He sighted on the sun and determined the points of the compass from its position in the afternoon sky, then rolled over and settled into a powerful, efficient crawl stroke toward where he estimated the nearest island to be.

Time dragged by. The hours spent in the university pool proved their worth, and Eric found a pace that helped keep his circulation up, but didn't tire his arms too much. His biggest problem was his injured leg. Although the breaks had nearly healed, the time spent in the cast had weakened his muscles, and his kick was unbalanced. He soon discovered a tendency to turn in a gradual but steady arc, and had to check the position of the sun frequently in order to keep his bearings.

The pain in the side of his head had receded to a dull ache, but the exertion of swimming aggravated it, setting up a dull, debilitating roar in his ears. Doggedly he stroked onward, trying to remain oblivious to the growing agony in his skull, and determined to keep alert through force of will alone.

Gradually a deadening mental lethargy set in. Although by instinct his arms maintained their steady, rhythmic stroke, his thoughts wandered, and his senses turned inward. Without realizing it, he lost touch with his surroundings.

Twisted memories arose in his mind, and he found himself back in *Mayflower's* cabin. He was seated across from a smiling Walt, watching him wolf down great heaps of eggs and bacon. Laurel lay cuddled against her father, her eyes hugely round, and her face pale and drawn.

Walt's face dissolved into Deanna's, and Laurel shrank to infant size, a squirming baby Amy in her mother's arms. Eric saw that they were in a tent, and somehow he knew there was a lake just outside, waiting for them all to go for a swim. Beside him, a toddler Becky tugged and pulled a tiny pink-and-white ruffled romper over her feet. *Don't help me, Daddy, I can do it myself!*

The children grew older as Eric watched, and scampered out through the tent flap, running for the water. Deanna laughed and took his hand, and she and Eric followed along. Amy, digging great pails full of sand with a tiny red plastic shovel. Becky, splashing in the water. Both children suddenly swimming in the ocean. Swimming toward the boat.

Deanna, standing at the rail, leaning over with her arms outstretched, calling to them and smiling. Amy, clambering up the ladder into her mother's embrace. Becky… Becky screaming!

Deanna's face dissolving into Stu Piersol's revolting leer, his huge muscled arms clasping a struggling Amy, then reaching out for Becky, reaching...

Reaching for Laurel...

Eric jolted back to reality. His head was buried in a cresting whitecap, and he swallowed a huge mouthful of brine. He came up coughing, and shook the water out of his eyes. The wind had come up, and waves blocked his vision of the horizon.

Looking around wildly, he was completely confused and disoriented. The sun was no longer over his shoulder, and he couldn't locate it. Panic threatened to overcome him.

As awareness of his surroundings returned, he regained control and rolled over to float on his back. The sun came into view, opposite where it had been, and he realized he had been swimming in circles. He had no idea for how long, but knew he was presently heading out to sea once more.

A sudden chill shook his frame. Reluctantly he extended his arms in an awkward backstroke, turning himself until the sun once more indicated he was swimming toward land. He breathed deeply and increased his stroke, fighting off the numbing cold that had begun to sap his strength.

All at once his weak leg cramped sickeningly. His body jackknifed, plunging his head beneath the surface. He managed to right himself long enough to take a deep breath, then folded forward into a jellyfish float. With his head under water, he clamped his hands around his tortured calf. Frantically he massaged the knotted muscles, managing to raise his head several times to take in more air.

Gradually the cramp eased until finally he could straighten his leg, but the throbbing pain persisted. He rolled over once more into a back float and lay exhausted on the surface. The torment in his muscles was intense, but the immediate danger of drowning was over.

Again he was wracked by chills, his body reacting to the shock of the cramp and no longer warmed by the constant exertion of swimming. He rotated to his left and began a slow and agonizing sidestroke, using his arms and one good leg, and dragging the useless one. He wondered if he was making any progress at all.

His mind drifted once more. He was alert only to the fading warmth of the late-day sun on the side of his face, which kept him oriented in the water and headed toward land. Stubbornly he resisted the encroaching fog of dreams and visions that threatened to steal his consciousness.

He tried to sing aloud, hoping it would keep him from falling asleep, but took in too much water and kept choking. He switched to mental music, revisiting first a favorite Mozart sonata, the lovely one in C major from the composer's productive middle period. Then, finding it too soothing, he called up Copland's *Fanfare for the Common Man*, the last movement of the Shostakovich Fifth Symphony, and finally a medley of all the movie themes he could remember that John Williams had ever written: *Rocky, Star Wars, Indiana Jones...* All the loud ones.

After what seemed like hours, he detected a subtle change in the sound and feel of the waves. Where once he had heard little more than the ripples of his own small wake and the splash of foaming whitecaps, now a faint rumbling invaded his consciousness. Larger swells lifted him from crest to trough and back again.

Roused by renewed hope, he redoubled his efforts. Shortly the vague rumbling sounds separated into the rhythmic beat of breakers, and he managed to raise his head enough to see the beachless coast of a craggy, cliff-bound island, with white-foamed waves crashing violently against it.

There seemed to be no safe place to land. In his weakened condition, Eric was caught by the powerful tide. He rode the crests of several waves, battering his knees on hidden rocks. Desperately he sought firm footing, but the steep and irregular slope of the bottom gave his feet little purchase. A vicious undertow dragged him out again and again.

Stroking as hard as he could, he swam parallel to the land, searching for an easier spot to go ashore. He was hit by another massive breaker and buried under foam and a blanket of smothering, foul-smelling seaweed. Rough gravel scraped his body painfully, as the wave dragged him first toward the shore, than back out again.

Three more times he was caught in the oscillating tumult, until at last the waves pushed him into the lee of a miniature cove. Briefly he managed to gain a footing, and was stumbling weakly through the shallows when a final massive breaker struck him from behind. It thrust him sprawling onto the shore, then tried to suck him out again.

Eric Kelman summoned his failing strength and dragged himself forward. His body throbbed in agony from a hundred scrapes and cuts, and the pounding in his head dimmed his vision and clouded his thoughts. He managed to crawl above the tide line, then collapsed onto the rough shells and rocks beneath him. Instantly he fell into a deep, dreamless sleep.

Fifteen

Eric awoke to darkness, roused by thirst and the torment in his battered body. Gradually he became aware of his surroundings, and memories of his escape and the swim to the island flooded back. He felt momentarily overcome with grief and apprehension over whatever fate Walt and Laurel must have suffered.

Stiffly he got to his feet and assessed the damage: multiple abrasions, one barely functioning leg, and constant ringing in his injured ear. *Not too bad*, he decided. *Nothing that won't heal.*

At first, he felt very little actual pain. He stood up, took a few steps, and was struck almost instantly by intense nausea, forcing him to his knees again. His stomach lurched, and he spewed forth a rank mixture of bile and sea water. He lowered his head and waited several minutes for the dizziness to pass, then cautiously regained his feet. This time his head remained a bit clearer, but every inch of his body began to throb. Much of his hide was scraped raw, and the sea salt burned in the open wounds.

His shoes were wet and clammy, but his shirt and swim trunks had nearly dried as he lay on the rocks in the early evening sun. Even with the onset of night, the late summer air remained fairly warm. Not knowing where he was, and reluctant to travel about the island in the dark, he moved from the shore to the edge of the forest to find a place to hole up until morning.

Eric realized he would need some sort of shelter if he were to be able to sleep and regain any of his strength overnight. Although he knew how to construct a rudimentary lean-to, his energy level was too low for the task. Aided by a nearly full moon, he began instead to gather brush and branches, and fashioned a compact nest in the soft reeds that lined the shore above the tide line. He lay down and pulled additional branches over him for insulation. Despite his thirst and discomfort, healing sleep came almost immediately.

Throughout the night, confused images crowded his brain, periods of near-wakefulness that alternated with almost coma-like oblivion.

Faces danced before him, and twice he lurched from his bed, crying out in torment and frustration as he saw his friends being torn away from him across a wild and unforgiving sea.

He awoke at dawn to find the world once again shrouded in heavy, chilling fog. The pain in his limbs had been replaced by a stiff and unyielding tenderness in every joint, and he gingerly extended his limbs and flexed them as much as he could tolerate. He crawled out from under the foliage, relieved himself, and addressed the most pressing of his problems: water.

He knew he lacked the strength to make an exhaustive search for a spring or stream. In any case, Walt had told him that few of the islands had a natural supply of fresh water. He turned his attention to the low-growing foliage that separated the shoreline from the pines and spruces further inland, and discovered several species of broad-leaved plants that were heavily coated with dew.

It took him quite a while to salvage enough water from the leaves to ease his throat, but the water revived him considerably. He stretched his cramped muscles, still stiff from sleep and the damp cold that surrounded him, and forced himself to attempt a few rudimentary exercises. Gradually his circulation improved, warming him from within.

As the morning light increased, he examined the land where it sloped downward toward the shore, and made a welcome discovery: a large patch of wild blackberry bushes, loaded with ripe fruit. *Not my normal breakfast*, he thought, *but as welcome right now as dinner at the Ritz.*

Although his joints and muscles still ached and burned, especially his injured leg, the food and water helped clear his mind for the task ahead. He was determined to find his way off the island somehow, and quickly. He had to alert the authorities to their situation, hoping for a miracle to save his friends. He walked toward the water and scanned the open sea, then looked left and right along the shoreline.

The fog that obscured his vision had begun to lift, and he could tell that the southern route was the least hospitable. A steep escarpment lined the sea in that direction, making travel by land all but impossible. To the north, the gravel slope on which he now stood disappeared, giving way to larger rocks and boulders. The dense growth of the forest prevented him from moving inland.

His only choices seemed to be either to follow the shoreline, or to try to swim along the coast. Fearing his strength would fail him in the cold water, he began stumbling his way through the jumbled rocks.

Eric picked his way along, carefully testing the slippery surface of the rocks before each step, in fear of twisting or spraining an ankle. The going was painfully slow. After nearly twenty minutes, he was barely out of sight of the place where he had spent the night. Then he caught the sound of running water, just audible above the now gentle waves that rippled softly on the shore in the still morning air.

Awkwardly he stumbled ahead, toward the distinctive sound of a brook that seemed to come from above him and to his left. He rounded a pile of large boulders and discovered a cascading stream cutting a shallow channel down the steep hillside.

Gratefully he knelt beside the stream and splashed his face and neck with the cool, crystal-clear water. It was cold to his touch, and he tasted it on his tongue. It was unmistakably fresh, with no trace of salt.

Neither knowing nor caring how pure it might be, Eric drank deeply, then stripped off his clothing and immersed his T-shirt completely. He wrung it out and used it to bathe away the salt from his abraded skin. Relief flooded his body as the brine sloughed away.

He sat down beside the stream, removed his boat shoes and socks, and dunked his swollen feet in the cold rushing water, leaving them there until they began to turn numb. He rinsed out his swim trunks and put them back on, followed by his T-shirt. Chills struck him, and he stood and beat his arms against his sides and stamped his feet. Gradually sensation returned, and some inner warmth combined with the strengthening sun to calm his shivers.

He turned his attention back to the coastline. It stretched ahead to the north in a nearly straight line, and where the sea crowded the shore, waves broke over rocks slippery with seaweed. He replaced his shoes and socks and started off, keeping his eyes fixed downward and carefully searching out flat surfaces that would ensure safe footing.

The wind began to rise again, directly onshore and pushing waves before it to crest against the jagged outcroppings. Breakers formed and splashed noisily over the uneven shoreline. The steep hillside encroached on the shore, and as he struggled onward, Eric began to doubt whether this northern route would continue to be passable.

One minute the landscape ahead seemed to be an impenetrable forest. Then, with his eyes still on the ground, he suddenly came upon and almost fell into a rushing inlet, obscured from view by a dense stand of birches. He could tell it would be almost impossible to see from a boat, or from either side, unless a person knew exactly where it was, or stumbled upon it accidentally as he had. It was a perfect hidden cove.

Although the incoming tide pushed a large volume of water into the strait, the sound of the breakers had masked the noise it made. It was somewhat narrow but appeared to be fairly deep, with an easily navigable channel. Eric debated swimming across, but did not dare trust his weakened body in the rapid current. Nor did he want to subject his raw skin to another salt bath. Instead he followed the bank, hoping to skirt around to the other side, or to find a shallow area where he could ford across.

Instead of diminishing, the inlet widened abruptly about fifty yards inland, and the current became less turgid. Eric soon realized that this was a substantial arm of the sea. Once past the constricted mouth, the channel curved fairly abruptly to the left, further obscuring the full extent of the cove when viewed from offshore. As Eric plodded along, he realized that the island must be shaped like a huge horseshoe, enclosing a broad and hidden natural harbor. The trees along both sides clung closely to its banks, but at the far end he could make out a narrow sandy beach.

Ahead and to the right, the birches and conifers stopped abruptly on the opposite shore. Coming abreast of them, Eric stared in wonder. At that point the cove appeared to be fully two thousand yards across. Almost in the exact center, her sails gathered haphazardly around the mast and boom, *Mayflower* lay quietly, riding the tide on her bow anchor.

Instinctively Eric stepped behind a thick spruce tree and surveyed Walt's boat for signs of life. For several long moments he watched her swing gently in the current. Although he couldn't be sure, it seemed probable that she was abandoned. There was no sign of Laurel or her father, or of the two men who had captured them. The little inflatable Zodiac was also missing from the stern.

He briefly considered swimming out to her, but quickly abandoned the idea. In his present condition, it could not be accomplished easily, and if the two pirates (which was how he now thought of them) were still on board, they could pick him off with their rifle as he approached.

Instead he continued to labor along the shoreline, careful to keep the screen of birches and evergreens between him and the boat. The fog had now dissipated entirely, and offered no concealment from anyone who might be watching.

As he moved along slowly, he scanned the shoreline for any trace of a small boat mooring. At first there appeared to be no sign of the speedboat that they had foolishly stopped to help, but he knew that there must be a boat somewhere. Whoever had anchored *Mayflower* would have needed some way to get ashore.

He almost missed it. Just south of the sandy beach area, a long and narrow artificial channel had been artfully cut into the shoreline, almost completely hidden by overhanging trees and bushes. It was just wide enough to hold the eighteen-foot powerboat and another skiff, a fourteen-footer with a small but powerful outboard clamped to the stern. Someone had carefully rearranged the reeds and grasses, so that it was hard to tell where the boats had been concealed.

Eric turned his attention to locating a path where the boat's occupants might have gone. He paced up and down the water's edge for twenty minutes, but could find no trace of any entry into the woods. He moved about a hundred yards into the underbrush, then walked along parallel to the shore.

The path was not far away, but was back the way he had come, so it took him a while to find it. It looked well used, although the trees and bushes kept it hidden from the shore. It was apparent to him that whoever was on the island, they had gone to considerable trouble to disguise their presence. If not for the yacht swinging gently at anchor off shore, no one would have suspected the island was inhabited. And the chance of anyone discovering the cove in the first place was remote.

Cautiously Eric moved into the woods again, reluctant to stay on the path itself in case some sort of lookout was posted somewhere along its length. Instead he blazed his own parallel trail. His progress was slow, made especially difficult by the way the land rose steeply upward from the water toward the center of the island.

He climbed carefully, returning occasionally to within sight of the trodden path to be sure he hadn't lost track of it. Eventually he came to the crest of the hill, and looked down into a thickly forested valley.

At first glance, the entire expanse of woods seemed deserted. Overhanging branches hid the path, and there were no clearings evident among the trees. He estimated the probable direction in which the path descended into the valley, and concentrated his attention on a more narrow area to either side of it.

Patiently he scanned from left to right, looking for anomalies that might signal human habitation, and finally spotted something out of place. A glinting reflection of sunlight caught his eye, in among some closely spaced pines just north of the lowest point on the valley floor. Moving from side to side along the crest of the hill, he maneuvered himself to a spot where the sunlight reflected most strongly. He was sure he was looking at a pane of glass in some sort of window.

Descent into the valley was somewhat easier than the climb up from the cove, and he stayed well away from the area where the path cut through the trees, still fearing a sentry. He circled around to the left, hoping to come upon the building from an off side. This put the sun behind him, and the reflected sunlight off the window helped him to keep his bearings, but still he could make out neither walls nor roof.

He almost stumbled upon the building before realizing it was there. Surrounded by thick conifers that grew densely right down to the ground, the structure was of A-frame design, and obviously not new. Its unpainted exterior blended in with the trees, as did its pyramidal shape. The steeply canted roof came to within two feet of the ground, and was sheathed in heavily weathered spruce shingles. Eric circled the building, carefully maintaining his concealment, and observed it in detail from among the trees.

The flat front and rear were only partially shingled. Torn tarpaper and exposed, diagonally arranged boards suggested that the building had never been completed, and had probably been abandoned years before. There was a single solid pine door in each end and windows up under the roof peaks, but the latter were boarded up. There seemed to be no way to see inside from the ground.

On both sides of the roof, pairs of heavy glass skylights were mounted about a third of the way down from the ridge, well beyond the reach of anyone standing below. Each skylight was propped open several inches, probably, Eric thought, to provide ventilation. A chimney protruded above the peak, but no smoke emanated from it. An old-fashioned well, complete with an octagonal peaked roof and a bucket hanging from a crank, stood a few paces from the front door.

The path through the woods terminated in a tiny clearing between the front wall and the well. In the rear, another short pathway led to a small, decrepit outhouse, situated downhill to avoid contaminating the water supply. A small stack of firewood stood next to it. Trees came to within a few feet of the structure on all sides, effectively cloaking it and making it appear part of the natural landscape when viewed from a distance.

Even though there appeared to be no sign of life, Eric sought out a hidden vantage point on the east side, where he could see both front and rear pathways, and settled down to wait.

Judging by the sun, he estimated the time to be well past noon. His dry throat ached, and he longed to make a trip to the well. Although at first the A-frame seemed deserted, he gradually became aware of small random sounds coming from inside: the scrape of a chair, a door closing, and once what seemed like a child's brief cry, followed by the sound of a slap.

Eric became increasingly agitated. He was virtually certain that Laurel and Walt were being held inside, but he could think of no way to approach their armed captors without putting himself, and therefore his friends, in further jeopardy. Without a weapon of any kind, he had little hope of helping them, even with the element of surprise on his side. Given that the men were armed, the odds were too overwhelming.

Forcing himself to remain calm, he settled back down to watch, and after about an hour the back door opened. The man called Mike stepped out, gripping a small girl by the upper arm. He closed the door carefully behind him, then dragged the child rapidly toward the outhouse and shoved her roughly inside. *Not Laurel*, Eric thought. *What's going on here?*

Mike leaned against the outhouse doorjamb and lit a cigarette. Presently the door opened tentatively, and he jerked it wide and hauled the child out. He half dragged, half carried her back up the path, and took her inside the building.

When the door opened again a few minutes later, Stu Piersol emerged with a protesting boy of about ten or eleven. The child dug in his heels and tried to break free of the man's grasp, but was rewarded with a smack on the back of his head, and another to his left cheek. He stumbled and nearly fell, but Piersol jerked him up cruelly by one arm and pushed him into the outhouse, then slammed the door behind him.

When the boy didn't come out again after several minutes, Piersol pounded on the door, shouting threats. Finally he forced it open and dragged the child out, eliciting a loud wail. Stu struck him again, and Eric nearly bolted from his hiding place to defend him. He realized, however, that he would be no match for two armed men, and would forfeit any chance to help the children, and Walt and Laurel too, if indeed they were in there. Unless their lives seemed to be in immediate danger, he would have to bide his time.

Five minutes passed before the door opened again, and Mike exited once more, leading a stoic and seemingly compliant Laurel. Eric breathed a sigh of relief to see her apparently unharmed. He could tell by her tense and rigid stance and walk that she was alert to any possible opportunity for escape.

Laurel still wore her boat shoes. Her T-shirt hung like a tattered rag from one shoulder, revealing most of her yellow bikini beneath. Eric could see no sign of major injury, although even from a distance, one side of her face seemed red and somewhat swollen. Unlike the other children, she made no effort to resist. *Just playing it cool*, Eric thought, proud of the courage he knew she possessed.

After a few minutes inside the privy, Laurel emerged. Mike reached for her arm, but she pulled back and avoided him. She started up the path alone, obedient but proud, her defiance almost palpable in the erect dignity of her posture. She opened the A-frame's door herself and went inside, followed closely by her captor.

Eric hoped to see Walt next, but there was no further activity around the building, except for a single trip by Piersol to the well. He resumed his watch, remaining hidden throughout the long afternoon and evening. When it was fully dark, he crept into the clearing and drank deeply from the well's bucket, then carefully circumnavigated the building, looking for some possible means of entering unobserved. Finding nothing, he returned to the woods and sat down to think.

Sixteen

As soon as they were satisfied that Eric had not come to the surface near the boat, the two men started *Mayflower's* diesel engine and motored away toward the distant shoreline. Walt sat tense and expectant under the unwavering guard of Mike's handgun. Laurel clung to him, sobbing uncontrollably over the loss of her friend.

Stu Piersol stood behind the wheel and compared the compass reading to the low-lying outlines of the far-off islands. He settled the boat on a course toward the largest of them.

"All right, *Daddy*," he said sarcastically to Walt, "make yourself useful. Get over here."

Slowly Walt disengaged Laurel's hands from his arm and rose off the hatch cover. He made his way cautiously to the console, and Piersol pointed to the compass. The teenager affected a tough demeanor, borrowed from every gangster film he had ever seen, trying to intimidate Walt.

"That's our heading, big shot. Just keep her right on target, and maybe you'll get to see tomorrow. But you screw around with me, and you and your little jailbait there are dead meat. You got it?"

"All right." Walt thought the boy sounded ridiculous, but he kept silent, pretending compliance. Faced with their guns, he had to figure out some way to outsmart the two men. He gripped the wheel and made a show of reading the compass, and Piersol turned away and joined his partner at the forward end of the cockpit. They whispered together, out of Walt's hearing.

Laurel lay huddled miserably in the starboard corner under the dodger. The men ignored her, and she stared balefully at her father. Walt managed a brave smile in her direction. His mind raced, but he could think of no way to improve their situation.

After a few minutes of quiet conversation, both men stepped back into the center of the cockpit. Piersol looked out around the port side of the dodger, satisfied that *Mayflower* was still on course. He nodded to Mike, who turned to face Walt, the gun still hanging from his right hand.

"Now this is how it's going to be," he began. "You just keep running this boat for us, and when we get where we're going, you and junior miss over there can get off. Do as you're told, and you'll be fine, but like Stu told you, screw around or try anything, and we'll put you off right here."

Walt had no hope the man was telling the truth. They knew he could identify them. Nevertheless he agreed.

"I want the kid out of here now," Mike continued. He turned to Piersol. "Stick her down below somewhere."

Piersol turned toward Laurel, and Walt spoke up quickly. "Laurel, go down in the forward berth and shut the door. Right now."

Laurel scrambled off the hatch and eluded Piersol's grab at her. She jumped through the hatch and disappeared from view, followed by the men's rough laughter. Mike turned to Walt again. "You got a lock on that berth she's going to?"

"No locks. But she'll stay put."

"She damn well better. Now get out from behind that wheel."

Walt stepped around the console on the starboard side, tense and, he hoped, ready for whatever was about to happen.

Laurel hurried into the forward berth, closed the door behind her, and climbed up on the triangular cushion, wedging herself as far back in the corner as she could. She drew up her knees and buried her head between her arms, grieving over the loss of her friend Eric, and fearing for her father's safety, and for her own. Long minutes passed. She could hear nothing but the steady rumble of the diesel engine, and the slap of the water against the hull.

Finally she crept over to the porthole on the starboard side, and was looking out just as a loud explosion echoed from the cockpit. Startled, she recoiled back into the corner, recognizing the noise as a gunshot. Half a minute later several more shots rang out. After a few minutes, when nothing else happened, she looked out again.

Toward the stern, and diagonally off the starboard side, she spotted their little Zodiac tossing on the waves. At that angle it appeared empty, and the far end sagged low in the water, partially deflated. She scrambled quietly down from the cushion and eased the door open, just in time to see Mike coming down the ladder into the cabin.

"Get back in there!" he growled at her. Quickly she closed the door and cowered behind it, expecting him to come after her, but all she heard were the sounds of cookware rattling, and the top of the icebox thumping down as if dropped. She climbed back into her corner and tried not to feel too afraid.

Not long after, the pitch of the diesel dropped, and Laurel felt *Mayflower* turn to port and slow down. The hull pitched from side to side in rougher water, and she peered out the starboard porthole again. Forested land lay not far from the gunwale, and she crossed to the port side and discovered the same thing there.

As she watched, the boat entered what looked like a wide lake, and slowed down even further. She heard heavy footsteps outside the cabin, and saw a pair of legs pass by on the way to the bow. The engine dropped to idle, then stopped altogether, and she heard the anchor splash into the water.

When her captors dragged her out of the cabin onto the deck, she saw that *Mayflower* was riding on just the bow anchor, instead of being tethered fore and aft. They were in the middle of a large, bowl-shaped cove, seemingly surrounded on all sides by tall stands of trees. She knew they had come through some sort of inlet from the sea, but couldn't locate where it was.

Her first thoughts were for her father, and she demanded to know where he was. Stu Piersol spun her around and slapped her sharply across the face. "Keep your mouth shut. We'll tell you anything you need to know. You want to get hurt, just keep yapping."

Laurel reeled from the blow and tried to pull free, but Piersol held her wrist firmly. He dragged her to the stern and lifted her roughly over the rail onto the ladder. Mike stood at the bottom in the speedboat, and he reached up and yanked her down beside him. She stumbled and fell into the bottom of the boat, rocking it sharply. Mike left her there and took his place near the transom. Stu joined them, taking his place on the center seat. Mike fired up the big outboard and steered the craft around *Mayflower's* stern and toward the shore.

Laurel briefly considered trying to jump overboard, but she was too uncertain of her swimming ability to risk it. Besides, she knew that they could easily run her down again in the boat. She kept as still as possible, waiting and hoping for a chance to get away.

Mike maneuvered the boat into a narrow cut in the shoreline, and eased up behind a smaller boat that had a little outboard tilted up on its stern. He stepped over the side and dragged Laurel onto dry land, passing her over to Piersol, who gripped her wrist tightly. Mike meticulously concealed the boat with foliage, hiding all trace of it from view. Then they located a path into the woods, and set off rapidly up over the hill.

The path was narrow, and they were forced to walk single file. Mike led the way, and Piersol let go of Laurel's wrist and pushed her ahead of him, in between them. They trudged up the path, and Laurel moved ahead passively, stumbling occasionally but keeping pace, hoping for an opportunity to escape.

Her meek and awkward compliance made the men inattentive, but Laurel was keenly alert to her surroundings. As they crested the top of the hill, preparing to descend into the valley on the opposite side, she saw her chance. The birches thinned out along the ridge, giving way mostly to acidic pines and spruces, so there was little underbrush. Abruptly she broke to the side and dashed off among the trees.

"Hey, Jesus!" Mike shouted. "Grab the little bitch!"

Caught by surprise, Stu Piersol was slow to react, and even with his longer stride and greater strength, it took him several minutes to catch up with her. Frantically she ducked around and between the trees, trying to keep them between her and her pursuer, but finally he wore her down, and managed to get hold of her arm.

Laurel turned and flailed at him, trying to scratch him and kicking at his shins. Stu tried to shield his face without letting her go, then twisted her arm painfully so that she doubled over to the side. Then he slapped the side of her face viciously, and the fight drained out of her.

Mike came through the trees just as Piersol struck her. "Lay off, Stu! You know the rules. We got to deliver them with no marks."

Piersol twisted Laurel's arm further, forcing her down on the ground at his feet. "Just letting her know who's boss, Boss," he laughed unpleasantly. Then he leaned down close, shouting his foul breath directly into the child's face. "You want some more? Huh? Just try that stunt again, why don't you?"

"Give it up," Mike said. "So she's got some spunk, that's good. That's what they want. Just keep a good grip on her this time."

"You got it!" He hauled Laurel brutally to her feet, then slung her over his shoulder like a sack, her head and arms hanging down his back. "Don't get any ideas, kid. You try anything more, and I'll smack you black and blue."

They started off down the path, the older man a half dozen yards in the lead. Before they had gone a dozen paces, Laurel felt Piersol's hand stroking the backs of her legs. She shuddered and squirmed, and he laughed nastily under his breath. He ran his hand roughly up her thighs and tried to force his fingers between them.

Laurel screamed and clamped her legs tightly together. She pounded her small fists on Stu's back. Mike looked back over his shoulder and saw Piersol's fingers shoved up under the child's swimsuit bottom, cruelly pinching her buttock. Laurel writhed in torment, kicking her feet ineffectually and screaming frantically.

"Goddammit, leave her alone!" Mike shouted. "You're getting to be as bad as the perverts we sell these kids to."

Stu continued his probing, and Mike strode back and slapped his hand away. "Jesus, I'm just having a little fun. She was asking for it."

"You start getting queer for these kids, and we're quits!"

"Come on, Mike. What's the harm in roughing her up a little? We ought to keep this one around a while anyway, save her until the next shipment. Let me break her in myself for a week or two."

"That's it! You want to play with the merchandise, get yourself a job with the pervs on the other side of the operation. I don't want to have anything more to do with you. Put her down!"

Piersol hoisted Laurel off his shoulder reluctantly and dropped her on the path. She tried to scramble up, but Mike seized her upper arm and held her down. He sank to his haunches and caught her chin between his fingers, digging into her jaw and forcing her to look at him. His voice was soft but menacing.

"Now listen, kid. From now on you're going to do exactly what you're told. And you know why?"

Laurel's eyes were wide and frightened. His fingers sank painfully into her cheeks, and she couldn't speak.

"I'll tell you why. If you give me any more trouble, I'm going to let this baby raper have you and…"

"Dammit, Mike! I ain't no…"

"Shut up!" the older man barked. Then he turned back to Laurel. "Step out of line once more, just *once*, and I'll let him do anything he wants to you, for as long as he wants. You understand?" He released her jaw and slapped her cheek.

Laurel was terrified. Her mouth sagged open and tears poured from her eyes. Mike slapped her again. "I asked you a question!"

She managed to nod her head.

"That's better. Now you're going to walk ahead of me, nice and quiet, and we're going to get along fine, aren't we?" He pulled her to her feet and gave her a shove down the path. Laurel stumbled and almost fell, barely able to see through her tears. She started forward meekly, all rebellion frightened out of her.

They reached the A-frame a few minutes later, and Mike unlocked and opened the door and shoved her inside. She looked up to see a large room with an unfinished interior. Above her was a very high peaked ceiling, with a skylight tilted open on either side of the ridge. There were rough beams for a loft, but it had never been floored.

Stu Piersol seized her arm again, and pulled her toward a door that was centered in the back interior wall. He opened it and sent her sprawling through, and she landed painfully on the rough pine floor. Then he slammed the door behind her.

With the wind knocked out of her, Laurel lay still for several moments, taking in her surroundings. The walls were lined with simple metal cots, eight in all, with thin ticked mattresses. They were bare of any sheets or pillows. A few coarse blankets were piled haphazardly on top of several of them. There were no other pieces of furniture, nor any windows, other than one that had been boarded up above a solid pine door in the back wall. The door was secured with a heavy padlock. As in the first room, air and light entered through a pair of skylights, each one far up on the slope of the roof and well out of reach.

Carefully she stood up and inspected her scraped arms and legs. Her T-shirt had protected her somewhat, and her injuries were superficial, but her face was sore. She wiped the tears away with the sleeve of her shirt. As her eyes adjusted to the weak light, she became aware of two pairs of bright round eyes watching her from a cot in the far corner.

She walked over closer. "Hi." She got no response from the two children who huddled there, one a boy a bit younger than she was, the other a girl of about eight. They looked as frightened as Laurel herself felt.

She sat down on the end of the cot. "What're your names?"

The boy regarded her solemnly, and identified her as a prisoner like himself, and therefore a possible ally. "I'm Benji. This is my sister Emily. Carter. That's our last name, I mean."

Laurel looked them over carefully. Emily Carter continued to stare at the older girl, terrified and unable or unwilling to speak. She clung desperately to her brother's arm, and he patted her absently as he continued to study the new arrival.

Emily wore a red and white checked playsuit streaked with dirt, and her arms and legs were bruised and grimy. Her hair was matted and disheveled, and her feet were bare. To Laurel, her eyes seemed unnaturally wide and bright, and appeared unfocused.

Benji was more composed. He was obviously taking the protection and comfort of his sister quite seriously. He was dressed in brown camp shorts, with a long sleeveless T-shirt hanging over them. He too was dirty, and there were several rips in his clothing, but unlike his sister, he wore socks, and had runners on his feet.

"I'm Laurel MacKenzie. Where are we, anyway?"

"I don't *know*." Benji was trying hard not to cry, but tears brimmed in his eyes.

"How'd you get here, then?"

"I can't remember. We were walking home from the playground, and this lady got out of her car and called to us. She told us our mother got hurt in an accident, and our dad sent her to get us, so we got in the car, and then somebody stuck something over my face that smelled real bad, and I guess I went to sleep, and I woke up here with Emily."

Fell for the oldest trick there is, Laurel thought to herself. Then aloud she said, "Don't you remember how they brought you here? Were you on a boat?" Laurel hoped they might have come by land. If they weren't on an island, and if she could get away, maybe she could find a road and go for help. Her courage was returning rapidly.

Benji seemed not to hear her question. He began to sob softly. "Do you think our mom's really hurt?"

"Not a chance," Laurel said, not unkindly. "They just told you that to get you to go with them. What's outside here?"

"Just trees and stuff. They leave us in here most of the time. The only time we get out is to go to the bathroom. There's a smelly old outhouse in the back there." He gestured toward the padlocked door. "And they bring us food sometimes, but mostly they just leave us alone."

"Have they hurt you?"

"Yeah, some. If we don't do what they tell us right away, they smack us around. I've tried to get Emily to do whatever they say, but every time they touch her, she starts to cry, and they slap her to make her stop. That doesn't work, so they just hit her some more." He looked down fondly at his sister, frustrated at his inability to protect her.

Laurel thought for a minute. "Is she here? The lady that took you in the car, I mean?"

"Nope," Benji replied, "just these two mean guys. They've got Emily awful scared."

Laurel again regarded the small girl's terrified expression, and tried to think of some way to reassure them both. "Look, you guys, I didn't get here by myself. My dad's around here somewhere, and my friend Eric." She fought back her own tears. Her last sight of Eric had been of his plunge into the sea, and he hadn't come up again. And she had no idea what had happened to her father. "They'll find us. And even if they don't, I'll figure out some way to get us out of here."

Emily burst out crying. "I want to go home!" she wailed.

"Me, too," Laurel reassured her, "and we will. I promise." But it was a promise she wasn't sure she could keep.

Seventeen

Laurel lay miserably on the bare mattress of one of the cots, hardly aware of the slow passage of time. Both Benji and Emily had fallen into a deep but restless sleep. She had explored every square inch of the big room, and had tested the heavy door in the outside wall. The huge padlock that held it shut was hung through a massive hasp, folded securely over the bolts that fastened it in place. Gamely she tried to pry the pins out of the three big steel hinges, but they were heavily rusted, and with nothing to use as a lever, she made no progress with them.

She avoided the interior door. Occasional sounds and low-pitched conversation came from beyond it, and she knew she had little hope of getting past the two men on her own. *Maybe when it gets dark...*

As the light coming through the skylight grew dim, she retreated to one of the cots and tried to think. *What would Dad and Eric do if this happened to them?* Thoughts of them brought fresh tears to her eyes, and she began to sob softly, not hearing the footsteps that approached the door.

As the latch depressed with a squeak, she came alert and scurried over onto the adjacent cot with Benji and Emily, inadvertently waking them both. The door opened abruptly, and Stu Piersol came in carrying a tray of sandwiches and three juice boxes. A large electric lantern hung from his other hand.

He set everything down on the floor and shut the door behind him. "You hungry?" None of the children answered him.

"How about you, little lady?" he said to Laurel. "You want something to eat?" He walked toward the cot. "Before I let you have your supper, suppose we get to know each other a little bit." He reached out and gripped her wrist, hauling her to the edge of the cot, then twisted her arm to force her to her feet. She tried to resist, but he handled her easily.

"Don't you pull away from me!" he said gruffly. "And it won't do you no good to yell. Mike's out in the crapper." He sat down on one of the cots and forced her to her knees in front of him. "You're going to make us a lot of money, you know that? How old are you, anyway?"

Laurel glared at him and didn't answer. Piersol slapped her face and twisted her arm again, so that she fell sideways onto the floor. He put his hand on the back of her neck and pressed her face down roughly against the warped pine boards. "Guess you've got to learn the rules, and I'm just the one to teach you. When I ask you a question, you answer me, and quick. You got that? Now how old are you?"

Laurel gulped and managed to say, "Twelve."

"Well, ain't that nice. Twelve whole years old." He pulled her back onto her feet with his left hand. "Let's get a good look at the rest of you." He dragged her roughly toward the door, into the light from the lantern. He bent her arm upward and spun her around, then pulled her back tightly against his own body. Not releasing her wrist, he wrapped his arm tightly around her neck under her chin, forcing her head up and back.

With his right hand, he grabbed the neck of her T-shirt and yanked down sharply. The thin cotton dug painfully into her shoulder, then tore down the seam and fell away from her neck. He twisted the material around his fist and jerked it left and right, opening up several more tears in the fabric.

"Well, look at this. Sexy little thing, aren't you, in that little bikini? Your momma let you run around like that?" Piersol released the T-shirt and clapped his hand over her small breasts, kneading them painfully. Laurel struggled in his grasp, but he held her fast. "Not much in the way of tits yet, but that's how the big guys like it. Don't know why. I like 'em when they grow big and round. But you got a nice little ass on you already." He dropped his hand to her bottom and pinched her sharply. His rough hand roamed over her flesh, probing and squeezing.

As he became preoccupied with exploring her body, Laurel managed to drop her chin inside his forearm, and sank her teeth deeply into his flesh. Piersol yelled and dropped her, then reached down and yanked her brutally to her feet. He backhanded her twice across the face, knocking her across the room where she tumbled down between two of the cots. She lay there dazed.

Cradling his arm, Piersol inspected the damage. His eyes narrowed. "You still got a lot to learn, you little bitch!" He strode over to the cot, picked her up and stood her on her feet. He thrust his hand between her breasts and grasped the center of her bra. Using it to hold her stiffly out in front of him, he drew back his hand to strike her again, and Laurel jackknifed her leg up squarely into his crotch.

Piersol shrieked and doubled over, tumbling Laurel back onto the floor. As he fell to his side and clutched himself, she vaulted up onto the cot and backed up into the corner, just as the interior door crashed back against the wall. Benji and Emily screamed and jumped down onto the floor. They scrambled quickly under the cot.

"What's going on in here?" Mike took in the scene before him in the lantern light, then reached down and hauled Piersol to his feet. "What the hell happened to you?"

Stu hunched forward miserably, unable to stand upright. He turned and glared malevolently at Laurel. "That little bitch! I'm gonna show her a thing or two!"

Mike laughed. "Creamed your balls, did she? Nice work, kid!"

"She *bit* me, too! She ain't gonna do *that* again." Still holding himself and bent over in a half crouch, he stumbled toward the cot where Laurel cringed, but Mike grabbed his collar and pulled him back.

"What's the matter with you, you stupid jerk? You want to queer our deal? We got a *contract*, for chrisake. We catch 'em, we feed 'em, and we deliver them to the boat in one piece. Intact and with no marks. Otherwise we don't get paid."

Stu Piersol was enraged. "Listen, Reynolds, I don't give a damn about our contract! No snot-nosed kid does this to me!"

"This one did, and you're not gonna touch her."

"Oh, *yes*! I'm gonna *touch* her all right. I'm gonna beat the living shit out of her first, and then I'm gonna show her how she's gonna spend the rest of her miserable little life, on her goddam *back*!"

Laurel plastered herself against the wall in stark terror as he started toward her again, but Mike Reynolds sank his fingers painfully into his shoulder and spun him around. "Think about it, stupid! Look at her! What is she, eleven, twelve? And virgin for sure. She's just what they're looking for, and we get double money for the ones that have never been laid, even more for a cute one like this."

"I'll give her double of something else, damn it..."

"Shut up! They'll get a fortune for her when they get her overseas.

They can charge the first guy who has her a carload of Euros. And when she's broken in good, they'll get years out of her. Chicken farm first, then on the streets. We can ask twenty big ones for this one, probably more."

Piersol was slowly coming to his senses. "All right, all right! Just keep her the hell away from me, that's all." He limped out of the room. Mike followed along, picking up the lantern as he passed. Then he put it down again and turned toward the terrified children.

"I'll leave you the light, let you see to eat your supper. Better eat it all, you might not get much more for a while. In a day or two, you'll be going for a nice ocean voyage. Real pleasure trip!" He laughed unkindly and slammed the door behind him.

Laurel's racing heart gradually slowed. She sighed with relief, amazed that she had escaped, a least temporarily, what Stu Piersol had been planning to do to her. She even knew the words "chicken farm" and what they meant: child prostitution!

Her father and mother had carefully explained to her the dangers young girls faced from certain types of strangers, and even from people she might know. She was plenty street smart, but it hadn't seemed quite real to her until now.

Vague terrors filled her mind as she imagined what was in store for her. Thanks to modern parents and her school health classes, she had a good working knowledge of the mechanics of sex, but knew little of its emotional ramifications and consequences, or of the violence that sometimes accompanied it. The words *rape* and *sex crime*, however, were commonly in the news, and she, like most children who were exposed to media overkill in such cases, associated it with brutality and even murder.

Naïve and carefree at twelve, she still thought the whole sex thing to be kind of disgusting, and wasn't looking forward to it. She giggled with her friends at their crude jokes, but secretly decided to put the whole thing off as long as possible. *Only now I might not have a choice.*

She examined her sore arm and gently patted her face, which was already swelling where Piersol had slapped her. She worked her jaw back and forth, relieved to find it not too painful. Stiffly she climbed down and went over to where Benji and Emily had hidden themselves under the cot.

The children lay clutching each other, stunned into silence by the scene they had just witnessed. Laurel extended her hand to them and drew them out, trying to appear calm so they would see she was all right. *And I am all right*, she thought. *I'm going to get out of this.*

"Come on, guys, we have to eat something." Gradually she coaxed them across the room and sat them down beside the lantern. They all tried to choke down the stale bread and tasteless meat. Laurel drank a bit of juice and at first her stomach lurched, but eventually it settled down a little. She managed to choke down about half of the warm liquid.

Leaving most of the food untouched, they crawled back to the cots. Laurel collected a couple of blankets, and all three huddled closely together. After a long time, they slept.

The following day, Eric Kelman made his way around the inland lake and climbed over the hill into the valley, discovering the location of their hidden prison.

Eighteen

Eric's watch had stopped. The crown had been torn out against the rocks at sea, but he estimated the time at somewhere around three in the morning. After drinking from the well, he had managed a few hours sleep, and now turned his thoughts toward formulating some sort of plan, desperate or otherwise. Despite the odds, he couldn't leave the children in there much longer without trying to help them. Unsure whether he could get from the island to the mainland, he didn't dare leave them to try to go for outside help. It was up to him to take some sort of action.

No light showed through any of the skylights, and he heard no sounds inside the A-frame. As silently as possible he approached the building, and circled around to the back door, the one the occupants had used when visiting the outhouse.

The door was stoutly reinforced with diagonal pine boards. The knob was made of heavy brass, and there was no keyhole. It opened inward, and so the hinges were hidden. Eric assumed it was probably padlocked from the inside. There was no way he could breach it, not without tools and a good deal of noise.

He looked above the door at the boarded-up window. The moonlight revealed just enough of the thick pine boards to suggest they would be equally difficult to break through, even if he could reach that high.

He edged around to the opposite side of the building. Although not reinforced, the front door was still substantial, with a heavy deadbolt lock set in above the knob. There was no other point of entry at ground level, and the four skylights were positioned high out of reach on the steeply sloped roof. There seemed to be no way to climb up to them without a rope and grappling hook.

He completed one more circuit around the building, this time looking up at the trees that encroached upon it. Several overhung the roof, and two of them were near enough to the skylights to suggest a possible means of entry.

Eric considered the probable layout inside the A-frame. They had used the back door to head for the outhouse, closing it securely behind them after each kid came out. When going to the well, they had left the front door open. That suggested a minimum of two rooms inside, with the captives imprisoned in the rear one.

Eric had little but the element of surprise on his side. He knew that the noise from any attempt to enter the building at night would quickly arouse the men, and that the poor visibility would hamper him as much as them. He decided to wait until the first light of dawn, and retraced his steps back to his hiding place in the woods.

For the next several hours he dozed fitfully, and shortly before dawn he fell deeply asleep. The sun was well up when the sound of a slamming door awakened him. Looking out through the branches, he saw Mike Reynolds striding up the path, carrying a small backpack. He disappeared into the trees.

Eric waited a full ten minutes, but there was neither sight nor sound of the man returning. He crept out from his hiding place and moved over to stand beside the sloping roof, out of sight of either door.

One of the trees he had observed the previous night, a fully mature oak, seemed to offer him the best chance of getting close to one of the skylights. A thick branch overhung the roof, just a few feet to the side of the rearmost skylight on the east side. He sized it up, analyzing various possible handholds in his mind, and worked out a route up into the branches. Then he started to climb.

The most difficult part was scaling the thick lower trunk. He was just able to jump high enough to reach the lowest limb, then braced his feet against the trunk and walked up it until he could swing first one leg, then the other, over it. He hung there momentarily, then levered himself up on top where he could reach out for the branches above.

Moving slowly and carefully, he progressed with little noise, and edged out along a substantial limb until he was lying prone, parallel to the skylight. The pane of glass was framed with rough two-by-fours, and stood tilted open about six inches. It lay just out of reach of his outstretched hands. He had hoped to gain silent purchase on the frame, and pull himself high enough to look inside without alerting Piersol. Now he could see that would be impossible.

He inched himself along the branch until he was above the top frame of the skylight, but also farther away. He gauged the distance, then carefully raised his body and balanced himself on his hands and one good leg. Taking a deep breath, he launched himself out into space and landed heavily on the roof, just inches from the skylight. Immediately he started to slide toward the ground.

Desperately he thrust out his hand and caught the lower corner of the frame. He swung in an arc against the rough shingles, tearing the skin on his knees and reopening some of the abrasions left over from his swim through the surf. He managed to grasp the frame with his other hand, and secured his grip somewhat. Below him and inside the building, he heard an interior door crash open.

"What the hell was that?" Stu Piersol's voice boomed in the room below. "Answer me!" Eric heard no sounds from the children. He hoped his hands were not visible to those inside, where he clutched the lowest crossbar of the skylight frame. Piersol shouted some more, then stomped out of the room and slammed the door. Eric heard him cross the floor and fling the front door open, and saw the top of his head emerge into the clearing. *No way he'll miss me hanging here*, he thought.

Piersol went around the west side of the building, muttering to himself. Eric looked down apprehensively, waiting for him to come around the far corner. When Stu finally appeared, he was looking straight ahead instead of up toward the roof. He took several steps forward and stopped below the rear skylight, then looked upward just as Eric let go of the frame.

Eric's body hit the younger man a glancing blow across the shoulders and back, breaking his fall. Piersol sprawled on the ground, and Eric was on him before he could get his breath back. The powerful teenager bucked strongly, trying to get his legs under him, and managed to throw Eric off to one side.

Favoring his bad leg, Eric struggled to his feet, and was ready when the young man charged him. He clasped his hands together in front of him, seemingly in submission, but when Piersol came within range he jerked the double fist up sharply under the boy's chin. The blow snapped Piersol's jaw shut, clipping off the end of his tongue. He howled in agony, blood spraying out between his teeth.

Seizing the advantage, Eric sank his clasped hands deep into

Piersol's gut just below the rib cage, doubling him over. Then he struck down on the back of his neck, knocking him nearly unconscious and unable to fight any longer.

Eric dragged Piersol into the A-frame and looked around for something to tie him with. Clothing littered the floor and the two cots that stood against the wall, and he grabbed a shirt from one of the piles. He heaved the nearly comatose man up onto a chair and twisted both arms behind him, then tied his wrists together with the shirtsleeves. As Piersol began to regain his senses, Eric strapped his legs to the chair with two more shirts. Satisfied that his opponent was immobilized, he sank down on one of the cots to catch his breath.

He looked around as Piersol came slowly awake, moaning in pain and with blood dribbling out of his mouth. The room was sparsely furnished, containing only the two cots, a table and a few chairs, a cook stove, and a dry sink. Food and other necessities lay scattered about. A substantial door stood to the right of center in a rough interior wall, closed and secured with a heavy bolt.

Ignoring Piersol's increasing agony over his partially severed tongue, Eric got to his feet and walked across to the door. He slid back the bolt and opened it, and found three frightened children huddled together on the floor behind one of the cots.

"Eric!" Laurel disengaged herself from the other two and flew across the floor, wrapping her arms around him and burying her face in his shirt. "I thought you were dead!"

"Not quite, runt. Had yourself a time of it, haven't you?"

She tilted her head back and turned her tear-stained face up to him. "Is my dad with you?"

"I'm sorry, Laurel. I don't know what happened to him. I was hoping he'd be here with you."

She slumped dejectedly against him. "Those creeps made me go down in the cabin after you fell overboard. There was a lot of shooting, and I saw the Zodiac floating away. They finally let me out when we anchored in this big lake, but my dad was gone. Then they took me ashore and dragged me over a big hill and down here."

Eric held her away from him and scrutinized her bruised face. He touched her cheek gingerly. "Are you okay? That looks nasty."

"It doesn't hurt much. The skinny guy tried to feel me up and I bit him, and then he hit me, and I kicked him you-know-where. He got the worst of it; you should have heard him yell. How did *you* get here? They told me you never came up."

"It's a long story. I was under the stern, trying to figure out how to get back on board without getting shot, when they started the engine. I had to dive to avoid the propeller, and decided to stay under as long as I could so they'd think I drowned. Then I swam here. It was just dumb luck I ended up on this island."

"I'm so glad you're okay. You *are* okay, aren't you? You look all scratched up."

"A little, and some bruises, just like you, but nothing serious."

Laurel's face fell. "Dad's not okay, is he?"

Eric gathered his courageous little friend into his arms and hugged her warmly. "I know it looks bad, but don't give up hoping. Your dad is tough. Until we know for sure, just keep believing that he got away, and is looking for you right now. Okay?"

Laurel managed a tear-stained smile. Then Eric turned his attention to the other children, both still cowering beside the cot. She released him and went over to help them up. "It's okay, guys, this is my friend Eric, the one I told you about. The one I promised would come and get us." *But I didn't tell you I really thought he was dead.*

Shyly, Benji and Emily got up off the floor and crossed over to him. Eric squatted down to their level and inspected them. Aside from the dirt and a few scrapes, they seemed to be okay, just frightened out of their wits. He asked them their names, and Benji answered for both of them.

"You're going to be all right now," Eric promised. "I'll take you home just as quickly as I can." He turned to Laurel. "Take them outside, but stay away from the guy I've got tied to the chair. Keep them hidden around back, just in case the other one shows up before I'm through in here."

"What are you going to do?" she asked.

"I'm going to have a nice, quiet conversation with our friend in the other room. Then we'll see about getting all of us out of here."

Eric shepherded the children through the outer room and out the front door, and saw them safely around back. He made sure they were out of sight of the path, then returned inside and pulled a chair over in front of his captive and sat down.

Piersol's mouth had stopped bleeding, but his shirtfront was heavily stained a dark red. His speech was slurred and somewhat indistinct. Eric slapped his face to get his attention, and then explained the ground rules. "You're going to answer all my questions, junior, or your bit-off tongue is just the beginning. First, where's your partner?"

Piersol groaned but didn't answer, and Eric cuffed the other side of his face, snapping his head sideways. He was not normally a violent man, but the sight of the terrified children, and especially Laurel's battered face, stirred him to unnatural anger. He had no pity for anyone who would treat children the way this man had.

Eric backhanded him once again, and as Piersol's head came around, his eyes cleared, filled with hatred. Then his face drained of color as he recognized the man he thought he had killed while on the sailboat. "Jesus Christ, man, you a ghost?" he mumbled around his swollen tongue.

Gradually the story came out, prompted by a few more well-placed blows, until Eric was sure he had the true picture. They were expecting the return of a ship sometime during the day, a substantial ocean-going cruiser that the pedophile ring used to smuggle their young victims out of the country. The ship was small enough to hide from the Coast Guard among the islands, and it could easily slip away out to sea under cover of darkness, but its hold could contain quite a few small passengers.

Laurel and the other two were to be part of the next shipment overseas. The other man (Piersol said his name was Reynolds) had gone out to meet the ship in the big powerboat, intending to try to negotiate an extra bonus for Laurel. He had towed the smaller skiff with him. Once the deal was struck, the plan was for Reynolds to leave the bigger boat at the ship, and return in the skiff to collect the children. Then the two men would ferry them out to the cruiser and receive their fee.

Eric estimated the time it would take for Reynolds to get out of the cove and find the cruiser. He checked the knotted shirts again, and tied another one around the chair back, securing Piersol's upper arms. Satisfied with the soundness of the bonds, he hurried out of the building and gathered the children together.

All three were happy to be out of their prison, and Eric found even the youngest one to be in better spirits. He could tell that Laurel was desperately worried over Walt's disappearance, but was trying not to let it show for the sake of the other two. He hoisted the little one onto his shoulders, and they set off up the path toward the shore.

Nineteen

Eric stayed on the path to make the going easier for the children, but he was constantly alert to the possibility that Mike Reynolds might return. Climbing up out of the valley with the eight-year-old on his shoulders, he was relieved to note that his injured leg seemed to be getting stronger, and that his various scrapes and bruises were troubling him less than they had the previous day.

Just before the crest of the hill, he stepped off the path and set Emily down behind a thick blue spruce. Laurel and Benji joined her, squatting down out of sight of the path, and Eric made his way through the brush until he could see the big cove spread out before him on the other side.

There was no sign of Reynolds or the skiff. From the high vantage point, Eric could see that the place where the boats had been concealed was empty. Both the skiff and the speedboat were gone.

Mayflower still lay peacefully at anchor in the center of the cove, her bow pointed in the direction of the sea against the incoming tide. Anticipating the absence of the two smaller boats, Eric's intention had been to hide the children somewhere along the shore, swim out to *Mayflower*, and radio for help. But once he reached the shoreline, he realized there was a major flaw in this plan.

When Reynolds returned and made his way to the A-frame, he would quickly discover his injured partner, and come looking for them. Even if Eric made radio contact right away, it would take too long for the Coast Guard to locate them. The only alternative was to get them all aboard *Mayflower*, and sail it out of the cove. However, he couldn't afford the time for repeated trips out to the yacht. He had to get all four of them aboard as quickly as possible.

He considered swimming out alone and bringing the boat in closer, but quickly abandoned the idea. When viewed from the crest of the hill, the water was much more transparent than it appeared from the shore. He could plainly see a thick scattering of rocks beneath the surface, extending well out into the cove. Although they lay submerged far enough for a skiff to pass over them safely, they would doubtless snag *Mayflower's* deeper keel. He didn't trust his own skill and judgment at the wheel of the larger boat, nor his ability to avoid grounding her.

In addition, he was unfamiliar with the operation of the boat's diesel engine, and might lose precious minutes figuring it out. Time was running short. The skiff could return at any moment.

He turned back to collect his charges, hoisted the barefoot Emily to his shoulders once more, and headed down the path to the shore line. He stood uncertainly at the water's edge, estimating the distance to the anchored boat. It seemed impossibly far, but he could see no alternative means of escape. He turned to the children. "Can anybody swim?"

"I can," Benji said proudly, "real good. My mom says I'm a natural." His face fell. "But my sister can't."

"That's okay," Eric reassured him. "I can take her with me." Then he turned to Laurel. "How about you, little buddy? Have you been practicing those swimming strokes Sara and I showed you?"

"No. I haven't been in the water since we got home from your cabin." She looked out at the vast expanse of water, much broader than Eric's lagoon had been. Her eyes were wide and fearful.

"No matter. It'll come back to you. Let's give it a try. You two stay right here," he said to the younger ones, "until I see what Laurel can do."

He looked apprehensively in the direction of the hidden strait that led to the sea, and strained to listen for any sound of an approaching outboard. Hearing nothing, he led Laurel down to the water's edge and spoke softly to her so the others couldn't hear. "We're in a little trouble here. The older guy, the one called Mike, is out there somewhere, and he could be back any minute. Even if Benji can make it on his own, it will take too long for me to ferry both you and Emily out to the boat one at a time. You were doing real well out at the lake, and I think you can make it on your own. Are you game to try it?"

Laurel gulped. "I guess so."

"That's my girl. This is going to be easy. Salt water keeps you up better than fresh, so if you just relax, you can't sink. Fill your lungs with air and roll over on your back if you get tired, and you'll bob like a cork."

Laurel smiled wanly. "But what if I can't stay up? If you're taking Emily, you won't be able to help me, too."

"We'll take some insurance with us. There's a small log back there along the path. We'll float it ahead of us, and if anyone gets in trouble, they can just hang on."

Laurel was still worried, but her trust in Eric overcame most of her fear. She and Benji went with him to retrieve the log, and all four of them entered the water.

Patiently Eric explained to Emily that she was to hang on to his shoulders, and he'd swim with her on his back. "But you mustn't grab me around the neck, okay? Because then I won't be able to breathe. That's *very* important."

Emily nodded, her dark brown eyes wide and solemn. Eric turned his back to her and placed her small hands on the points of his shoulders. "Like this, see? Now wrap your legs around my back and squeeze." She dug her heels into his ribs, and he twitched beneath her and laughed. "Whoa! That tickles! Now just hold your head up out of the water, and you'll be fine. Let's practice." He stretched forward and glided out into the water, then stroked several yards away from shore. The child clung securely to his back, her head well above the waves. He turned and swam back a few strokes.

"How's that? Fun, wasn't it?"

"You're really strong," Emily said, the first words Eric had heard her speak. He smiled at her over his shoulder. Then he called to Laurel and Benji. "Okay, you two, shake a leg!" He tried to keep his tone light, to avoid infecting them with his own anxiety.

The two older children pushed off from the shallows, Benji swimming strongly and Laurel with the log stretched out in front of her. She started kicking. It soon became apparent to Eric that the boy didn't need any help. He moved with a sure, clean precision that spoke either of raw talent or many hours of lessons. But Laurel wasn't making much progress. Her inexpert kicks were ineffective, and she feared letting go of the log, so that her arms were of no use to her. Eric called to Benji to slow down, then moved to her side.

"This isn't working, runt. You aren't getting anywhere. You need your arms, just like you were doing out at the lake a couple of weeks ago."

"I'm scared to let go of the log. This water is so much rougher, and it's a long way to the boat. And it's *cold!*"

"I know, squirt. But you can *do* this. I *know* you can. I'll take the log with me, so you'll have it if you need it. Give it a try."

Reluctantly she pushed the log away, and immediately took on a face full of water. She sputtered and thrashed out, and Eric caught her arm and lifted her. He maintained his own buoyancy by treading water with his other arm and legs, conscious of keeping Emily above the surface.

"Remember the straws? Breathe out when your face is in the water, and do that stroke that Sara showed you, the breaststroke thing. That's the best one to keep your head up."

Laurel tried again, scissoring her arms forward and out in a clumsy breaststroke, and surprised herself by moving forward.

"That's the idea!" Eric praised. "Again."

She settled into a steady rhythm, and soon they were beginning to close the gap between the shore and the boat. Emily actually seemed to be enjoying her ride, and Benji was thoroughly at home in the water, far out ahead of the others. Eric, however, began to tire. The strain of supporting the child, maneuvering the log ahead of him, and keeping even with Laurel's slow pace were beginning to sap his strength.

As they approached the boat, he caught the high-pitched sound of an outboard, echoing from the island's cliffs off shore. Benji had already reached the hull, but he and Laurel still had fifty feet or more to go. He glanced toward the stern and saw that the boarding ladder was not in place.

Eric shouted to the boy not to try to get on board, but to swim to the stern, opposite the strait that led to the open sea. If Reynolds caught sight of the child trying to climb over the side, they were in real trouble. Benji did as he was told, disappearing from view.

The sound of the outboard grew louder as the skiff maneuvered through the outer reaches of the inlet. Eric knew they didn't have much time. Laurel was tiring, and there was no chance they could reach the sailboat before the outboard came into view. Reynolds would surely see their heads in the water.

Taking a risk, he left Laurel clinging to the log and stroked strongly toward the sailboat. Rounding the hull, he found Benji clinging to the end of a slack line that was hitched to the stern railing. He swung Emily off his shoulders and anchored her small hands on the line. "Keep your hand on her," he instructed the boy, "and make sure she doesn't go under. Take care of your sister, okay?"

"I will!" The boy wrapped his arm securely around Emily's waist, holding her well above the waves, and clung to the rope.

"Good man! I won't be long." Eric plunged back toward Laurel and quickly reached her side, his strength born of desperation. The sound of the outboard suddenly boomed across the water as the skiff left the narrow inlet and entered the cove.

He had no time to explain in detail what they had to do. Quickly he issued a set of terse instructions. "Laurel, trust me, and do exactly what I say. Take five really deep breaths, right now." As she did as she was told, he continued, "I'm going to take you under water until the boat passes, and I won't let you go. Just hold your breath as long as you can. When you can't hold it any longer, let it out through your nose a little bit at a time. When it's all gone, pinch me and I'll know to bring you back up. Okay?"

Her eyes widened in terror, but she nodded. He looked back at the rapidly approaching skiff. Its bow was pointed high in the air, obscuring the helmsman, which meant that they probably had not yet been seen.

"Grab on to me and close your eyes so the salt won't burn them. Now let out all your air and take another really big breath, and *hold it!*"

Laurel wrapped her arms and legs tightly around him, squeezed her eyes shut, and gulped a huge draught of air. Eric gathered her close in one arm, breathed deeply himself, and dipped beneath the surface, treading awkwardly with his other arm to gain some depth.

The sound of the outboard was muffled underwater, but he could sense when it drew abreast of him and began to pass them by. He felt Laurel's chest begin to heave. He stroked her back reassuringly, and she clung even more tightly to him, her legs wrapped around his hips. When he sensed she was at the end of her endurance, he kicked upward, and their faces broke the surface, both of them gasping.

Reynolds' boat was nearing the shore, and he was looking away from them. Once he landed, however, they would likely be spotted.

Eric looked toward *Mayflower*. Having passed the sailboat, Reynolds would now have a clear view of the stern, but Benji and Emily were nowhere in sight. Eric searched the water desperately, then spotted the small boy just emerging from the opposite side of the boat near the bow, his little sister clinging to his shoulders. He had managed to get her to the bow anchor line, which was hidden from view of the shore.

Laurel seemed exhausted. Eric told her to take a deep breath for buoyancy, then rolled her over on her back and hooked his arm under her chin. Keeping low in the water, he towed her toward *Mayflower* and helped her take hold of the line beside the other two children. She hung on limply, completely spent.

The sound of the outboard died abruptly, and Eric peered carefully around the bow, his eyes barely above the surface. Reynolds was concealing the skiff in its place among the rushes. He hoisted his backpack out of the bow, swept the last of the concealing foliage into place, and set off into the woods.

Eric waited a few moments to be sure the man was gone, then guided the children around to the stern. Hand over hand, he hauled himself up the dangling line, and reached through the opening in the stern rail to grasp the boarding ladder. He swung it down into place, and helped the children to climb aboard.

Emily and Benji were chilled and lethargic from lying motionless so long in the water. He took them both down into the cabin and told Benji to remove his wet clothes. Emily was limp and unresponsive, and he quickly stripped her playsuit off and wrapped her in a thick towel. He rubbed her briskly to stimulate her circulation, then turned his attention to Benji, handing him a second large towel. When they were both reasonably dry, he set Emily down in the forward berth, located his duffel, and slipped one of his own oversized sweatshirts over her head. She lay down and curled her legs up tightly against her stomach. He bundled her into his sleeping bag, and she went immediately to sleep.

Eric found Walt's duffel bag and dug out a second sweatshirt for Benji. Finding his friend's kit saddened him. The implications of its continued presence on the boat were not good. He shook off his feeling of helplessness and handed the sweatshirt to the boy. Benji discarded his towel and put it on, then sat at the table, more tired than he wanted to admit. Eric opened the food locker and handed down a jar of peanut butter, some bread and jam, and a package of cookies. He dug a knife out of a drawer. "There's stuff to drink in the ice box over here, juice and milk. Can you make yourself a sandwich?" Eric asked.

"Sure," Benji answered.

"Check on your sister. When she wakes up, make her one, too."

"Okay."

Eric had reacted with fear and apprehension when he saw the boy towing his sister in the open water toward the bow. The small girl could easily have pulled him under, drowning them both, but Benji apparently knew his own ability. His determination to hide them from view of the shore showed both courage and intelligence. Eric took the time to praise him.

"You did really well out there. You saved your sister's life, in fact. Nice work!" Benji's face lit up with pride; he was coming back to life.

As soon as Benji finished making himself a sandwich, Eric dug huge gobs of peanut butter from the jar and slapped them onto several slices of bread. Taking them with him, he made his way toward the hatch, then noticed for the first time a series of gaping rectangular holes in the paneling above the chart table.

The Global Positioning System receiver was missing, as was the depth sounder. Most important, the ship-to-shore radio had also vanished. *Those jerks probably have a thriving business in stolen property*, he thought. He concluded they had probably planned to scuttle *Mayflower* in order to hide their crimes, but her hardware would bring good prices when fenced. On impulse he opened the cuddy above the cooler, and was relieved to find his Pentax binoculars still on board.

He closed the cabinet and climbed back on deck, where Laurel was checking out the boat's gear. She had discarded her soaked and torn T-shirt, and the sun had dried and revived her. She seemed to be running on pure adrenaline. Eric handed her some of the food, and they quickly gulped it down. Then he surveyed the boat. The ignition key was still in place, as was the winch handle. The sails had not been properly stowed and covered, but appeared to be undamaged.

"You did good, champ," he praised her. "A world's record for staying under water, for sure. I knew you could do it."

Laurel's smile shone. "And I didn't even have to pinch you to come up, did I? Did you call the Coast Guard? Are they coming?"

"Bad news, I'm afraid. Our friends back there have already started stripping her. All the electronics are gone."

She looked stricken. "What'll we do, then?"

"We've got to sail her out of here, right now, and get to a phone on shore."

"We can't do that without Dad!"

"Why not? You know how everything works, and you're good at this. *Really* good. It's not just for us, either. We have to get Benji and Emily back home, too."

Tears filled her eyes. "But I don't know these waters. What if I hit some rocks? I need Dad! What's happened to him?"

Eric squatted down in front of her and placed his hands gently on her upper arms. He stared straight into her eyes, calming her with a relaxed smile. "We can do this together. Your dad taught you, and you taught me, and if we're ever going to find him again, we have to save ourselves first. Those two guys will be coming back here any minute, and we have to get moving. Right away."

Laurel took in a huge lungful of air, sighed, and shook herself. "You get the anchor. I'll get the engine started."

"Not quite yet. I've got something to do first. Stay put." Eric mounted the rail and dove cleanly over the side. He stroked powerfully toward shore, his fatigue forgotten in his determination to get them away safely. To do that, he had to capture the small outboard boat, so that Reynolds and Piersol couldn't follow them.

Reaching the shore, he quickly located the hidden inlet and brushed aside the leaves and branches. He cast off the bowline, stepped aboard and shoved it out into the lake. Turning to the outboard, he grasped the starter cord and pulled, but the engine failed to catch. He tried twice more, then realized the fuel tank was missing, no doubt taken ashore by Reynolds.

He scanned the boat for oars or a paddle, but the hull was empty. The small boat drifted slowly, parallel to the shore. He unclamped the small engine from the stern and heaved it overboard, then hoisted himself up on the gunwale and rocked the boat so that water cascaded inside. As the hull swamped, he dove overboard and struck out toward the sailboat.

Behind him he heard angry voices coming down the path. He dug his arms in and kicked strongly, determined to reach *Mayflower* with his last reserves of strength.

Reynolds and Piersol emerged from the forest when Eric had covered about half the distance to the sailboat. They headed for their boat, and quickly discovered it was missing, making it impossible for them to give chase. Piersol lifted his rifle and fired at Eric's retreating head.

Eric heard a soft plop as the bullet entered the water just slightly to his left, followed quickly by the gun's report in his ears. He executed a shallow surface dive and turned abruptly right, then left again, continuing under water until his lungs cried out for air. As soon as he surfaced, another shot rang out. He plunged below the waves again, but Piersol began firing at the water where he had disappeared. Eric felt a sharp tug at his side, but ignored it as he zigzagged toward *Mayflower's* hull.

He pulled himself over the stern to find Laurel lying prone on the deck, out of the line of fire. The range was too great for accurate shooting, but shells continued to fly in their direction, some of them hitting the hull.

Keeping his head down, Eric plunged through the hatch into the cabin, and was relieved to see the two smaller children uninjured. He scooped them up and stuffed them into the after berth, putting the engine between them and any bullets that might possibly penetrate the fiberglass hull. He told them to stay put until he came for them.

He climbed swiftly back on deck and ran forward along the gunwale. With one sharp pull, the bow anchor came free from the rocky bottom, and he hauled it aboard as Laurel fired up the engine and slammed it in gear. Within moments they were headed out of the cove, and away from immediate danger.

Eric made his way back to the cockpit, then felt suddenly very dizzy. He slumped against the cabin wall. Laurel was concentrating on the color of the water, trying to gauge its depth, all the while keeping her head as low as possible in case the gunman got lucky. Then she spotted the trail of blood spattered across the deck.

"You got hit!" she called out to him.

"Not serious," Eric gasped, now thoroughly out of breath. He pulled up his sodden T-shirt. A few inches above the waistband of his swim trunks, an angry, blood-filled wound creased his rib cage, with the flesh peeled back on either side. It stung like fire, aggravated by the salt water.

Laurel throttled back to idle and moved to help him, but he held up his hand. "You've got a job to do, First Mate. Get us out of here. I can take care of this if you tell me where the first aid kit is."

"You're sitting on it." She hesitated, deeply concerned, and then advanced the throttle again. Eric stood up and opened the locker door beneath him. Not surprisingly, given his architect's attention to detail, Walt had stocked the kit in anticipation of a wide variety of emergencies. Eric found a bottle of peroxide and some cotton balls. He cleansed the wound, then wondered how to close it. The kit contained sutures, but he had never stitched anyone's flesh before, especially his own, and this didn't seem a good time to learn.

He dug down deeper and found a package of butterfly bandages. It took six of them to draw the sides of the wound together. Then he covered them with a broad band of adhesive tape, hoping it would hold the smaller bandages in place when he moved and stretched.

Laurel divided her attention between her concern for him and running the boat. They reached the mouth of the cove and entered the narrow inlet, and *Mayflower* lurched and heeled over as her keel dragged on the bottom. Laurel throttled back, and the hull drifted free.

"You need a lookout?" Eric asked. "How about if I sit on the bow and watch the bottom for rocks?" Without waiting for an answer, he climbed onto the gunwale and started forward, ignoring his nausea and the pain in his ribs. Stretching out full length on the foredeck, he peered over the side of the hull next to the bowsprit. The thick sea water was nearly opaque, but he could make out shades of color that indicated rocks and sand not far from the surface.

As Laurel steered cautiously through the twisting channel, he called back to her, helping her to avoid the worst of the undersea obstructions. Twice more the keel caught briefly in the sand, but each time their momentum dragged it through.

Finally they reached the open water. Eric returned to the cockpit and sat down carefully, mindful of his wound. He suddenly became aware that the diesel was laboring, and Laurel leaned over the stern rail and peered down toward the water line.

She straightened and looked over at him. "We've got another problem."

"What's up?"

"There's almost no water coming out the pipe, and the engine's overheating." She shut it down, and the boat wallowed in its own wake.

"Can we fix it?" he asked her.

"I don't know how. The last time it happened, Dad had to take it apart. It had a bunch of goop in it, seaweed or something, and the filter had gotten clogged. It must have happened when we dragged the keel back there."

"So we sail, then." Eric climbed to the top of the cabin and threaded the main halyard onto the sail. Then he returned to the cockpit, put the line on the winch, and started cranking. The big mainsail raced up the mast and filled. Quickly he unfurled the jib and secured its line to the winch, and the big boat began to run before the freshening wind.

Twenty

Once they were under way, Eric checked on the children down in the cabin. He brought both of them up on deck, fearing the onset of seasickness in the stuffy enclosed space. He took the helm while Laurel went below, emerging shortly with two sets of her own lightweight T-shirts and shorts for the children to wear. They were somewhat too big for Emily, but more comfortable and less awkward on her than Eric's huge sweatshirt, and definitely cooler in the dense, humid air. Laurel dressed her on deck, while Benji went below and changed out of his sweatshirt in privacy. Then he came back topside.

Laurel returned to the console, and Eric dug life vests out of the locker for the two children and helped them put them on. Then he took out two more vests, one for Laurel and one for himself, a precaution against what looked like some unsettled weather ahead. The heat was becoming oppressive, and Laurel put the bulky vest on directly over her swimsuit, complaining bitterly about its weight and the way the collar rubbed against her neck.

"I think it looks quite glamorous," Eric teased her gently, earning him another stuck-out tongue. "Do you have any idea where we are?" he asked her.

"Yup. I've been here with Dad a couple of times, but he did most of the sailing through this part." She pointed to a passage between two steep escarpments. "We have to go through that channel up there, and on the other side is a big bay. I know the water once we get there. When we cross the bay, we come to that island next to The Narrows. We have to sail out to sea to get around the rocky shallows on the other side. Remember how Dad showed you?"

Eric remembered the spot well. "Isn't there any place we can put in to shore along here? The sooner we find a telephone, the quicker the Coast Guard can start after those guys."

"I don't think so. You can get the chart out and look, but Dad always said the whole coastline was mostly rocks, and there aren't any towns along here anyway. The first place to put in is the Coast Guard station we passed on the way here. If we had the Zodiac, we could anchor and go ashore." She thought for a moment. "Where *is* the Zodiac, anyway? How come they cut it loose?"

Eric was halfway down the hatch. "Beats me."

Seconds later he emerged with the chart, and spread it out on the floor of the cockpit. Benji flopped down beside him and peered at the lines and numbers. Between the chain of islands and the mainland, the chart indicated dangerous waters. Eric could see no harbors or navigable inlets anywhere along the coast, and the shallows extended too far out to allow them to get close enough to swim ashore.

Laurel entered the channel between the two tall islands, and the wind shifted and became more turbulent as she passed under the shadow of the cliffs, becoming more turbulent. She called to Eric to trim the sails, and he reset the traveler and adjusted the jib as she instructed. *Mayflower* became slightly more stable, but Laurel still had her hands full maintaining a heading.

"Dad motored through here twice," she said. "We only sailed it once, on a really calm day, but he said it wasn't easy. The darn cliffs whip the wind around every which way."

Eric stared upward, and Laurel followed his gaze. Behind them, towering white clouds lined the northern horizon, but the sky ahead and to the south was rapidly becoming overcast and gray. "Wish we had those BPFs in front of us," she observed.

"BPFs?"

Laurel smiled at him. "That's a highly technical term for the big white clouds, according to my dad. It stands for Big Puffy Fellows, and they mean good weather."

"Any other important scientific terms I ought to know?"

"Sure! The sails are BFTs."

Eric puzzled over the acronym, but couldn't work it out.

"Give up?" Laurel asked. Eric and Benji both nodded. "BFTs! Big Flappy Things!"

They all enjoyed a good laugh, but Laurel remained tense under the strain of guiding the big boat in the uncertain, erratic winds. She and Eric relaxed somewhat when they finally cleared the channel and emerged into a wide bay.

The hot wind whipped the surface more strongly now, and

Mayflower was overpowered and hard to handle. Laurel called for a reef in the mainsail. Eric had no idea what to do, but she talked him through it. He lowered the sail enough to tie off the bottom part of it. With less surface presented to the wind, the boat settled down, driving forward at a clean six-and-a-half knots.

As he stood on the cabin top reefing the sail, Eric glanced out toward the far horizon and saw the outline of a sleek cruiser. It appeared to be motionless. Once the sail was set, he retrieved his binoculars from the cabin and made his way to the bow.

Through the powerful lenses, the distant ship seemed fairly large. Eric had no way of estimating its length, but the number of portholes and the relative size of figures moving around on the deck suggested a vessel capable of trans-oceanic travel. He spotted a speedboat tethered at the stern, and was fairly sure from the shape of it that it could be the same one they had stopped to "help" two days earlier.

He returned to the cockpit. "Back on the island," he asked Laurel, "did you ever see those guys using a radio or a telephone?"

"Nope. Why?"

He turned to Benji, who shook his head, but Emily said shyly, "I did."

Eric dropped down beside her. "When did you see it?" he asked her gently.

"Once when the big man took me to the bathroom, he had a telephone in his hand. It was one of those little ones that fold up, and he was talking to somebody named Georgie."

Eric squeezed her shoulder and smiled at her affectionately, then stood up again, bracing himself against the motion of the hull and staring out to sea. "A cell phone. That's what I was afraid of."

Laurel caught his worried tone of voice. "What's wrong?"

He turned to face her. "There's a cruiser lying out there. If it's the same one Reynolds and Piersol were talking about, and if they've all got cell phones, we could be in some trouble. They've got that fast speedboat, too."

Mayflower was already halfway across the broad bay, and her sails made her clearly visible from a long way off. Laurel had begun to ease off the wind, preparing to swing out to sea to avoid the rocky flats that extended out from the next island.

Eric considered their situation. If the cruiser belonged to the pedophiles' organization, and if Reynolds and Piersol had alerted them to his escape with the children, they were probably already under scrutiny. It was unlikely that the cruiser would come in close to shore, but the small speedboat could easily overtake the relatively slow sailboat at any time. If Laurel took them out to sea, she'd sail right into their hands.

"Hey, runt, isn't there any other way to get around those rocks?"

"Sure, but I can't do it. The Narrows, remember?"

Eric thought for a moment. "Didn't your dad say they were passable?" he asked.

"We did it once, but not in *Mayflower*. We were in a powerboat, and it was pretty scary. There isn't any room to maneuver, and the water moves really fast through there. And the way the wind keeps changing is unbelievable! I wouldn't know how to sail through it."

"I'm going to ask you to try it."

Laurel reacted strongly. "No way! We'll pile up!"

"That might be better than the alternative," Eric said. "If we try to go around the long way, that cruiser will nail us for sure. We can't outrun their speedboat, and they'll have guns. We have to take the chance."

"I can't!"

Benji and Emily sensed something was wrong, and were becoming agitated. Eric squatted down beside them and smiled, touching the little girl's hair with gentle affection.

"Maybe you can't..." he said, addressing Laurel. "But maybe *we* can, the two of us together."

Laurel was clearly frightened. Dark clouds had descended over the islands ahead of them, and her confidence faltered in the face of the worsening weather and the challenge of navigating the cramped passage. The Narrows scared her. Worse, they threatened her with the loss of her beloved boat.

"Laurel," he began tentatively, "do you have any idea who those people on the cruiser might be?"

She stared at him, her eyes wide. "When I kicked that Stu guy in the balls, he got so mad, he was gonna kill me. If the other guy hadn't stopped him, that is. He was yelling all kinds of things he was gonna do to me, sex things, and what was going to happen to me when they took me to the ship. I got the idea, all right."

Eric stepped to the console and placed a comforting hand on her tense shoulder. "So you know why we at least have to try to get away from them. They've got guns, and there are probably a lot of them. We can't outrun a speedboat, so our only chance is to try to fool them. Get closer to the Coast Guard station, or to some other boat, before they run us down."

"But I can't go through The Narrows!" She was upset and fearful. "I'll bet *nobody* can in a sailboat. It's just too rough and shallow."

"You're a fine sailor, just about as good as your father, maybe even better."

She looked up at him apprehensively. "No I'm not. He's the best."

"Even if that's true, that makes you second best, and that's pretty darn good. We'd at least have a chance in The Narrrows. We won't be any worse off than here, and a lot better off than if they catch us."

"Oh, yeah? We could get *dead* going through there!"

"That's not going to happen." He tried to give her confidence. "We've got life jackets, and three-fourths of us can swim. Besides, I've got a good feeling about it. I think you can get us out of this."

Laurel was close to tears. "What good will it do? They'll just come after us in the speedboat and get us on the other side."

"It'll buy us some time to figure something out. Who knows what might happen? Maybe the Coast Guard will be waiting for us over there. Your mom and Deanna must have reported us missing by now, so they'll be out looking. Or maybe the speedboat will try to follow us through The Narrows, and pile up on the rocks. What do you say?"

Laurel looked around, almost frantic. "We're too big! I need lots more room to turn than a speedboat does. And I don't know where the channel is. I can't do it, Eric. I just *can't!*"

Mayflower raced onward, still committed to the long way around and certain capture. Eric understood her problem. Their boat was a displacement hull, drawing at least six feet of water and slowed down by the effort of pushing the water aside to move through it. The speedboat was a planing craft, and could almost fly over the surface, with only a few inches of hull and the propeller shaft beneath the water. It could maneuver much more easily in the close confines of The

Narrows, and was much less likely to strike the rocks.

He had almost given up trying to persuade her to try the dangerous passage. About to acquiesce, he turned to her and saw that she seemed to be deep in thought, all traces of panic erased from her face. She looked back and forth between the open sea ahead and the treacherous channel that lay close to the coast. She stretched up on tiptoe to peer over the bow, her brow furrowed. "Maybe... Maybe we can fake them out."

"How?"

"Just suppose we can get through. I don't see how, but I sure don't want somebody like that slimy Stu putting his hands all over me again!"

Eric rejoiced silently. Her courage was returning. "If we wait until the last minute," she continued, "then make a quick run for The Narrows, they'll probably try to follow us. I'll bet they won't know they can go around and wait for us at the other end. They won't take a chance on us getting away. Then, if we get through all right before they catch us, and if they come right behind us, there's lots of deep water straight ahead."

"What good will that do?"

"There's that big shallow field of rocks that sticks out from the island. The tide's pretty low. If you turn into it too soon, you go aground, even in a small boat."

Eric was beginning to catch on. "But how can you get them to turn that way?"

"Suppose we come about, just as soon as we clear the rocks. If they're not too close to us, maybe they'll try to head us off by cutting the corner."

"Won't they see the rocks?"

"Probably not," Laurel answered, becoming enthusiastic. "They're a lot harder to see beneath the surface when you're going fast. If they're after us, I bet they won't be paying much attention to the water anyway."

Eric left the decision up to her. "So are we going to try The Narrows?"

A visible shiver of apprehension ran up her back, and he patted her shoulder. She thought about her prison on the island, and the plans those men had been making for her and for the two younger ones. She glanced at them, huddled miserably in the corner under the dodger.

She made up her mind. *It's up to me to get us out of this, I guess.* "Coming about!"

Eric flew to the winch and released the jib. He hauled it in on the opposite side as the mainsail slammed across the cockpit. Benji and Emily scrambled to hold on as the boat heeled over and plunged toward the jagged end of the island. *Mayflower's* speed rose a full knot.

Expertly Laurel played the wind, and once Eric saw that her heading would miss the point of land, he raised his binoculars and looked out over the rail. He could just make out some movement on the deck of the cruiser. Tiny figures were heading toward the stern, and as he watched, they hauled the speedboat in close to the hull. A few minutes later the sound of the big outboard engine reached them faintly across the water. *Here we go!* he thought. *Now if we can just keep from killing ourselves, maybe we'll get lucky.*

Twenty-One

Mayflower entered the mouth of The Narrows slightly overpowered, but Laurel couldn't risk taking another reef in the sail at the speed they were traveling. She was unprepared for the small amount of clearance to both port and starboard, and startled by the clarity with which she could see rocks and sand bars barely below the roiling surface. Quickly she discovered that her forward visibility was too restricted in such a narrow channel. With the sun canopy over her head, she couldn't stand tall enough to look out over the dodger and the cabin roof.

"Eric!" she shouted. "I can't *see!*"

He quickly sized up the situation, and unsnapped the heavy canvas from Walt's improvised canopy supports that were bolted to the stern rail. Freed of the canopy, Laurel stood on tiptoe behind the wheel, her face a taut mask of concentration as she strained to see past the dodger and mast. She still couldn't watch both sides of the bow at once. In calmer, open waters this was no problem, but in such close quarters she feared she couldn't anticipate hazards in time to avoid them.

Eric watched her straining to judge the location of the channel ahead. Then he got an idea. He plunged down the hatch into the cabin, missing the bottom two rungs of the ladder and landing heavily on his weak leg. Ignoring the pain that lanced all the way to his hip, he hauled his empty cooler out of the locker, whirled, and limped quickly back up on deck. The wound in his side throbbed painfully.

Eric dropped the cooler beside the console. He scooped Laurel up in one arm without dislodging her hands from the wheel, and kicked the cooler over next to the console where she had been standing. Then he lowered her carefully, steadying her until she found her footing again.

"Oh, yeah! That's better!" she said. "Thanks, and no runt jokes, please."

"Wouldn't dream of it."

A strong tide was running through the cut, and the wind gained force between the two land masses that rose precipitously on either side. *Mayflower* hurtled on with too much sail aloft, and no way for them to take the time to reef her. Benji and Emily clung to the sides of the dodger, and were tossed about as the ride grew rougher.

While Laurel struggled to avoid the many hazards in the channel, Eric pointed his binoculars aft again. *Mayflower* sailed behind the island just as he spotted the speedboat pulling away from the cruiser's stern. He knew it would gain on them rapidly. He turned his attention to Laurel and watched her with admiration, a tiny dynamo focused entirely on forcing the big boat to obey her hands. He wished he could help in some way.

But Laurel was tiring. The overpowered boat threatened to tear the wheel from her grasp. Suddenly a gust of wind slammed against the mainsail, threatening to backwind it, and Laurel spun the wheel to fill it again. *Mayflower* heeled abruptly, and her feet flew off the cooler. She landed painfully on her left hip, but still clung to the wheel.

Eric sprang to her side and took the wheel, giving her time to recover. Knowing he couldn't maneuver the boat well enough himself, he extended his hand and pulled her to her feet. "You okay?"

The breath was knocked out of her, and she rubbed her sore hip as she climbed back up on the cooler. "Guess so. Gonna have a good bruise there. Look out!"

She grabbed for the wheel, and Eric let go. She spun it to port, narrowly missing a gravelly sandbar, and the boat yawed violently, throwing her off balance again. Eric caught her by a strap on her life vest and kept her from falling. The turbulent wind slammed the sail once more, and the big boat shuddered, it's keel grazing the seabed. Laurel was tossed about, unable to maintain enough purchase to control the wheel, and the boat bucked and plunged.

Eric moved quickly behind her and braced his back against the stern rail. He spread his legs wide for balance and gripped Laurel's waist firmly, just below the life vest. Thus anchored and supported, she regained control of the pitching vessel, and brought it back to the center of the constricted channel.

The strait widened somewhat as they approached the mid point of The Narrows, and Eric could see clear, deep water on both sides, but *Mayflower* continued to roll violently in the unpredictable winds. Laurel was clearly exhausted, her slim arms trembling under the strain of fighting of the big boat's constant pitching. He released his grip on her waist and reached around her on both sides, seizing the wheel. "Let me do this for a while. Just stay ready to take over if you see something coming that you think I can't handle."

Laurel released the wheel and sank back gratefully, her life vest bumping against his chest. She shook her arms and rotated her wrists, easing the stiffness out of them. "You've been doing great!" he told her. "Just rest a little."

She stepped down off the cooler and ducked out from under his arm. Sinking down on the port seat, she leaned out over the rail to scan the water ahead. "It's gonna get a lot worse in about three minutes," she told him. "The far end isn't much wider than the boat, and it squirts you out like water from a hose. There's rocks on the left and sandbars on the right, and you have to keep going perfectly straight until you're in the clear. I'd better take it through when we get there."

Eric wasn't about to argue; he knew the limitations of his recently acquired sailing skills. Over the sound of the wind, he could hear the engine of the pursuing speedboat echoing off the islands' hills as it entered The Narrows. Because of the twists and turns in the strait, he couldn't tell how far behind it was, but from the sound of the engine, he knew they had throttled back.

The smaller boat would have a lot less trouble getting through, but he was betting they wouldn't know the waters, and would take it pretty slow to avoid the rocks. Thinking the slower sailboat was trapped, they had no reason to hurry. *Mayflower* still had a chance.

"They're coming, aren't they?" Laurel asked, glancing astern.

"You know the old one about crossing bridges before you come to them?"

She smiled up at him, fatigue etching deep lines in her youthful face. Eric wondered anew at her amazing courage and resiliency. But the awful responsibility of their predicament was his alone, and weighed heavily upon him. He had talked the child into taking this terrible chance, and now he had to rely on her sailing ability to pull them through. *But did we really have any other choice?* he thought.

He felt the surge of the tide, and as the wind shifted again, *Mayflower* heeled hard over. A wave washed over the gunwale and he ordered the two younger children down onto the floor of the cockpit.

He looked behind briefly, but the approaching speedboat was still concealed by the bends in the cut. Nevertheless he could hear the engine, louder now but still throttled back in deference to the rough water. He tried to guess how long it would be before they were overtaken.

Laurel stiffened alertly as the channel began to close in on them. "My turn again." She ducked back between his arms and climbed up on the cooler, taking over the wheel once more. He stepped back.

"Stay there, Eric, please. It's gonna get really rough. Don't let me fall again."

He resumed his wide stance against the rail and steadied her once more, squeezing her shoulder reassuringly. She craned her neck to one side and strained to see the tight passage ahead.

The current roared in the cut, pushing the hull ahead of it. To Eric, *Mayflower* seemed to be flying. Whitecaps foamed on the waves, and he could no longer see beneath the surface. They were moving too fast to avoid rocks anyway, at the mercy of the wind and tide, and had to trust to luck. Laurel clung desperately to the wheel, just trying to keep them centered in the channel. At one point they could almost reach out and touch the cliffs on either side.

The wind buffeted them back and forth, and a sudden gust hammered the mainsail, knocking them viciously to port. The keel struck some underwater obstruction, and the big boat nearly foundered, her mast dropping perilously toward the waves. The wheel whipped from Laurel's hands and spun uncontrollably back and forth as the waves crashed against the rudder. She screamed.

Eric wrapped his left arm around her and held her firmly, tight against his body. He caught the wheel to stop it, then lost his footing and started to slide sideways on the tilting deck. He tried to brace his foot, but the knee of his weakened leg buckled under the strain.

Benji and Emily were tossed across the cockpit floor, and piled up against the locker. Their extra weight, added to Eric and Laurel's, tipped the port gunwale beneath the water. Eric released his grip on the wheel and lunged upward toward the starboard rail. Catching hold of it, he hauled himself and Laurel across the slanted cockpit to the high side.

With her balance improved, *Mayflower* labored to come back

upright, but with no hand on the helm she swung once more to port, dangerously close to the rocks. Laurel reached out and managed to grasp the wheel. Hanging from the crook of Eric's left arm, she spun it around to the right, and the boat lurched to starboard and heeled over alarmingly. This time the gunwale stayed clear of the waves, and as the big boat gradually righted, Laurel eased her back into the narrow channel. Slowly the mast rose away from the churning sea.

Eric braced his feet again as the deck leveled out, and set Laurel down on the cooler, his hands locked firmly on her waist. Twice more the violent motion lifted her right off her feet. She hung suspended in mid air in Eric's strong grasp but never lost control of the wheel, keeping them centered between the threatening shoals on either side.

Abruptly they burst into the clear. *Mayflower* shot out from between the islands as if fired from a gun, and plunged into calmer water. The wind fell off and the graceful hull slowed and righted. Laurel pointed her up into the wind and strained to see signs of the treacherous shelves that radiated from the two parallel headlands just below the surface. Somewhere ahead, Eric knew, the narrow channel gave way to deeper water all around.

Their plan now seemed desperate and foolish. A hundred things could go wrong. The speedboat could overtake them before they reached clear water, or its driver could see through their plan and avoid the rocks. Even worse, Laurel could misjudge the distance, and put *Mayflower* onto the dangerous flats. The responsibility was awful, especially for a twelve-year-old, and Eric regretted once more having let her assume the burden of their safety.

Behind them, the speedboat's roar suddenly increased. They both turned to see it just emerging from the entrance to the cut, riding high on a plane and coming on fast. Three men were aboard, and the one in the bow was holding a rifle.

"I need you at the winch!" Laurel shouted. "When we come about, crank in the jib *fast!*"

"Keep your head down! They might start firing any minute." Eric gave her a quick squeeze of reassurance and stepped out in front of the console. Despite his warning, he didn't think their pursuers would risk shooting until they were a lot closer. They wanted the children kept safe and unharmed, but he knew he himself wouldn't be so lucky.

He wrapped the free line loosely around the winch, then grabbed the handle and slapped it into the socket. He whirled and released the jib sheet on the opposite side, but continued to hold it taut on the drum with his hands, keeping the sail full. *It's all up to her now*, he thought, then aloud he shouted, "Just say when!"

Its big engine screaming, the pursuing speedboat closed on their stern, less than a hundred yards away. Eric saw the armed man trying to level the rifle at him. Laurel strained forward over the wheel, her eyes fixed on the surface. "Ready... Ready... Coming about!" she shouted.

She whipped the wheel and Eric dropped the line. He lunged across the cockpit and hauled in the opposite sheet, yanking it snugly around the drum. The big boom snapped the mainsail across, and almost simultaneously Eric cranked the jib in tight. Both sails filled with a thump, and *Mayflower* heeled over and dug in, tacking off on the very edge of the rock-filled shelf.

Eric thought they had made it, but the keel caught the bottom near the edge of the channel. The big boat stumbled. Laurel screamed, and Eric threw himself on the lower rail. His weight levered the keel up out of the mud, and *Mayflower* broke free, righted, and plunged on.

The speedboat howled after them, less than two dozen yards behind. *Still sailing*, he thought, *but about to be caught. Damn!*

The speedboat's pilot saw the mainsail come across *Mayflower's* cockpit. Without thinking, he spun his wheel to cut them off, just as the man with the rifle fired. The bullet went wide, missing Eric's head by inches, and ricocheted off the boom.

The pursuing boat swerved violently in the choppy water, its stern sliding sideways. The propeller came up out of the water, and with its load suddenly released, the engine screamed. The pilot corrected the wheel and the careening hull slapped hard down onto the water, smashing the propeller on a jagged outcropping just inches below the surface.

The hull lost its edge and the bow hammered down, splintered on another rock, then rebounded scant feet from *Mayflower's* gunwale. Eric watched in amazement as the slender craft flew up into the air and cartwheeled end over end, spilling its three occupants into the water. It fell back with a splintering crash, right on top of them, and the engine burst into flames. Seconds later the water erupted in a violent explosion as the gas tank split open and ignited.

The shock wave hit them hard, smashing the big sailboat over on its rail. Shrapnel and burning wreckage pelted the deck. Eric fell across the two children on the cockpit floor, shielding them with his own body as fragments from the wreck rained down on his back. Laurel fought the wheel, trying desperately to keep the sails out of the water and avoid a knockdown. Gradually she coaxed *Mayflower* upright.

Eric scrambled to his feet and began stamping out the flaming debris. Benji and Emily were terrified but unhurt. He turned toward the console to see flames shooting upward from a fuel-soaked spike of fiberglass that had impaled itself in the back of Laurel's life vest. Unable to find the buckles, she was tearing frantically and ineffectually at the straps.

Eric stumbled to her side and hammered the shard from the vest with his fist, knocking it over the stern. He whirled her around and crushed her against his own vest, smothering the flames. As Laurel at last freed the straps, he peeled the smoldering vest off and dropped it overboard. He quickly inspected her bare back for burns, and was relieved to find her uninjured.

The sails luffed, and Laurel grabbed the wheel again and hauled *Mayflower* back into the wind. As they pulled away from the accident, Eric scanned the wreck for any sign of life. The slick of burning fuel spread out in all directions, sending clouds of heavy, acrid smoke skyward. He debated trying to circle back, then decided that no one could have survived such a tremendous detonation.

Battered and scarred but still vital, *Mayflower* sailed on, bearing them to safety.

Twenty-Two

Relieved at their narrow escape but sickened by the havoc and slaughter behind them, Eric refocused on the open sea ahead. Laurel's concentration on sailing had spared her the sight of their pursuers' deaths, and the two younger children had seen little from where they lay on the cockpit floor.

"Want me to take her for a while?" he asked Laurel. She was obviously exhausted, clinging to the wheel but letting the big boat seek its own route through the deeper, safer water.

She stepped down off the cooler, and Eric moved it aside out of the way. She smiled up at him with tired eyes that still held a glint of mischief. "Think you can handle her, old Doc?"

"I sure can. I had a great teacher. The best."

The hot, humid air had given way to a chillier wind, and Laurel went below to find warmer clothes. She reappeared a minute later in a long-sleeved pullover and shorts, and carrying extra things for Benji and Emily. She took off their life vests and bundled the youngest child into one of her own sweatshirts, three sizes too large. Emily looked like a forlorn waif. Benji fared a little better; Laurel's extra sweats fit him nicely.

She disappeared down the hatch once more, and after several minutes she was back with extra towels and a jacket for Eric, which he put on gratefully. Then she turned to Emily, who had drooped down onto the cockpit floor.

"Cheer up, squirt," Laurel said to the little one. "We're going home. Bet your mom and dad will be glad to see you." She gathered the child up in her arms, carried her to a forward corner of the cockpit, and collapsed onto the seat beneath the dodger. She rested her head against the taut canvas, and cuddled Emily warmly against her side.

The wind dropped, and *Mayflower's* speed fell below four knots. Benji stretched out on top of the port side locker and tucked his life vest under his cheek. Eric took one of the spare dry towels and wrapped it around the boy's bare legs, and in a few minutes he was sound asleep.

Not wanting to disturb the children's rest, Eric tied the wheel and climbed up onto the cabin's roof. He released the reef from the mainsail, and returned to the cabin and cranked it up the mast to take full advantage of the lighter air. Then he stepped behind the console and untied the wheel again. He sank back wearily against the stern rail.

He was physically spent and drained of feeling. With little to do but watch the compass and maintain a constant heading, his thoughts drifted aimlessly. His conscious mind resisted any review of the past two days. *Mayflower* plodded on in the general direction of the Coast Guard station some miles ahead.

Gradually he became aware of a soft and plaintive sound, penetrating the rippling noise of the water that passed under the hull. He glanced at Benji, who was still sleeping on the seat to his left. Then he looked forward to where Laurel sat under the dodger, holding a sleeping Emily.

Emily's head rested in Laurel's lap. Absently fingering the younger child's hair, she sat forlornly gazing over the rail. Tears flowed freely down her cheeks, and her breath caught raggedly in her throat in tiny sobs.

Eric stirred from his lethargy, and tried to put aside his own emotional exhaustion. He called to her softly, "Hey, sweet one. Come on back here with me."

Laurel lifted Emily gently and squirmed out from beneath her. She folded a towel and laid the child's head down on the seat, then crept miserably toward the stern and slumped down in the starboard corner. Eric moved over beside her and sat down. He lifted his good leg and rested his foot on the bottom rim of the wheel to hold the boat on course, then gathered the weeping child into his arms.

Laurel clung to him and buried her face deep within the folds of his jacket, her small shoulders shaking as she gasped between sobs. She drew her knees up and tucked her feet beneath her, desolate in her grief over her missing father.

Eric held her tightly and stroked her hair, trying to soothe her. Gradually her crying subsided into occasional hiccups, and the trembling in her body ceased. Eric thought she had fallen asleep, and was surprised when her tiny voice drifted up to him.

"He's dead, isn't he?"

Eric knew she meant her father. "No, he's not," he said confidently. He wished he felt as sure as he sounded.

She lifted her head and wiped her eyes on the back of her hand. "He isn't?"

"On Sunday, when those guys boarded us and one of them knocked me overboard, what did you think?"

"I was sure they'd killed you."

"And here I am, right?"

Laurel gazed at him in wonder. "I didn't have time to think about that much. I still don't understand how you kept from drowning. Didn't that guy knock you out?"

"Well, for starters I had one heck of a headache. The cold water woke me up, though, and I swam under the boat and came up under the stern. I heard them when they were looking over the rail, trying to find me, and I stayed out of sight. I was trying to figure out how to get back on board when they started the engine. If I hadn't dived under, the propeller would have made hamburger out of me. When I came back up, the boat was pulling away, and nobody was looking for me any more."

"So how did you find us?"

"Luck, mostly. First I had to swim to shore."

"How did you do that? We were miles out."

"Sometimes you just do what you have to. You just have to decide not to give up, no matter what, and keep on trying. Like not giving up on finding your dad."

"But how did you find the right island?"

"That was just dumb luck, although if you think about it, it made sense that those pirates would have come from the nearest landfall."

"How did you know where to come looking for us?"

"I didn't. I spent one cold, miserable night on the beach first. The next morning I was trying to find a road or something, when I practically fell into that inlet. I was too tired to swim across, so I followed the shore where it went inland, and all of a sudden, there was *Mayflower*, right in front of me."

He smiled inwardly, suddenly remembering Deanna's gentle teasing the night he had taught Laurel how to swim. "Then I climbed into a phone booth, changed into my tights and my red cape with the great big 'S' on it, and flew off to rescue you."

He was rewarded with a small giggle, and then a poke in the ribs. "Come on, what really happened?"

"Part good luck, and part common sense. I went exploring along the shore of the cove and found the path to that A-frame where they took you. Then I just holed up in the woods and watched, and eventually I saw you kids being taken to the outhouse."

"How did you get us out? Those guys had guns."

"When the older one went to get his boat, I climbed a tree and jumped onto the roof. That was the noise you heard, that big thump, and that's why that Piersol guy came into your room yelling and swearing. When he went outside to look around, I slid off the roof and landed on his back. He never knew what hit him."

Laurel giggled again, then turned serious. "But Dad wasn't with you. What's it all got to do with him?"

"You thought I was dead, right? And instead, your old Doc turned up safe and sound. If an ancient fossil like me can do it, your dad *must* be out there somewhere, still okay and trying to get home to you. Maybe he's there already. Maybe he's got the Coast Guard out looking for us. In fact, I'll bet he's got the FBI, the Royal Canadian Mounted Police and even the Queen's Palace Guard all galloping to our rescue right now."

Laurel managed a wan smile. A glimmer of hope shone in her eyes, with just a touch of impishness. "Old fossil, huh?"

"That's me."

She sighed. "Maybe you're right, but I think you're just trying to cheer me up."

It was his turn to be serious. "Of course I am. But that doesn't mean I don't believe what I just told you. You don't *know* what happened to your dad, so there's no point in imagining the worst. Concentrate on all the ways he could be safe."

She unfolded her legs and sat up straighter, taking a deep, shuddering breath. She turned a warm smile on him and hugged him briefly. "Thank you."

"My pleasure."

Benji sat up and kicked off the towel, rubbing his eyes. He wrapped his arms around himself, huddling deep within the warmth of his sweatshirt. In spite of his jacket, Eric felt chilled himself. He gave Laurel's hand a squeeze, patted her bruised face gently, and stood up behind the wheel again. "Hey, Benji. Want to steer for a bit?"

The boy's eyes lit up and he came fully awake. He hurried over to the console. "Sure. You think I can?"

"Piece of cake," Eric said. The wind had dropped even further, and *Mayflower* was on an easy heading, slightly off the wind and maintaining little more than three knots. Eric pointed to the compass. "See this dial? When you turn the wheel, the compass rotates like this."

Benji watched the dial in fascination as Eric eased the big boat left a few degrees, and then back to the right. "All you have to do is keep the compass right here, on 170 degrees. In fact, make it a perfect 172. That'll keep us pointing almost due south, which is where we need to go." Eric pointed out the calibrations on the dial. "Think you can do it?"

The small boy eagerly took the wheel, staring at the compass with fierce concentration. At first he turned it too far and *Mayflower* oscillated back and forth, but he quickly caught on. "Now you've got it," Eric praised. "Keep us right on this heading, and you'll be a Bosun's Mate in no time. If you get in any trouble, Laurel will help you."

The sea ahead was broad and empty, with nothing to threaten their progress. Wearily Eric moved to the hatch and went below. All the tension of the past hours drained out of his battered body, and he felt every one of his sixty-one years. He located his duffel bag, stripped off his jacket, T-shirt and swim trunks, and retrieved the sweatshirt he had earlier wrapped Emily into. He dug out a pair of jeans and a clean shirt, put the sweatshirt on top, and sank down on the cushioned seat beside the table. His side throbbed painfully, but the bandage was still intact.

Mayflower swept onward, driven slowly by the gentle wind and only slightly heeled to starboard. He was tempted to fall into the forward berth and close his eyes for a few minutes, but the boat and his three young companions were still his responsibility, and no one else's. He sighed and climbed back onto the deck.

Laurel had recovered her spirits somewhat, and she was standing beside Benji, showing him how to read the sails and ticklers. The boy's eyes shone with excitement. Emily had not awakened. Eric stepped over the rail onto the gunwale, then turned and mounted the cabin's roof. He peered out over the bow and spotted the unmistakable outline of a Coast Guard cutter, far in the distance but heading directly toward them. He returned to the cockpit.

"Visitors coming," he announced, pointing a few degrees to the right of the bow. "Coast Guard cutter at one o'clock. Break out the tuxedos and evening gowns, and pour the champagne. Looks like we're about to be rescued, *runt!*" Eric emphasized the tease.

"Looks like we already rescued ourselves, *Doc!*" she came right back. Benji stared at them curiously, not understanding the joke. "Let's get the fenders, so they can come alongside." She turned back toward the console and affected an official tone. "New heading, Bosun's Mate Benji. Change course, 180 degrees."

Proudly the boy turned the wheel, easing off expertly as the dial slowly rotated to the new reading, and the boat's speed dropped a half knot. "Well done!" Laurel praised. "Maintain your course."

"Aye, aye, sir!"

Laurel bent to the port locker and handed the fenders out to Eric. She showed him the proper hitch to secure them to the rail, and they tossed them over the side to protect the hull. By the time they were finished, the cutter had more than halved the distance between them, and was slowing down.

Laurel took the wheel from Benji and brought the boat about, letting the sails flutter. Eric lowered the main and furled the jib part way, leaving just enough sail for them to maintain way. With the engine crippled, they needed some sail to enable them to maneuver.

The big cutter loomed over them, and Eric tossed a line to a crew member to keep the two boats abeam. An officer stepped to the rail and called down to them. "Ahoy, *Mayflower*. We're glad to see you. We've been searching for you. You were due back in port last night."

"I know," Eric shouted back. "We ran into some trouble, pirates of a sort. Some of them just blew themselves up on the rocks."

"We got a report of smoke and an explosion near the mouth of The Narrows. Any survivors?"

"I don't think so," Eric answered. "There wasn't much left after the gas tank blew."

"I'm Captain William MacDonald. Are you Walter MacKenzie, sir?"

Eric glanced down at Laurel's stricken face as she absorbed the implications of the officer's question. If the Coast Guard thought Walt was still on board, that meant he hadn't been found. He leaned down and encircled her shoulders in a quick hug. "That doesn't mean anything," he told her. "He could be stuck on some island, just like we were. We'll find him. Don't give up. Don't *ever* give up!"

He turned his attention back to the Guardsman. "Eric Kelman, Captain. Mr. MacKenzie was taken off our boat two days ago, and we haven't seen him since. There's a lot we have to tell you."

"How many souls aboard?"

"Four of us," Eric answered. "We picked up two children from an island up the coast, where they were being held prisoner."

This caught the Captain's attention. He stared curiously at Eric, but held his tongue. He glanced astern toward a second cutter that was approaching from the southeast. "I'm putting a man aboard your vessel, Mr. Kelman. He'll take your statement while we escort you into port. Our sister ship will head out to investigate the accident. Who's piloting your craft?"

Eric gestured toward Laurel at the wheel. "First Mate Laurel MacKenzie."

The officer cocked his head to one side and regarded the youngster. Then he scanned the sea astern, assessing the direction from which *Mayflower* had come. "You didn't bring her through The Narrows, did you?"

Eric nudged Laurel, and she answered, "Yes, Sir."

He stared at her almost in disbelief. "By yourself?"

"Eric helped me."

"I just followed orders, Captain," Eric corrected her. "She did it."

MacDonald's astounded gaze wavered back and forth between them. He was trying to absorb the fact that one so young could have the skill required for such a dangerous passage. Finally he smiled at Laurel broadly and gave her a smart salute. She glowed.

A second officer was called to the deck. He conferred briefly with

Captain MacDonald, who then turned back to Laurel, acknowledging her unofficial rank. His tone held no trace of condescension. "This is Lieutenant Michaels, First Mate MacKenzie. Please invite him aboard to take your statements."

Laurel accepted her role with pride and seriousness. "Yes, sir, come aboard please."

As the transfer was made, Eric explained to the Captain about the stolen radio, and asked him to contact their families.

"That's being done as we speak, Mr. Kelman. They'll be waiting for you at our dock."

"Perhaps you should also notify the parents of these two children. They must be very worried." Eric gestured toward Benji and Emily, who were staring wide-eyed at the bigger vessel. "Bosun's Mate Benji, please step up and give the Captain your name and phone number. And don't forget your sister," he added unnecessarily. The boy came forward shyly but excitedly, plainly in awe of the military display before him.

After taking the child's information, the Captain addressed Eric again. "Do you want a tow, or will you follow us in?"

Eric looked at Laurel, and she shook her head. "We'll sail her, thanks," he called to the cutter.

"Very good. Cast off." The crewman tossed their line back on board, and Laurel and Eric raised and reset the sails. They gave Benji the job of retrieving the fenders, leaving them on the deck and tied to the rail for use when they docked.

Once they were underway and following along just outside the wake of the big cutter, Eric sat down with Lieutenant Michaels and related the events of the past few days. It took quite a while. Laurel handled *Mayflower* with her usual expertise, and when they entered the harbor, the cutter signaled them to tie up alongside the dock. Eric explained to the lieutenant about their crippled engine, and he offered to take the wheel to bring the boat in under sail.

Eric glanced at Laurel. "Do you want Lieutenant Michaels to take her in for you?"

She stood on tiptoe and strained to look over the bow at the approach to the dock, then checked the wind direction. "I think I can do it."

"Looks like your services are not required, Lieutenant," Eric said with a smile. He turned back to Laurel. "Carry on, First Mate."

"I hope she knows what she's doing," Michaels whispered to Eric. "This is a valuable piece of hardware she's playing with."

Eric grinned at him. "It's her hardware, and she's not playing, believe me. She just brought us through The Narrows, then fooled a boatload of bad guys into smashing onto the rocks. I'd say she knows what she's doing, all right."

Eric collected Benji, and they dropped the fenders over the side. He took up his place by the winches, ready to handle the sails. He furled the jib, and Laurel sailed into the harbor on just the main.

Without benefit of the engine, she sailed right up to the dock and brought *Mayflower* smartly about, issuing brisk commands to Eric. Their teamwork flowed smoothly, and the fenders barely kissed the dock as they tossed their lines ashore. Several Guardsmen standing nearby watched her performance critically, then broke into spontaneous applause.

Twenty-Three

Eric lifted Emily over the rail and set her down on the dock, delivering her into the care of the nearest seaman. Benji and Laurel scrambled ashore, and she spotted Fran's Volvo just pulling into the parking lot. She took off running, and flew into her mother's arms almost before she was out of the car.

Eric left *Mayflower* in the custody of the dock crew, and followed Captain MacDonald toward the Coast Guard station. Then he spotted Deanna getting out of Fran's car. She ran over to him. "Are you okay? I was so worried."

"Tired and a little beat up, that's all," he answered.

Deanna embraced him, squeezing his wounded ribs. He winced and couldn't stifle a soft groan, and she dropped her arms instantly. "You're hurt!"

"Caught a bullet in the side, that's all, just grazed me. I've got it taped up. Nothing serious."

"I'll bet!" Deanna had little patience with her husband's stoicism. Then the import of what he had said hit her. "A bullet! What have you been doing? What happened? I'm getting you to the hospital, right now!"

"It'll have to be later. I promised the captain that I'd go over my statement with him in more detail. It can't wait, if they have any chance of catching those guys."

"What guys? And does this captain know you've been shot?" Deanna was both angry and fearful for his safety.

"No, and please don't tell him yet. Some sort of international pedophile ring got hold of Laurel and the other two kids I brought back. They might be the ones who murdered that scout counselor, too. I'll tell you the rest later. Has there been any word of Walt?"

"Not yet. I feel so badly for Fran. She's holding up really well, just as if she knows he's all right, but it's tearing her up inside."

"Laurel's the same way."

"Are the kids hurt?"

"A little bit bruised and dirty, that's all. Nothing serious."

Captain MacDonald came up to them. "Sorry to interrupt, but it's important that we get some more information from you, so we can get moving on this."

"Of course, Captain," Eric replied. "This is my wife, Deanna." He gave her a warning look that said, *Don't say anything about the bullet wound.* Deanna grimaced, but kept silent.

"Pleased to meet you, ma'am," MacDonald said. "I'll let your husband get back to you just as soon as I can." He turned back to Eric. "We'll need to talk to the little girl again, too."

"That's no little girl! You should have seen her wrestle the boat through The Narrows. And how about giving her a little more time with her mother? She's lost her dad, and she's a little bit fragile, emotionally, right now. You can get started with me." Eric kissed Deanna once more, then turned and followed MacDonald into the Coast Guard station. She stared after him in exasperation.

The interview lasted almost an hour, as Eric recounted everything that had occurred after they stopped to help the supposedly stranded speedboat. Laurel joined them after the first fifteen minutes, plainly exhausted but driven to help if she could by fear over her father's safety. Several other law enforcement officers sat in on the meeting.

Periodically the Captain issued orders to his staff. They were already engaged in a search of the island where the children had been held captive, and had managed to detain the cruiser that had been lying off shore. All of those on board had been arrested, and were being brought to shore for questioning and detention.

MacDonald quizzed Laurel closely as to what might have happened to her father. She told him how Eric had been knocked into the sea, after which the men had shut her in the cabin so she couldn't see what was happening. She also told him about the gunshots, and seeing the crippled Zodiac out through the porthole. All she knew for sure was that when they finally let her out, Walt was gone.

Finally satisfied that they had covered everything, the Captain said, "I guess that will do it for now, but if either of you can remember anything else, please let us know immediately."

"We will," Eric answered. "What about the two kids we brought back with us?"

"They're being looked after downstairs until the parents get here. I'm sure they'll want to thank you in person. In addition to saving them, you've performed a valuable service for us. We've been trying to get a handle on this operation for months now, but haven't had a single lead. There are more than a hundred missing kids on our list that we suspect are victims of the sex trade, and I intend to try to get them back, now that we have something substantial to go on."

"What's being done to find Walter MacKenzie?" Eric asked.

"Everything possible, believe me. We have a Search and Rescue copter in the air already, and half a dozen boats are covering every square inch of the coast line and islands." He turned to Laurel, trying to sound more confident than he felt. "We're going to find your dad, don't you worry."

The authorities impounded *Mayflower* for examination, in case Laurel's abductors had left anything behind that might help the investigation. It was well after midnight when Fran dropped Eric and Deanna off at the emergency room of the hospital. She offered to stay and drive them home afterward, but Eric refused her kindness, and she headed for home to put Laurel to bed.

An intern removed the butterfly bandages and cleaned and examined Eric's wound. His ribs were intact, and although his flesh was badly abraded, the doctor assured him the only lasting effect would be a rather spectacular scar. He closed the gash with sutures, administered a tetanus shot, and offered to write a prescription for Demerol, which Eric declined.

Deanna called a taxi, and as soon as they arrived home Eric tumbled into bed, almost incoherent from exhaustion. His troubled sleep was haunted by memories of his missing friend.

Eric Kelman awoke early, unrefreshed, to an overcast, unseasonably chilly day. University classes were scheduled to start the following day, but thanks to his advance preparation, nothing remained for him to do. He decided to stay away from the office. He checked in with the departmental secretary, then sought some distraction by working on his model railroad. The wound in his side began to throb painfully, however, and he gave it up and sat in his recliner, uncharacteristically doing nothing.

Shortly after ten, Deanna called him to the phone. Captain

MacDonald was on the line from the Coast Guard station. "Dr. Kelman, we've finished with your boat. I had our men do a general cleanup, and they cleared out the water pump intake for you. There appears to be no damage to the engine, but the hull needs some repairs. There are a few bullet holes, but they're all above the water line. The rest is mostly cosmetic."

"Thank you, Captain," Eric replied. "Is there any word on the search for Mr. MacKenzie?"

"I'm sorry to have to say no. The team is still working, but there doesn't seem to be much hope after all this time."

Eric sighed. "Thank you. I appreciate all you've done for us."

"I have some other news, too, good news this time. Your chief of police, Carmichael is it?"

"That's right."

"He told us of your involvement in the disappearance of a small group of scouts from the national park, and the murder of a counselor. We've found those kids."

Eric was greatly relieved. "That *is* good news. Where?"

"That cruiser you spotted was a floating prison. When we boarded her and took the crew into custody, we didn't think that there was anyone else on board. But when we started searching her, we uncovered a hidden hold just above the bilges. There were more than twenty kids crammed in down there, not one of them over fourteen, and most a lot younger. I'd say the three you saved were supposed to be the last of a full load. The crew was probably heading for the open sea as soon as it got dark."

"Good timing all around, I'd say."

"I'm sorry to trouble you further, Doctor, but could you make arrangements to have your boat moved? Dock space here is at a premium."

Eric didn't bother clarifying *Mayflower's* ownership status. "Of course. I'll come down right away."

He broke the connection, then dialed the MacKenzie's number. When Fran came on the line, he relayed some of what he had heard from the Coast Guard. "I can bring the boat back for you. There's no need for you to come."

Fran's voice was sad and strained. "Do you want Laurel to go with you?"

"Not necessary. I won't use the sails. The Coast Guard repaired the diesel, and they'll brief me on how to run it. I can handle it alone. Let her rest; she's done more than her share."

"I think she'll want to help," Fran said. "She didn't sleep late this morning, even though she's pretty wrung out. She's been fretting about *Mayflower* ever since she got up. She seems to think the boat is her responsibility now that Walt's... Eric, I'm sorry, have I even thanked you for everything you did? If not for you, I'd have lost them both."

"Forget it, Fran. I was just in the right place at the right time. And don't give up hope for Walt yet. They're still out searching."

"But it's been days..."

"I know... I'm so sorry, Fran."

"You brought Laurel back to me. I'm so very, very grateful to you, you know that. If you could have saved Walt, too, I know you would have. Hang on while I check with Laurel, and see if she wants to go with you."

Eric heard voices in the background, and then Fran came back on the line. "She wants to go. She says her father would want her to." Her voice broke. "Eric, she's given up too!"

He had no words of comfort for her. "I'll be over in just a few minutes."

Twenty-Four

Deanna quickly packed some sandwiches, took a few cans of cola from the refrigerator, and put everything in a bag for Eric to take with them. Then she drove him to the MacKenzie's house. After taking the boat back to Stillwater Basin Marina, he planned to drive home in the Pathfinder, which he had left parked there at the start of their sailing adventure.

They picked up Laurel, who huddled silently and miserably in one corner of the back seat on the drive to the shore. Deanna dropped them off at the Coast Guard station. Eric checked in and picked up the keys to the boat, and thanked the seaman at the desk for the repairs to the engine's cooling system. Then he and Laurel walked out onto the dock.

Mayflower sat forlornly alongside, her scarred paintwork reflecting their mood and the gloom of the gray sky. Laurel climbed aboard and started the engine, and Eric cast off the lines and joined her in the cockpit.

The air was heavy and still as they motored out of the harbor, making the sails useless. Laurel sat listlessly on the port side, her right hand lax on the wheel, as the little diesel pushed them along at five knots. Eric busied himself coiling lines and stowing fenders. Then he dug the sail cover out of the forward hatch and snapped it into place.

When he returned to the cockpit, he sat down beside her and gave her a hug. She turned toward him and buried her face in his shirtfront, sobbing miserably. Her hand dropped from the wheel, and he rested his foot between the lower spokes, keeping the boat on course.

As he had the day before, he held her close and stroked her hair. Gradually she quieted and lay limply against his side, staring without seeing out of sad, reddened eyes. Finally she took a deep breath and looked up into his face.

"My dad's really dead, isn't he?"

Eric wanted to reassure her, but the words stuck in his throat. It was time to be honest. "I hope not, little pal. But we have to accept that he probably is."

"What's it like to die?"

"We don't really know." He searched for words of comfort, but came up empty.

She was thoughtful for several minutes. Then she stiffened and looked up at him with concern. "Are you going to die soon?"

Eric tried for a lighthearted answer. "Why? Do I look sick?"

"Don't tease me!"

"I'm sorry. No, I'm not going to die soon. But I will some day, and you know what? It doesn't really bother me. It used to, but not so much any more."

"Why not?"

"Because I've had so many good years, and I expect to have some more, maybe even a lot more. And when the time comes, I'll be ready to rest."

"How old are you?"

"This is my sixty-second summer, runt."

"Wow!" She hadn't really thought of age in that way before. "It's only my twelfth."

"You can't count."

"Huh? I'm twelve, you know that."

"I know. And you were born in June, right?"

"Right. You know that, too."

"So you were just a couple of months old during your first summer, and the next June, when you were one year old, that was your second summer. And so on."

"Oh, yeah." She sighed. "That explains it."

"What?"

"Everything that happened since my birthday. My thirteenth summer. Thirteen is an unlucky number."

"Nuts!" Eric exclaimed. "There's no such thing as an unlucky number. That's superstition."

"*I* believe in it. This summer proves it, doesn't it?"

Eric searched for an explanation. "Remember all the fuss about the Millennium coming? Some people predicted all sorts of terrible things happening, even the end of the world, just because of a year that ended with three zeros. And what happened?"

"Nothing much."

"You've got it. It was all superstition. And it's silly!"

"Why?"

"Because the way we count the years is our own invention, and it's artificial. We called the year leading up to the new Millennium 'two thousand' because someone started counting it from when they thought the Christ Child was born. But they got that wrong, too. He was probably born three years earlier, maybe even as many as eight. Scholars figured that out by studying history, and the dates when other things happened back then."

She was puzzled. "So the year two thousand really should have been called two thousand and three?"

"Maybe. Or two thousand and eight, or some other number. It doesn't really matter, because what year it is doesn't have any effect on luck, or on the universe, or cause disasters, either."

"Are you sure?"

"Remember out at my cabin, when we were talking about the huge size of everything, all the billions of stars, and how small we are in comparison?"

"What does that have to do with two thousand or thirteen being unlucky?"

"Think about it. Our planet is just a tiny little speck in the whole big universe, and humans are only one of all the millions of kinds of living things on it. Do you really think any force or intelligence out there pays the slightest bit of attention to how we count our years? Or bothers to cause us bad luck because of it?"

"But it *is* my thirteenth summer, and all that stuff happened to me."

"And to me, too, and to all those kids. But it's Benji's tenth or eleventh summer, and Emily's eighth or ninth, depending on what month they were born. And my sixty-second, don't forget. So are they all unlucky numbers?"

She thought for a moment. "I guess not."

"If thirteen were unlucky, then *everybody* would have bad luck during their thirteenth year. And I remember my thirteenth year. I had my first girl friend then. It was *great!*"

Laurel managed a wan smile. "What was her name?"

"Never mind! You're a nosy little runt."

"So is *anything* unlucky?"

"Believing in luck is like believing in astrology, that the stars have this great big influence on us. People read their horoscopes, and every day there are twelve predictions about what will happen to them according to the month they were born in."

"Lots of people believe in that. My mom reads her horoscope every day. She's a Capricorn."

"So am I," Eric said, "but does that mean that she and I have the exact same kind of luck every day? I'll bet she doesn't really pay much attention to it. Horoscopes are just entertainment. Look, there are about six billion people in the world, right? So divide that up by twelve predictions, and that means that whatever the horoscope says for Capricorn, for example, should apply to half a billion people. *Five hundred million people, all with the same fortune.*"

"It *is* pretty silly, isn't it?"

"I think so. But on the other hand, I also know some very intelligent people who believe in it, and a lot of other things that I think are illogical. Maybe they're right and I'm wrong. So most of the time, I just keep my mouth shut. It saves lots of arguments."

She lapsed into silence for a while. Then: "My dad's thirty-four. His birthday's in February, so that makes this his thirty-fifth summer, right?"

Eric noticed she still spoke of Walt in the present tense. "Right. And thirty-five is just a number like any other, eight or ten or even thirteen. It doesn't mean a thing."

"Except he won't have any more," she said in a tiny voice, again burying her face against his chest. Eric had no answer to give her.

Mayflower labored on through the calm sea. Shortly after one o'clock they ate the sandwiches that Deanna had made. As they sat in the stern with their soft drinks, Laurel seemed lost in thought. Her eyes were red from crying, but she was now composed, becoming more and more resigned to the loss of her dad. Eric was staring absently over the starboard rail when he heard her voice, too soft for him to understand the words.

"What was that, runt?"

"I was just thinking," she replied. "I can't figure out what makes people act that way."

"What do you mean? Who?"

"Like why did those guys board our boat, and how come they took me and all those other kids? What did we ever do to them?"

"You didn't do anything."

"So how come they wanted to hurt us?"

Eric searched for an answer. "Remember that owl, out at the cabin, when we were sitting out under the stars?"

"You mean the one that ate the mouse? Gross."

"That's the one. What do you suppose the mouse did to the owl, to get himself eaten like that?"

"That's dumb. The owl was just hungry. The mouse was in the wrong place at the wrong time."

"So, did the owl sit up there in the tree and think to himself, 'I'm going to catch me a mouse, and I know it's wrong, but I'm going to eat him anyway'?"

"You're kidding me again, right? Birds and animals don't think like that. He was hungry, so he ate something. He didn't care about right or wrong. Anyway, what's that got to do with what those guys tried to do to us?"

"They were hungry."

"Huh?"

"People are animals too, Laurel. We're more than *just* animals, at least I hope we are, but we have things that drive us, biological things. We have to eat, we have to drink, we have to have shelter, and so forth."

"I don't get it."

Eric tried to make it clearer. "In some ways we're just like other animals, but in some really important ways, most of us are different. If a fox is hungry, it kills a chicken. But it doesn't feel sorry for the chicken. A fox, like most other animals, lacks compassion. It has no empathy for the creatures it eats."

He wondered if the words he chose made sense any to her, but he could tell from her thoughtful expression that she had no trouble following him.

"But *we* do," she said. "We care about animals and stuff, like if a dog gets hit by a car, we take him to the vet."

"Right. Now back up to the fox again. He kills a chicken and eats it, so he isn't hungry any more. And the important thing is, he doesn't kill any more chickens until he's hungry again. But some people have a different kind of hunger, not just for food, but also for other things, and they can't ever get enough. As far as we know, we're the only species that uses money, and some people want as much as they can get, more than they can ever use."

"So those guys tried to kill you, and my dad, just so they could make *money*?"

"Laurel, I know you understand what they were planning for you and Benji and Emily, and all those other kids."

"Yeah, the sex thing." She was suddenly angry. "That's what I mean! Why do people *do* things like that to each other, especially to little kids?"

"That's a different kind of hunger. People who want to have sex with children are twisted. It's kind of like being hungry, only worse. They don't see kids as people, and they convince themselves that it doesn't matter what they do to them, as long as it satisfies their appetite. And because it's against the law, they have to pay a lot of money to criminals like the ones who took you, Reynolds and Piersol, to get what they want."

"But *they* didn't try to hurt me that way. Oh, that Stu guy tried, but the other one wouldn't let him. And I fixed him good, too. You should have seen him rolling around on the floor after I kicked him."

Eric grinned at the image, and at her bravado. "Reynolds left you alone because all he wanted was the money. He knew he could sell you to the sick ones for a whole lot more if you were... if you..."

Laurel shuddered. "I know what a virgin is! If they'd hurt me like that, I'd have killed myself or something."

Eric went on quickly. "I didn't mean to scare you, sweetheart. Most people in the world are good and decent. Most of them have those feelings of empathy and compassion I told you about, and they really care about kids, and about keeping them safe. But there will always be some sick ones, and there will always be the greedy ones who will do anything to get rich, no matter who gets hurt."

Laurel chewed that one over in her mind. "Eric..."

He waited for her question, but she couldn't seem to form it. She stared down at her feet. "I don't know how to say this."

"Just try. Whatever it is."

She took a deep breath. "Why does sex have to be so awful?"

"It doesn't *have* to be. In fact, it can be pretty wonderful, when it comes at the right time of life, and with someone you love."

"I'm scared of it."

He smiled at her. "That's okay. Most people are, at first. In fact, that's probably good. It keeps you from jumping into it too quickly."

"Can I ask you something? It's kind of embarrassing."

Eric thought he knew what was coming, and gritted his teeth. "Sure. Fire away."

"Do you think my mom and dad have sex?"

He barely kept from bursting out laughing. That wasn't what he had been expecting. "Just where do you think *you* came from? The stork?"

"Oh, I know all that, but that was *then*. I mean *now*."

"We're drifting into some pretty personal stuff here, you know." He was uncomfortable with the direction their conversation was taking. He didn't feel it was his place to try to talk to someone else's child about such things. However, he was pleased to hear that she was again talking about her father, still in the present tense and without such intense grief. The healing had begun. He decided not to try to evade her questions, but considered his answer very carefully.

"This isn't something your mom and dad would ever talk to me about, or anyone else, probably. For most people, sex is a private thing. But I can tell you this. In the short time I've known all of you, it seems pretty obvious to me that your mom and dad love each other very much. And when people really love each other, they want to do things for each other, and make each other happy in any way they can."

"So..."

"So sex is one of the most beautiful, wonderful things that two people in love can do with each other."

She thought this over. "So they do it."

"Not my business, and not really yours either."

"I think it's gross."

"That's one of your favorite words, isn't it?"

"Well, it is. I mean, my *mom* and *dad*? I mean, they're sort of old..."

This time he couldn't keep from laughing. "You'd better not let them hear you say that."

Laurel was silent for a long time. Finally she approached the question from a different angle, the one Eric had originally been expecting. "You and Mrs. Kelman are even older, right?"

"Right, and I know where you're going with that one, so you can stop right there, my nosy friend." He tried to sound indignant.

"I'm sorry."

He smiled. "That's okay, I'm just teasing you. But I'm not going to answer any really personal questions, and that's that."

"You still love each other, don't you? I mean, *really* love each other?"

"I don't mind answering that. Yes, we really do. And if you say 'gross' again, I'll toss you overboard."

She ducked her head, a small, secret smile on her lips. Two spots of color appeared on her cheeks as she thought about all the implications. *Maybe sex isn't so bad after all. Probably pretty special, in fact.* "Wow!" she whispered aloud. Then she grinned up at him. "Can I change the subject?"

"I'd definitely advise it, unless you really want to find yourself turned into shark food."

"You said those guys on the boat didn't care who they hurt, as long as they got rich, right?"

"Uh, huh. So?"

"So is it wrong to want to be rich?"

"It is if you get that way at somebody else's expense. Decent people make their money by doing things *for* people, not *to* them. Like your dad designs houses, and because he does it really well, he makes a good living for the three of you, and the people who live in his houses get a really nice place to live. Everybody wins."

"We're not rich."

"Well, not like Bill Gates, maybe. But you aren't exactly starving, either. And I bet your folks think they're extremely rich, the same way Deanna and I are."

"Really? Are you rich?"

"Sure am," he answered. "Fabulously wealthy, in fact."

"Have you got a million dollars?" Thanks to TV, that was every kid's yardstick of economic prosperity.

"Nope. Nowhere near, unless you count my pension fund, and that's got to last me the rest of my life after I retire."

Laurel looked at him with a puzzled expression. "You're *not* rich, then."

"Oh yes I am. Being rich is having everything you need, and I do. Come to think of it, I've got *more* than that. I've got *two* of all the important things."

She raised her eyebrows sarcastically. "Such as?"

"Let's make a list. I've got two houses, if you count the cabin, and I can only be in one at a time, so I've got more than I need. Doesn't that make me rich? And I've got two cars, and can only drive one at a time. I've got two cats, two tanks of fish…"

"I've got one cat! Does that make me half rich?" she teased him.

"Okay, the cats don't count. They're probably a liability, in fact. Both of them scratch the furniture." Laurel laughed gently. "Now for the important stuff," he went on. "I've got two great kids, and there isn't enough money in the world to replace them. Next, two perfect grandchildren, ditto. I am very, *very* rich."

"I get it. How about your wife, though?"

"Oh, yeah. Just one of those. I got that right the first time."

Laurel was quiet for a moment. Then she turned her sad eyes to his face, but a tiny mischievous smile turned up the corners of her mouth. "And you've only got one friend like me, I bet."

He gave her a quick hug. "I got that right the first time, too."

Twenty-Five

As they rounded the final headland that sheltered the marina from the open sea, Eric remembered his conversation with Walt about Laurel's musical talent. "Hey, runt, want to know what your dad and I talked about while you were getting a tan last Saturday?"

Laurel roused herself, curious about anything her father might have told Eric. "Sure. What?"

"You really enjoy playing in the band, don't you?"

"Yeah, I do," she answered.

"And he told me you practice just about every day, even in the summer when you don't have to."

"Well, sure. That's the only way to get good. Besides, it's fun."

"He also said your teacher thinks you might be able to make a career out of it. I suppose you haven't thought about that very much yet, but there's a lot to be said for spending your life doing something you really love. And I suspect you really love music."

"You mean be a college professor, like you?"

"Not necessarily. There are many, many things you could do. Be a performer, for instance. Or you could teach school like your band director. I can't remember her name…"

"Mrs. Walling. I wonder if she thinks I might be that good."

"That's what she told your dad. And you could be a composer, or an arranger, or a conductor, or a technician… Or lots of other things, once you have a really good education. But I suspect what you like best right now is playing the clarinet."

"Uh, huh."

"Anyway, when your dad told me all this, it occurred to me that you might be ready to go to a really good teacher."

"Mrs. Walling's good. Our band sounds *great*, and we won first place at the festival last spring."

"I know she is. I didn't mean to insult her. But she isn't a clarinet specialist. I think maybe you need to study with an artist performer. Your dad does, too."

"I don't know anybody like that."

"I do," Eric said. "His name is Alexander Knowlton, and he lives in the Capital. He used to play with the very best orchestras, and now that he's retired, he teaches. Of course, he only teaches the best, most serious students, the ones who really want to work hard."

Laurel was keenly interested. "Do you think he'd teach me?"

"I can't promise. But your dad and I both think he might give you a chance, once he hears you play. And I can arrange for that to happen."

"What's he like?"

"He's quite an old man, now, and a really nice one. And he knows just about everything there is to know about the clarinet. He started playing professionally back before the Second World War."

"Wow!" She thought about it for a few moments. "Is he anything like you?"

Eric laughed. "Maybe a little. He'll make you work really hard, but you'll learn a lot from him."

She looked at him seriously. "If he's like you, I want to do it. Did my dad really think I could? Get to study with him, I mean?"

Eric deliberately chose the present tense. "Your dad thinks you can do anything. He's very proud of you, and if you choose music for a career, or anything else for that matter, he'll always be very proud of you."

Her eyes brimmed with tears, but she managed a brave smile, and hugged him tightly as *Mayflower* approached the northern dock at Stillwater Basin Marina.

Eric dropped the fenders over the side as they coasted gently up to the dock with Laurel at the wheel. He stepped over the rail and tied off the bow and stern lines, and she stopped the engine. She started down the hatch to gather up their gear, and Eric was about to climb back on board to help her when he spotted the marina manager heading toward the end of the dock.

"Dr. Kelman?" the man called out. "Your wife phoned about ten minutes ago. Said you should call her just as soon as you got in."

"Thanks very much. I'll be right there." He turned and shouted down into the hatch. "I'll be right back, runt. I have to go up to the office and call home." He left the boat and walked the length of the dock, wondering what Deanna wanted.

Eric entered the marina office, located the receiver, and dialed his home number. Deanna picked up on the first ring and her excited voice came over the wire. "They found him! They found Walt! He's in St. Michael's in the Capital!"

"Is he all right?"

"He's been shot, and he lost a lot of blood, but they say he's going to be okay."

"What happened? Do they know?"

"He was picked up two days ago. The crew of a cargo ship spotted the Zodiac, drifting and half sunk, and they pulled it aboard. Walt was unconscious. The ship's doctor did what he could, and they changed course right away and made port in the city."

"Two days ago!" Eric was incredulous. "Why didn't they notify someone?"

"Typical bureaucratic screw up," Deanna answered. "Walt didn't have any ID on him. They'd been looking for a drug runner who escaped from the Coast Guard and stole a Zodiac early last week. Apparently they thought Walt was him."

"It's a wonder they didn't shoot him themselves. Does Fran know?"

"She's sitting right here next to me. He finally woke up about two hours ago, and when they found out who he was, they called her right away."

"Did he tell them what happened?"

"Just the general outline," Deanna said. "He was still pretty weak, but the police got most of the story straight before the doctor chased them away. After you got knocked overboard and Walt sent Laurel down into the cabin, one of those men held a gun on him. Then they stood him by the stern rail and shot him in the back. He fell overboard and landed in the Zodiac. They cut it loose and shot a couple of holes in it, then took off in the sailboat. I guess they expected it to sink, but it didn't."

"Separate floatation chambers, that's why," Eric explained. "You have to shoot holes in more than one of them to scuttle it."

"Anyway, Walt must have regained consciousness, at least for a bit. The bullet shattered a couple of ribs and tore him up some inside, but it missed his lungs and heart. He managed to wad up his shirt, and he laid down on it before he passed out again. The pressure helped limit the blood loss."

"Which hospital did you say they took him to?" Eric asked.

"St. Michael's. Fran wants to go into the city as soon as Laurel gets back. Can you come right away?"

"Why don't you two go on ahead? I'll collect the runt and drive right to the city, and we'll meet you there. That'll save us all some time."

"Wonderful! We'll take off right now. Love you."

"Love you too, sweetheart. Oh, and do me a favor. Tell Fran I said, 'I told you so!'"

Eric dropped the phone and set out on a run for the dock. Laurel was nowhere in sight when he reached the top of the gangway. He shouted at the top of his voice.

"Yo! First Mate Laurel MacKenzie! All hands on deck!"

Laurel's head popped out of the hatch, her eyebrows raised and curiosity shining in her eyes.

"I told you thirteen summers could be lucky," Eric told her joyously. "Start the engine, and let's put this thing on its mooring and get out of here. Your dad wants to see you!"

* * *

Also by Peter H. Riddle:
TWELFTH BIRTHDAY
the first Eric Kelman/Laurel MacKenzie adventure